THE REDIRECTION
of *Damien Sinclair*

a pine bluff *novel*

NANCEE CAIN

Serrated Edge Publishing

Serrated Edge Publishing
PO Box 969
Jasper, AL 35502
www.nanceecain.com

First published September 2018

This is a work of fiction. Names, characters, businesses, places, events and incidents are either the products of the author's imagination or used in a fictitious manner. Any resemblance to actual persons, living or dead, or actual events is purely coincidental

ISBN: 978-0-9995362-0-9

10 9 8 7 6 5 4 3 2 1

Editor: Jessica Royer Ocken
Line Editor: Coreen Montagna
Cover Design by Shannon Lumetta
Interior Book Design by Coreen Montagna

Printed in the United States of America

To Jessica Royer Ocken, for your patience and humor.

Prologue

"Demon Sinclair, you bastard! I thought you were my friend!"

Ignoring this outburst, Damien Sinclair straightened his gray-patterned tie and buttoned his coat as he prepared to leave the courtroom. He wouldn't say he and Jim Viner had ever been friends—just acquaintances. This was evidenced by the fact that he hated that nickname. No one who knew him used it. Just the press.

"This was business, Jim," he finally said.

"Business, my ass!" The irate ex-friend/acquaintance turned toward his much younger, now-ex-wife. "Lisa, this was all a mistake. Baby, that girl meant nothing to me. I'll buy you anything you want. Just come back home."

Lisa smiled smugly. "After today, you don't have much left, old man."

Jim lunged, but Damien grabbed his arm. "Don't make this any worse," he hissed. "It's over. Just leave."

Jim shrugged out of his grasp. "Thanks a lot. I'll see both of you in hell."

"Don't be a sore loser," Lisa taunted.

"Lisa," Damien cautioned.

He felt a presence behind him and turned to meet his father's eyes.

"Well done, son," Sebastian Sinclair said. "See you back at the office." He patted him on the back, bustling out of the courtroom.

Fingering her pearls, Lisa smiled and leaned against the table. "Thank you, Damien. You pretty much handed me Jim's balls on a silver platter. I see a nice vacation in my near future. Maybe someplace warm, like Belize."

"Just doing my job. Enjoy your trip." Damien placed his file folders in his briefcase, lining them up perfectly. He tucked his Montblanc pen in the side pocket. He never put a pen in his shirt pocket; it ruined the line of the coat.

"You worked so hard, you deserve a vacation, too." Lisa ran her manicured hand down the sleeve of his jacket. "Crazy rumors are swirling around the country club. One says you and Lauren are engaged, but another says you're no longer together. And now that I'm free and single…" She bit her lip and gazed up at him, the implication more than clear.

Damien smiled. No way in hell would he get mixed up with her. While she'd hidden her tracks better than her ex-husband had, he had no doubt she'd done just as much cheating in that marriage.

"I don't discuss my personal life, and I don't mix business with pleasure," he told her. "Shall we?" He motioned her toward the door.

She sighed. As they walked through the courthouse, several people stopped to speak to him. To his annoyance, Lisa stayed right by his side. He'd just gotten rid of one clingy woman; the last thing he needed was another.

As they finally exited through the front door, she asked, "Walk me to my car?"

He had an appointment with Samson for a haircut in thirty minutes, but his mother would roll in her grave if he wasn't a gentleman. Smoothly, he hid his irritation. "Of course. Where are you parked?"

She laughed and pointed. "I used Jim's handicap placard, over there."

Damien's lips thinned. There were people who genuinely needed that spot.

Downtown Atlanta was bustling as it neared noon. As they started down the stairs, a taxi leaned on its horn and a bus pulled away from the bus stop, leaving behind its distasteful fumes.

He loved the energy of the downtown area.

"You can't leave me!"

A shot rang out, and Lisa sagged against him. Around them, people began shouting and running. Damien caught Lisa and turned to see Jim sobbing, still pointing the gun.

Another shot rang out, and his world exploded.

Chapter One

"You're going to be all right, son."

Damien heard his father's voice from far away. *Where am I?* A cloud of pain enveloped him. Somebody pried his left eyelid open, and he was blinded by a light. The darkness returned, only to have the other eyelid opened and the bright light again. Somebody moaned.

Or was that me? Just leave me the hell alone.

Sleep offered a respite from the discomfort…

A soft hand held his, and the sound of a woman crying pulled him out of murky oblivion. He squeezed the feminine fingers, trying to stop the crying.

"Don't leave me," a voice whispered.

Despite his current state, he could tell this wasn't Lauren or Renata.

He forced his eyes open, but the room spun, and the pounding in his head made him feel seasick. Before he'd even had much of a chance to focus, he closed his eyes again.

But he knew what he'd seen.

Why is Harley here?

The next voice he heard was his younger brother Angel's. "Damn, you'll do anything for a headline."

Annoying little shit.

Damien attempted to roll over but gave up as another wave of nausea engulfed him.

"I hardly think that's appropriate," Dad replied.

Damien opened his eyes and blinked, trying to get the room to focus. His mouth was dry, and his voice sounded as gravelly as it felt. "Where am I? What happened?"

His brother frowned. "Is that normal, Dad?"

"Why don't you go find Maggie and quit bothering your brother?" As usual, his father sounded annoyed with his youngest son.

Angel stood with his hands stuffed in his pockets, looking like he wished he was anywhere but here…wherever here was.

He also looked different, more put together than usual.

"What happened to your dreads, Angel?"

"I cut them off—last month for mom's funeral…" He frowned. "Dad? This isn't normal. Do we need to get a nurse or a doctor or something?" Angel ran a hand through his blond hair, the sleeve of his shirt slipping to reveal his tattoos.

Mom's funeral? Damien rubbed his eyes with the heels of his hands. He tried to sit up, but the room spun, and he found himself tethered to machines.

"Easy now. You're in the hospital, Damien. You were shot yesterday after you won the Viner case."

His father looked terrible. His gray hair was uncombed, and it stood on end as if he'd run his hands through it. Damien couldn't remember the last time he'd seen his father unshaven.

The memories became clearer. "That's right, Mom died…cancer." He frowned. "The Viner case…" He remembered going into court… but nothing else. "I won?"

"You're Perry Mason. Do you ever lose?" his brother quipped.

His father glared at Angel. "Yes, you won. As you were leaving the courthouse, Jim Viner shot Lisa, then you, before killing himself."

"Shot? Lisa? Is she okay?"

His father shook his head. "She didn't make it."

"Dead? Both of them? He shot me? I'm not dead?" He felt like he was in a parallel universe. These things didn't happen to *him*.

"The bullet hit your shoulder, but the doctors are more concerned about the fact that you hit your head pretty hard. Thank God, you're going to be okay," his father reassured him.

Angel grinned. "The Devil didn't want to deal with the Demon in hell."

"This is the neatest room on this floor," the night nurse teased. "Keep this up and you'll have a job in housekeeping."

"I like things neat. And orderly." Damien bit back his observation that her hair clips were two different colors. "What's the date today? You forgot to mark it." He pointed at the dry erase board that listed his nurses' names and had the ridiculous faces for how he was feeling—which was like shit warmed over.

"It's New Year's Eve. You've been here three *long* days." She nodded at the clock next to the television mounted on the wall. "And it's almost midnight. I can bring you some apple juice to ring in the new year, if you'd like. Or you have the orange juice and cranberry juice left over from your *breakfasts*."

He glared. "Yippee."

"Hey, what can I say? We love to live it up around here. Do you need anything?" She shoved the bedside computer against the wall.

"The food here is inedible."

The evil nurse laughed. "All hospital food is. You think I haven't heard that complaint before?"

"I want to go home."

"Got big plans?"

"No. I mean, if I wasn't stuck in here, I'd be at a party…" With people he didn't really give a shit about. But even that would be preferable to this mind-numbing, endless boredom.

"We want you to go home, too. Call me if you need me."

She left with a wave, leaving him wondering whether she'd meant it in a we're-sick-of-you way, or if that was just a nursey-reassuring thing to say. He hadn't been *that* bad of a patient. He'd only sent his breakfast back once this morning.

Doesn't anyone know how to scramble an egg?

He sighed. Having a severe concussion, he'd been forced to lie in a dark room, forbidden to watch television or read. He couldn't concentrate on an audio book, and he found music depressing, it reminded him of his mother. This left him alone with his thoughts, which were anything but pleasant. Like, why had he survived? He hadn't particularly liked Lisa, but she was *dead*. And he felt guilty as hell. Over and over he'd tried to review the case, but pieces were missing, and Dad had refused to bring the files for him, citing the stupid order to rest.

He'd never forgive himself for missing how mentally unstable Jim was. He should've protected his client. And Dad said the resulting publicity had only increased the demand for his services as a divorce lawyer, which he found more than a little disturbing. Yesterday a shrink had come to see him and talked about survivor's guilt and PTSD.

In his opinion, shrinks were only good for swaying juries. He'd politely taken her business card and tossed it in the garbage after the woman left.

Why hadn't Lauren even called to check on him? Sure, she'd broken things off the day after Christmas — probably underwhelmed by her gifts, and he'd been glad, relieved even — but they'd dated on and off since high school, and her father was part of the same law firm. Being in Paris was no excuse. Hell, Renata was visiting her family in Brazil, and she'd sent flowers and called. Unlike Lauren, Renata was almost the perfect woman — uncomplicated and fine with a scratch-the-itch relationship that had no permanent ties. He hadn't wanted ties since...

Nope, not going there.

Staring at the ceiling, he wished for the millionth time they'd replace all of the tiles. The one with the stain on it bothered him. And what *caused* that stain? *Yuck.*

He picked up his phone, tempted to call Angel. Since Mom's death, he'd grown closer to his younger brother. He and his girlfriend, Maggie, had left yesterday. Angel didn't like hospitals — or Dad. It was likely Maggie who'd made him come in the first place. Before they left, they'd invited him to come to their bed and breakfast on the lake in some Podunk town in Alabama. *Dammit.* He should know the name. Angel's friend Emma Devine lived there, too...*Shit, what's her new last name?* He added those to the growing list of stuff he couldn't remember. Regardless, he didn't think he'd ever be that bored...

The door opened, and he bit back his groan. *Fuck, now what?*

How did they expect anyone to ever get well in a hospital when they never left you alone? He hoped it wasn't for more damn blood-work. He looked like a junkie. The nurse had changed his dressing earlier...

A hand holding a cell phone appeared and the sound of "Auld Lang Syne" filled the room. To his surprise, Harley Taylor crept in and closed the door behind her. She was the last person he'd expected see. Her parents worked for his, and they'd basically grown up together, but until she came home to help care for his dying mother before Christmas, he'd had little contact with her for more than ten years.

Damien frowned. "Why are you barefoot and wearing sunglasses?"

"Shhh, I'm incognito. I slipped by the nurse's desk. I think they're having a party in the break room, judging by the laughter. The rest of this place is quiet as a morgue. Oops, sorry. I mean...Um, never mind." She picked up the two leftover juices and two Styrofoam cups. Shrugging out of her coat, she plopped down in the chair beside his bed. She shivered and propped her bare feet on the mattress.

"Hospital floors are disgusting. Get your nasty feet off my bed, and get a pair of socks out of that cubby hole they call a closet."

"My feet are not nasty. Do you like this color polish?" She wiggled her dirty, but red-polished toes in his face.

"Gross. Why are you here?" he grumbled as she dug a pair of black socks out of the closet.

Twisting her long blond hair into a bun, she took a pen out of her purse and used it to secure her hair as if it were a single chopstick. She sat back down, wiggling her now-covered feet.

"That does feel better, thanks. I, uh, broke my heel." Digging through a handbag the size of a mini-suitcase, she pulled out the broken shoe and its mate and threw them in the garbage. She continued rummaging. "I thought I'd stop by because no one should be alone on New Year's Eve. I knew your dad was at a party—he looked handsome in his tux, by the way—and my parents are out on the town and staying overnight somewhere. They said having a kid back home 'cramped their style.'" She wrinkled her nose.

Elise and John? He shook his head, not wanting to think about their "cramped style"; they were like second parents to him. And Harley was hardly a kid, she was two years younger than he was, which made her twenty-nine.

"Why aren't you with Claire?" he asked her. Claire Lassiter was Harley's best friend. Her parents were good friends with his, and he saw her several times a year at different events.

"Because she's with Charlie. Who wants to be a third wheel? Woot, there it is!" Smiling widely, she pulled out a miniature bottle of Grey Goose. "It won't be enough to get pissed because we'll have to split it, but bottoms up! Cranberry or orange juice?"

"Isn't this against the rules?" His eyes darted to the door.

She shrugged. "Remember the time we snuck into your dad's liquor cabinet?"

"That wasn't me; that was Angel. And he was only twelve!"

"That's right. Of course it wasn't you. You *always* live by the rules." She studiously poured half the vodka into each of the Styrofoam cups.

Was she being snarky?

"Choose your poison, Damien Daredevil," she said, not bothering to look at him.

Definitely snarky. He took the orange juice. "Take off those sunglasses; you look ridiculous. It's practically midnight."

"I think they make me look like Holly Golightly from *Breakfast at Tiffany's.* Your black silk pajamas make you look like a young Hugh Hefner. Pretend we're at a costume party."

He raised one eyebrow. Her dress was black, but the similarity to Audrey Hepburn ended there. Like her Norwegian-born mother, Harley's skin was fair and her hair naturally platinum blond. She squirmed under his perusal.

Something clattered outside the door, and he jumped. Laughter followed.

"It's midnight!" Touching her cup to his, Harley quickly downed her cranberry and vodka. "Happy New Year, Sin."

She was the only one who still called him that. He liked it only marginally better than Demon.

"Happy New Year, Harley."

With a furtive look at the door, he quickly drank his mini screwdriver. He put the cup down and stuck his shaking hand under the covers. His heart was still racing from the noise in the hallway.

"Remember how Mamma used to give us that fake champagne grape juice? I always wanted the pink, but you and our brothers insisted on the white. I was dreadfully outnumbered as the only girl in the bunch."

Damien nodded. He didn't really relish the thought of tripping down memory lane. Not with Harley.

The silence grew awkward.

"So, you're really okay?" Her voice trembled, and she reached out and smoothed the covers. "I can stay if you want me to…"

"I'm fine. Thanks for stopping by."

She stood. "Well, I, um, guess I'll, uh, head home. When do you get out of here?"

"Not soon enough."

"Damien?"

"Yes?"

"I don't suppose you have some cash on you, do you?"

"No, why?" He sat up. "Take off those glasses." The only person who ever hit him up for cash was Angel, back when he was using. And he could always tell by his eyes if he was high.

"Never mind!" Harley bent over to take off his socks, and he grabbed her huge sunglasses.

His shoulder protested, but he ignored the pain. He slumped back in bed, horrified. "Holy shit, Harley. What happened?"

The blue eye that wasn't blackened and swollen shut filled with tears. "It's nothing, just a little black eye," she said. "It's late, and I need to get home, but I don't have enough money for a ride."

"Harley." He gentled his voice, but his heart hammered. As a divorce lawyer, he'd seen plenty of pictures of battered women. "Who did this to you? Have you been to the police?"

"Nobody. I tripped. Look, I need to go. I'll, um, find a way home…"

He reached for his cell phone on the bedside table and sent a quick text. His phone beeped an immediate answer.

"Don't you have a credit card?" he asked.

"I only use cash. I kept losing my debit card and ran into trouble with my credit. What are you doing? Who are you texting?" Her voice quivered.

Now that he really looked at her, she seemed incredibly fragile.

"I don't have any cash. Dad took my wallet home. There will be a limo downstairs in ten minutes to take you home—or better yet, to the police. Has anyone checked your eye? I'll page my nurse."

"No! Stop. I mean, thank you. I just want to go home. A limo is a bit much. A ride share or cab would've been fine. I'll pay you back, when I hit the lottery."

"Ever the optimist. It's not necessary to pay me back. That's what friends do. And put the socks back on. Do you want to die of some horrid disease?"

"Thanks, Sin. Someone would think you care."

She was out the door before he could reply.

Chapter TWO

*W*hat was that?

Damien gripped the bathroom door and listened, his heart racing like a meth addict's. He'd been released late yesterday but had been too tired to shower when he got home — and that was saying something. Pneumonia had delayed his release, and his ability to get a good night's sleep, by a week.

Dammit!

The sound came again. It wasn't his imagination. Rubbing the annoying stubble on his jaw, his heart hammered as the female shriek grew louder. Why was this happening right outside his door? That shrill sound likely just sent every dog in the building running for cover. Should he call security? The police? The voices rose.

Wrapping a towel around his waist, he padded through the living area, now recognizing the woman's voice. *What the hell is Harley doing here? How did she get past security and all the way up to my floor?* He hadn't heard a word from her in a week. Her father, who was his father's estate manager, had driven him home from the hospital yesterday, but Damien hadn't known how to ask casually if Harley was okay after her New Year's Eve black eye.

He threw open the front door to find Harley and Jerry, the three-hundred-pound security guard, escalating their argument to a roar reminiscent of a packed SEC football stadium. If asked who might win, he'd place his money on Harley without thinking twice.

"Stop!" His command might as well have been whispered for all the attention it received.

Shrugging out of her coat, Harley threw it on top of a duffel, a rolled-up yoga mat, and her purse.

"Don't tell me I can't go in there." Her blue eyes flashed as she pointed at Jerry's massive chest. "You're not the boss of me, you wanker. If you lay one finger on me, I'll grab your balls and twist them so hard you'll sing soprano for the rest of your life. Do you hear me, you *drittsekk?*"

Whoa. She'd just called Jerry a dick and an asshole. Whenever she mixed British and Norwegian insults, it meant trouble. Damien knew this from experience.

"Miss, you can't just barge in here. We have protocols to be followed. Even if Mr. Sinclair gave you the code to get up here, you have to check in with security first."

"*Ms.* Get in this century. Damien, can I slap a harassment lawsuit on him or something?"

"What? No! Calm down. And how did you get the code to get up here?"

"Mamma gave it to me."

Her chest heaved, drawing Damien's attention to the tight blue T-shirt that read *Bite Me*. He snapped his eyes back to Harley's flushed face. Tossing her blond braid over her shoulder, she looked like a modern-day Viking goddess.

"Please tell this *faux po* I'm not a criminal. I'm your *friend.*" Wide blue eyes beseeched him to intervene.

Get ready for it…here it comes… Sure enough, her lower lip poked out into a slight pout. Dammit, even as a kid he'd been a sucker for that look.

Jerry's chest puffed, and he spoke through clenched teeth. "Look, *Ms.* I'm not an officer. I'm chief of security—"

Damien winced in sympathy for the unsuspecting chump. *Here we go.*

"You call this security? *Puh-lease.*" She rolled her eyes. "How much does Mr. Sinclair pay in association fees? You probably need to give him a hefty refund. I mean, if I can breach your so-called *security*, it's pretty pathetic, don't you think? After all, I'm just a *girl*."

Ouch. She'd even used finger quotes to punch her sarcasm.

"Now, wait just a minute…" Jerry shifted, pulling himself taller as he placed his hands on his expansive waist.

Damien bit his tongue to keep from laughing. The scene reminded him of that cartoon where the rooster berates the chicken hawk. But unlike the cartoon, it wasn't likely to end in laughs if he didn't intervene. The bewildered guard didn't stand a chance against Harley. It was time to intercede before the man either had a stroke or physically hauled her off the premises.

"I've got it from here, Jerry. Thank you." Damien met the defeated man's frustrated gaze with a look of apology.

"I'm sorry about this, Mr. Sinclair. I don't know how she got past the desk downstairs." Running a beefy hand through his thinning brown hair, Jerry shuffled back and forth.

"No problem. I apologize for the disruption. Next time Ms. Taylor visits, she'll be sure to stop at the desk, per protocol." He gave Harley a pointed look, then nodded curtly to dismiss the guard.

"You're not my father. I can give my own apologies."

Jerry gave her a smug smile. "Apology accepted."

Harley's eyes zeroed in on the departing guard like a sniper ready to pull the trigger. Damien gave her a gentle push toward the door before round two started.

"Wanker."

Damien raised his brow, unsure if she'd directed the insult toward him or Jerry. With a loud *humph* of displeasure, she blew her bangs out of her eyes. Picking up her things, she bounced through the door and into his penthouse like she owned the goddamned place.

He closed the door and followed her into the living area. Standing with his hands on his hips, he used silence as his weapon of choice.

Harley paled, and she bit her lip as she eyed his colorful bruising and healing wound. He crossed his arms, feeling exposed and uncomfortable. She looked away for a second, blinking as if something was in her eye.

He frowned. *Is she upset?*

Before he could ponder the thought, she started in on him.

"Damn, Sin. You look like hell. Go put some clothes on, for heaven's sake. What if that towel falls? I don't wanna see your dangly bits."

I look like hell? He noticed she'd carefully concealed the remainder of her black eye.

"Why are you here?"

After she'd left him at the hospital, he'd had an uncomfortable night recalling their shared past. He'd done a careful self-check to put her firmly back behind a closed door.

He pressed a remote, and the blinds rose to unveil a spectacular view of downtown Atlanta. Refusing to get dressed just to irritate her, he sat on the gray couch. He stopped short of propping his feet on the chrome-and-glass coffee table, not wanting to risk flashing his "dangly bits."

Where does she get off calling them bits, anyway? She knows better. Don't go there...

When he looked over, a definite smirk lingered on her full mouth.

Do her lips still taste like cotton candy? Dammit. *Where the hell did that thought come from?*

He looked out the window for a second as he gathered his scattered wits. That pain medication must still be fucking with his mind. No, he hadn't had any in a couple of days...

"I'm gonna crash here for a bit," she announced. "I'm worried—um, I mean, your father and my mother are worried about you being alone. They sent me to help. You know, just until you're back on your feet. Mamma said your housekeeper quit because she couldn't handle all your OCD quirks."

His gaze returned to hers. She smiled as she plopped on the couch next to him.

"W-What?" Mystified, his mouth dropped open.

"You heard me. You almost *died.* You need help." She stroked his leather sofa like it was a cat as she looked around his living area.

What the fuck?

He snapped out of his stupor. "So they sent *you?*" he croaked. "And I'm fine."

Harley couldn't take care of a houseplant, much less another human being. Hell, when they were kids, her goldfish would've died if he hadn't fed it.

And what about whatever happened to her on New Year's Eve?

Her brows knit together. "Of course. Who knows you better than me? I'll just ignore your unreasonable demands. Plus, I can cook, clean, and do errands. Your wish will be my command—as long as I want to do it."

"I'm yours, Damien, always and forever." The memory of her naked flesh beneath his surfaced. *That's over. Keep her in the friend zone.*

He jumped as she ran a finger over his injured shoulder.

"Stop it! You know I'm ticklish." He shoved her hand away. "I don't need help, and I want to be left alone. I'm perfectly capable of taking care of myself." Frustrated, he pinched the bridge of his nose.

"Oh, sure, I just bet." Harley hopped off the couch and marched into the kitchen.

Reluctantly, he followed, watching her rummage through his somewhat bare, but perfectly organized pantry.

She shook her head and snorted. "Do you plan to live on air? Seriously? You take the labels off your canned goods, print the names on them, and line them up in alphabetical order?"

"What? I just got out of the damn hospital. I like them to match, and of course they're alphabetized, how else would you know what's in there?" he mumbled.

If his housekeeper hadn't quit just before Christmas, he wouldn't be in this position. His father must have mentioned it to Elise, Harley's mother.

She glanced over at the refrigerator and raised one eyebrow. Its glass doors betrayed its almost-empty state. Throwing open the door, she dove in, pulling out rotten food.

"Ew!"

He sighed.

She turned and motioned at the food—if you could still call it that—now scattered across the counter. "Mamma would be horrified. Look at this! All you have to eat are toaster tarts, an outdated carton of milk, some horrible moldy science experiment, frozen pizza pockets, and a jar of peanut butter, no bread. Who eats this stuff?"

She wrinkled her nose, dropping the Ming Dynasty-era Chinese leftovers into the garbage. Then she poured the clabbered milk down the sink, gagging at the stench.

His skin crawled as he surveyed the mess on his spotless counters. "*I do,* and I have access to home delivery of anything I want to eat. Put that stuff back the way you found it and go home. I don't need help —"

"You're getting fat."

Was she smirking? *Definitely.* And after she'd foraged through the refrigerator, it was obvious she wasn't wearing a bra.

He sucked in air like a drowning man. *Jesus, what the hell is wrong with me?* Goddamned celibacy, that was the problem. *When will Renata be back?*

Wait. What the fuck? *Did she just call me* fat?

"I beg your pardon?" He used the voice that made witnesses squirm under cross-examination. And the arctic death glare he cast would've made anyone else turn and run — or at the very least stutter an apology.

Not Harley. She leaned in and pinched the skin above his towel.

"You're getting soft in the middle. I know you've been laid up on your arse in the hospital, but eating junk food isn't going to help. That's where I come in: Harley to the rescue. Lucky for you, I'm still between jobs." She smiled, patted his cheek, and breezed past him, headed toward the living room.

As far as he knew, she was *perpetually* between jobs. She had the attention span of a four-year-old. Damien stormed down the hall into his bedroom, swearing under his breath. In his closet, he pulled on a pair of black jeans — going commando in his haste, something he *never* did. Perusing the row of black, gray, and white T-shirts folded with military precision, he decided on a gray one. Before putting it on, he paused to look at himself in the full-length mirror.

Getting soft in the middle? She's insane. He sucked in his stomach. He could probably stand to lose a couple of pounds. Elise's holiday goodies, followed by his hospitalization, had taken a toll. Okay, maybe five tops.

Sonofabitch, she's right. I'm a porker. He groaned and ran a hand through his hair, which was in desperate need of a cut.

He winced as he shrugged into the T-shirt and began mentally preparing his argument to get Harley to leave as he returned to the living room. He found her standing at the window, watching the traffic below. Her pale blond hair shimmered in the sunlight, giving her an angelic appearance.

Her devil horns must be hidden.

Collapsing on the couch, he reached for a remote, and Albinoni's "Adagio in G Minor" filled the room.

"Don't you have anything from this century you can play?"

"If you don't like it, leave."

"It isn't like you're seventy years old," she grumbled, sitting next to him and curling her feet under her butt. "Even your father listens to Aerosmith when he's by himself."

"He does?" He gently but firmly pushed her feet off the couch.

Lifting her red tennis shoe toward his face she grumbled, "They're clean."

He shook his head.

"Fine, Calvin Clean." Kicking off her shoes, she tucked her feet back underneath her.

They sat in a companionable silence for a few moments, listening to the haunting music.

"I always think of your mother when I hear this music," she commented.

He gave her a sad smile. "Me, too."

Sometimes Harley surprised him with her sweetness, like when she'd sat with him right after his mom died, and stopped by the hospital so he wouldn't be alone on New Year's Eve. Usually she was hell on wheels.

Good God, I'm becoming a sap.

"I'm glad you got shot after she died." She winced. "I mean, I'm not glad you got *shot...* " Her face flushed. "But I don't think your mother could've taken the stress. She was so weak at the end."

Harley had been a huge help in caring for Mom during her losing battle with cancer last month. "I know what you meant."

Her gaze met his with a shared sorrow. She leaned over and wrapped her arms around his neck, resting her head on his good shoulder.

"Please let me stay for a bit. Everyone's worried about you."

He sighed. Had he ever really had a choice? "Fine."

She sat up and smiled. "Great! So, ready to go grocery shopping? Or do you just wanna trust me?"

"Trust *you?* Hell, no. I'm not eating tofu and granola."

"Whatever. Which room is mine?"

Damien frowned. "You do realize staying 'a bit' doesn't mean moving in, right?"

"I don't anticipate being here more than a couple of months."

"A couple of months? I was thinking a couple of days."

She shook her head, slowly.

This must be what it felt like on the Titanic, *knowing drowning was inevitable. Dammit.* She should seriously consider a job as a union negotiator or lobbyist.

He sighed. "Down the hall. But only for one week. I'm going to go brush my teeth and comb my hair."

"Okay, O benevolent boss." Bouncing off the couch, her eyes sparkled as she moved past him.

He rolled his eyes. Harley and her alliterations…*Shit, have I just been played?* He ran a hand through his hair. If he had to deal with Harley, he'd need to be on top of his game.

Damien went to his bathroom and grunted at his image in the mirror. He looked like a refugee from the zombie apocalypse. He brushed his teeth and haphazardly ran a comb through his hair, leaving it damp. It hurt too damn much to do anything else. He rubbed his hand across his two-day beard. First thing tomorrow he'd visit Samson for a haircut and shave before going in to the office.

Harley peeked into the guest room and shook her head. Everything in Damien's home was a muted shade of gray, white, or black, with a little chrome and glass for accent. *Really, the man needs some color in his life.* The room was large, with a balcony view, and at least twice as big as her room at home. She threw her things on the bed. Standing at the window, she took a moment to collect her crazy, convoluted feelings.

Seeing his injured shoulder had unnerved her more than she'd anticipated. When he was in the hospital, it had been covered by a bandage or his pajama shirt. It took every ounce of self-control she possessed not to break down crying in front of him. A few months ago, the thought of him dying was unthinkable. Two weeks ago, it had almost happened.

When her father told her Damien had been shot, it was the second worst day of her life. Losing a loved one was her greatest fear. That night, when she'd been allowed to visit him after his surgery, she'd wept the entire ten minutes. As she was leaving, his eyes had fluttered open and he'd squeezed her hand, as if *he* were comforting *her*.

Harley began unpacking. She needed to focus. Yesterday she'd overheard Mr. Sinclair telling Mamma that Damien had refused to see a psychiatrist. Worried, she'd decided to check on him herself. It wasn't like she had a real job. And her parents had been hinting it was time she move on and be an adult. Which was true…But she'd be able to adult much better after she made sure Damien truly was okay.

He meant more to her than he'd ever realize. But her dreams were carefully tucked away, and had been for years. Still, she couldn't begin to imagine the world without Damien Sinclair in it. She'd loved him since she was five years old.

Everyone knew that.

Except Damien.

Chapter
Three

"Not no, but *hell, no*. I escaped death once; I refuse to risk it again."

"Shut up, Damien Downer. You're the one who said you *didn't* almost die. We *have* to take my van. I'm in a no-parking zone. See? I already have a ticket. Can you pull some strings and take care of it?" Harley batted her eyelashes like some sort of demented Southern belle.

"Do you have something in your eyes? Give me the keys." He held out his hand, giving her his best lawyer death stare.

"*Oh, hell no,*" she mimicked. "It's my car."

A couple of older women walked by and smiled. Damien thought they lived in his building but couldn't be sure. A white-haired man wandered up beside them.

"Which way to the T?" he asked.

"The T? I don't think you're supposed to be out here, Mr. Gavosovich. Where's your daughter?" Damien replied. He only knew the man's name because he talked nonstop about the same shit every time he saw him.

"Who?" His white brows drew together over his dark eyes.

"Your daughter." Damien couldn't remember the woman's name and impatiently motioned to Jerry. He didn't have time to deal with crazy *and* Harley.

Harley hooked her arm with the confused Mr. Gavosovich's.

"What is the T?" she asked as she guided him toward Jerry.

"The subway. I need to get back home to Lynn."

"Is Lynn your wife?"

"No! It's where I live. Lynn, Massachusetts."

Jerry met Harley and took the confused man's other arm.

"Jerry will make sure you get there." She kissed the older man on the cheek before returning to her van. "Where will they take him?" she asked, biting her lip as she watched Jerry cajole the old man inside.

"He lives on the floor below me with his family. Give me your keys."

"Is he okay? And why can't I drive?"

"He has dementia, I believe. Fine. Pay your own damn ticket."

Damien put two fingers to his lips and blew a loud New York whistle. To his surprise, it worked. A cab pulled to the curb, screeching to a halt.

"Okay, okay. You can drive Velma." She slapped her keys in his hand.

"Velma? You named this camper on crack Velma?"

"It's not a camper. It's Velma Van. Don't you think it's cute? Come on, you loved *Scooby Doo* as much as I did. Like the artwork Angel threw up on it? He did it when he was here after you got shot. He's so talented. It's exactly what I wanted."

Damien looked over the vintage VW van painted with bright, retro-looking graffiti. *Throw up* described exactly how he felt about being seen in the ridiculous thing.

"Uh, we can take the Jag. It needs to be run," he offered in one last, desperate attempt to retain control. His car was his favorite toy. Black and sleek, the motor purred like a well-satisfied woman.

Harley reached over and plucked the ticket off the windshield. Another older couple walked by and nodded before entering his building.

"Do you live in a retirement home or something? Don't be hatin' on the van. I camped out on the beach in it last summer." She frowned and read the traffic violation. "Yeesh, I wasn't in there that long. They never cut me any slack. This is my fourth one since I've been back in Atlanta."

She handed him the ticket, which he shoved in his pocket.

"No, I don't live in a retirement home. But there are a number of retired people who live here. It's nice and quiet."

"How old are you again?"

"Thirty-one." Damien held out his hand. She knew damn well how old he was. *I like peace and quiet. What's the big deal?*

Rummaging in her purse, she offered him a piece of bubble gum, which he declined. Gum smacking followed smoking on his list of annoying habits. Next was chattering.

Jerry returned and stood at the front door, glaring at Harley. Damien decided it best to move the damn thing. The poor guard could only take so much. Plus, he didn't relish the thought of facing the homeowner's association and trying to explain Harley Taylor. There was simply no easy way to explain her.

He opened the door and groaned. "Was Angel on an acid trip? I thought he was clean."

The inside of the bus was also painted in bright colors.

"Of course not. You know how he and your Dad tangle. This kept him busy when he wasn't visiting you in the hospital. He had a blast, and it spared your Dad's garage. Remember what he did last time?" She shrugged out of her hoodie, tossing it on the floor.

Buckling up, Damien started the van and jumped when the music blasted from the radio. He turned it down, only to have Harley crank it back up. She sang along with some woman about her humps. Pinning her with his patented *shut-the-fuck-up* look, he waited for her to stop caterwauling. His look was famous. He used it to turn witnesses on the stand into quivering puddles of confusion.

Ignoring him, Harley had the audacity to smile and blow a bubble.

Sighing, he pulled out, and she pointed for him to turn left from the right lane.

"This isn't the way to the grocery store."

"We're going to that new organic store."

He grimaced. When she hit a particularly painful note, he mentally added off-key singing to his list of annoying habits.

"What? You don't like The Black Eyed Peas? This song is a classic."

"Who?" He returned the obscene gesture flipped by the driver he'd cut off.

Harley turned the radio down. "The Black Eyed Peas, the group singing on the radio."

"Never heard of them. I thought black-eyed peas were those disgusting legumes you're supposed to eat on New Year's Day."

"You need to expand your horizons and listen to something besides classical music and the stupid Rolling Stones. Besides, everyone knows The Beatles were better."

Turning the radio back up, she sang at the top of her lungs. His eyes were drawn like a magnet to *Bite Me* as she jiggled and bounced along with the song. Tits like those should be illegal; he was at risk of distracted driving.

"I do listen to other music," he protested, trying to keep his eyes on the road. He'd forgotten how she brought out his argumentative side. Quarrelling with her when they were kids had helped hone his skills for the courtroom.

"And The Stones are the best rock and roll band. *Ever,*" he added.

"What*ever*." She rolled her eyes, her head nodding with the beat of the bass.

Did she really just roll her eyes over The Rolling Stones?

Not having it in him to argue over music, he turned the radio down and changed the subject. "How are Byron and Keats?" He'd always liked her older brothers.

"They're fine. Keats defends his thesis in a few months for his doctorate in English. Byron just got promoted to detective. I really think Keats should have majored in Japanese or mathematics. English was too obvious with his name. I don't know why Mamma allowed Daddy to choose our ridiculous names. Or why she didn't at least insist I be named Elizabeth Barrett Browning Taylor or Shelley Taylor. I mean, seriously? They named me after Daddy's stupid motorcycle and a poet."

"I never knew you hated your name. It could've been worse."

Harley snorted. "What could possibly be worse than Harley Blake Taylor?"

He grinned. "Ready?"

"Tell me."

"Kawasaki Coleridge Taylor."

Harley guffawed and drum-rolled the dash. He chuckled along with her. It felt good laughing together, just like old times.

After parking at the grocery store, he eased out of the car, trying not to jar his shoulder. He still managed to move it wrong. *Sonofabitch.*

"Are you okay?" She grabbed his hand and peered up at him.

Damien pulled her braid. "I'm fine. Let's get this over with. Where's your jacket?"

"In the car, *Daddy*."

"Brat."

He looked at the size of the store and sighed. It was huge, and he was already exhausted. He couldn't even remember the last time he'd been in a grocery store. It must've been with Lauren right before Thanksgiving, when she'd insisted on trying to cook. The meal had been memorable, but not in a good way, and they'd ended up ordering Chinese. Prior to quitting, his housekeeper had shopped for him.

Pushing the cart, he followed Harley through the store, offering a clipped *yes* or *no* to her ideas for meals. Standing in the frozen food section, he looked around, frowning. *What the hell?*

"What's wrong?"

"Where are the damn pizza pockets?"

"Right there." She pointed to some healthy version of his favorite snack.

"Those look disgusting. Where are the real ones?"

She patted his back. "They don't carry processed food, Sin. It's bad for you. Everything here is organic and free of additives."

She spoke to him like he was three years old, which was fucking annoying. *I'm an adult, dammit.*

"Oh, yeah? Well, I bet it all tastes like grass, and not the illegal kind." He sulked.

"Ha! How would you know?"

"I went to college."

"Uh-huh. I bet you never got your nose out of a book long enough to smoke a joint, much less eat a Jamaican brownie."

It irked him how well she knew him. It could've happened…

Not really, you're boring as fuck.

He opened a freezer door, picked up a gallon of organic, gluten-free, probably tasteless coffee ice cream, and threw it in the cart. Harley started to protest, but he raised one eyebrow and used his best badass prosecutor glare.

"Fine," she huffed. "Look, why don't you go have a cup of real coffee and wait on me? I have to completely restock your pantry and fridge. This could take a while."

Damien swung around without hesitation, but warned, "Leave the ice cream."

He took a complimentary cup of fair trade coffee and sank onto the bench, feeling like a chewed up, spit out piece of gum. *God, I'm weak.* Not that he would ever admit that to Harley. If he did, he'd never hear the end of it.

A loud bang startled him. His heart started pumping like he'd just run a four-hundred-meter sprint, and his limbs felt like lead. No matter how hard he tried, he couldn't seem to get enough air into his lungs. He whirled around until he spotted an employee shoving shopping carts together, but his discomfort didn't ease.

I'm dying. I'm fuckin' going to die in a goddamned grocery store that doesn't even carry real pizza pockets.

The bubble of panic tightened his chest and blurred his vision. Feeling lightheaded and nauseated, his hand shook, and he spilled the coffee. He slammed the cup into the garbage, rubbing his damp shirt and jeans, praying no one noticed.

Where the hell is Harley? What's wrong with me?

Elbows on knees, he covered his eyes and struggled to collect himself. Goddammit, he was famous for his ability to work a room, or a courtroom, to his advantage. He'd hosted parties with hundreds of people. Why was he now hyperventilating in a fucking wholesome food store?

I want out, now. He looked up, searching for Harley.

Sweat dripped down his back, and the overwhelming sense of doom remained. Mopping his brow, he shrugged out of his coat and waited, clenching and unclenching his fist. Patience was not his middle name. Finally, he spotted her wheeling the cart around the corner, almost hitting three people in her haste. If he got out of here without having to defend her in a lawsuit, it would be a fucking miracle. She was as flighty as ever. His eyes followed *Bite Me* as she bounced toward him.

His only rational thought was to wish she'd go back down the frozen food aisle.

Harley rushed through the store, stealing furtive glances at Damien sitting on the bench. Pale and shaky, he watched her with an unnerving intensity.

Glaring, he mouthed: *Hurry.*

Guilt pricked her conscience as she scurried to finish the shopping, more than once almost running over someone on the way. It hadn't crossed her mind to ask him if he felt well enough to do this today. *Bloody hell, I bet he isn't supposed to be driving, either.*

Damien met her at the checkout, and she breathed easier seeing some color return to his face. His eyes darted back and forth, seeming to scrutinize everyone in the store. She nudged him when it was time to pay, and he jumped, clearly startled. For a brief second, he looked confused, before pulling out his wallet and scanning his debit card.

"I'll drive home. I don't think you should be shifting. It's too hard," Harley offered, wheeling the cart toward the van.

"Yeah, it is kind of hard." He scanned the parking lot like he was some sort of Secret Service agent.

"That's what she said," Harley quipped, laughing when his face flushed.

Ignoring her joke, he muttered, "Never mind. I'll manage. Better to arrive alive."

"Don't say that; it's bad luck. You have no sense of adventure. Live like a pirate. You already look like one with your hair and scruffy face. I like it not cut so short."

"I don't think the life expectancy of pirates was very long. I'll drive."

They loaded the groceries.

"But it's my car. Why can't I drive?"

"Because you can't drive worth a damn."

"Fine." She sat in the passenger seat, slamming the door shut. "When's the last time you rode with me?"

"Um, I don't know…ten years ago, or more?" He started the car, heading home.

"Thirteen years ago, when I was sixteen and you taught me how to drive a stick shift, dumbass."

"I can't imagine you've improved much."

"You certainly don't give me much credit." She wouldn't mention the number of tickets she'd received for speeding — no need to add fuel to his chauvinistic thinking. Harley cranked up the radio.

He was entirely too serious. He always had been. She blamed his parents, who'd never failed to remind him of his role as the firstborn Sinclair heir. Image was everything in their eyes. She had a sneaking suspicion they were part of the reason Damien had dumped her all those years ago. She hadn't been good enough for him, because she was the daughter of the help. Her mother managed the Sinclair household, and her father managed the estate. They lived in a house at the end of the property.

Ten minutes later, he pulled into the garage. "You go on up. I have to register your vehicle and let the front desk know you'll be here for a few days."

"Weeks."

"Days. Tim will help you load the groceries on a cart."

She listened with barely concealed mirth to his endless instructions for operating the keyless entry system on his front door and where to put every item purchased. When he'd finished, she gave him a smartass salute, laughing when he scowled. She was happy to leave Damien with the ridiculous amount of paperwork required to register one dumb car, though she wished she could see the look on Jerry's face when he realized she'd be in residence for a while.

Tim, the parking garage attendant, smiled and hurried over.

"Hi, Tim. There's no need," she told him. "I can do this."

"No, ma'am. That's what I'm here for."

He chatted affably as he helped her, and she learned he was a married college student with a baby girl arriving any day. She decided she'd crochet him a baby blanket. There was a new pattern she'd been wanting to try.

After unloading the groceries, Harley raced into Damien's room to do a little snooping. She looked around and shook her head. What should be the most intimate room of his home was cold and austere, not warm and inviting. If she didn't know it was his bedroom, she'd think it was another guest room. The only personal items within view were his violin and an out-of-date music player. There was no need to peruse his playlists. She knew full well they held nothing but The Rolling Stones and classical music.

Against the center of the wall was the largest bed she'd ever seen. Wrought black iron, with four posts, it dominated the room. *The naughty things Sin could do to me in that bed...*

Shoving the daydreams away, she ran her hand over the soft, gray duvet. On impulse, she turned the cover down and pressed her cheek to his pillow. The lingering scent of her late-night fantasies made her sigh. Damien always smelled clean and masculine with a hint of spice, reminding her of a crisp fall morning.

His bedroom overlooked the city and accessed the same balcony that ran in front of the living area and her bedroom. A treadmill stood by the door to the balcony, positioned so he could either watch the big screen television on the wall or look out over the city. Everything was neat and in order. The man even had a coin machine for his spare change.

Harley bit her lip, listening to make sure Damien hadn't returned. Not hearing anything, she tiptoed to the closet and opened the door. Slack-jawed, she stared. It was bigger than her bedroom at home.

His clothes matched his home — varying shades of black, gray, and white. Every hanger faced the same direction, and Mr. OCD had marked the rod to make sure his clothes were spaced apart in exact increments. The only color to be found in his clothing was in his silk ties, but even they were conservative in hue. Running a finger over a gray striped one, she wondered if he'd read her favorite book. She looked at the ties and back at the bed…

Harley fled the room before getting caught.

In the kitchen, she opened drawers and cabinets, familiarizing herself with where things were stored. She wasn't sure what to prepare for a late lunch or early supper. Damien had to be hungry, but she decided it would be prudent to ask and avoid the argument. As sure as she made a salad, he'd want a sandwich, just to be difficult.

Concerned, she glanced at the clock. It shouldn't be taking this long to add her vehicle to the registry — unless that daft security guard was raising hell about her staying. Would he deny her access after the incident this morning? Or did he run her tag and see she had several outstanding parking tickets?

Where is Sin?

Registering Harley's car for a lousy parking space was an ordeal Damien hadn't anticipated. It took him thirty minutes to persuade the high-strung security guard that Harley didn't pose any kind of threat to other residents or employees. Being an adept lawyer, he'd had no qualms skirting a direct assurance. Completing the paperwork, he promised to send her down with her driver's license to conclude the process. He was ninety-percent sure this was required so Jerry could read her the Riot Act in person.

Exhausted, he plodded toward the elevator, wanting nothing more than another shower and a nap. He had the energy of a hundred-year-old sloth. *Do sloths even live that long?*

A loud noise echoed through the quiet garage, and raw fear exploded in his chest. *Not again! Blood…so much blood. People running, screaming…* He dropped to the ground and spots danced before his eyes until he remembered to breathe. The sudden movement made his shoulder hurt like a motherfucker, but fear silenced his groan. Scoping out the garage in a panic, he tried to determine from where the gunshot had been fired.

Sonofabitch. He crawled to the concrete pillar and crouched beside it, trying not to wheeze like an asthmatic. Another bang sounded, followed by laughter.

The noise had been nothing more than a car door slamming shut.

His hand shook as he mopped the sweat from his brow, berating himself for being such a dumbass. It was imperative that he pull his act together before facing Harley. If she saw him trembling like a ninety-year-old Parkinson's patient, he'd have to answer twenty questions, and he wasn't up to it. Worse, she'd probably call his father. Image was everything to Sebastian Sinclair, and having a son afraid of his own shadow wasn't an option.

Damien stood and slowly made his way to the wall of the garage. He leaned against it, wanting to bash his damaged brain against the brick.

Must get my shit together, must get my shit together…

The elevator dinged, and he opened his eyes.

Fuck.

Harley stepped out, looking around, worry creasing her brow. Damien regulated his breathing with the rise and fall of *Bite Me* as he prayed for an invisibility cloak. He slid down and crawled back to the pillar, trying to hide. No such luck. When she spotted him, her eyes grew large and her hands covered her mouth.

Fuck, fuck, fuck!

"Sin!"

She ran toward him, *Bite Me* bouncing with each step.

"Are you okay? Did you fall? Oh, snap! I don't have my phone. Help! Someone, help! Call 9-1-1!" she screamed, jumping up and down, causing *Bite Me* to jiggle even more enticingly.

"Stop it!" he snapped. "I'm fine."

"I need to get you to the hospital. Don't you dare die on me!" She collapsed next to him, tears streaking down her face.

"Jesus H. Christ, Harley. *Stop.* I'm not dying!" The last thing he wanted was another scene. Jerry and Tim came running around the corner. *Fuck me to hell and back.*

Huffing and puffing after the exertion, Jerry proceeded to check his pupils. "I think we need to file an incident report, Mr. Sinclair. Are you okay? Do you need an ambulance?"

Jerry's delivery was clipped and precise. He stopped his physical assessment when Harley shoved his hands away.

"I've got this. You call the ambulance." She proceeded to mop his forehead with her shirt, giving him a flash of under boob, which didn't help his control issues.

Great, all I need is a hard-on to increase my embarrassment.

Damien brushed Harley's hands away. "I'm fine."

Jerry pulled out his phone.

"I don't need an ambulance," Damien barked.

Jerry frowned but put the phone back in his pocket. Harley continued her triage, running her hands up and down his body.

"Oh geez, Mr. Sinclair, I didn't see you fall. Please don't have them fire me; I've got to have this job to pay for school." Tim's myopic blue eyes widened behind his thick glasses.

Harley stood and poked an accusing finger into Jerry's massive chest. "You call yourself security? Why don't you do something besides walking around harassing innocent people? I told you to call an ambulance."

The massive man growled with frustration.

"I don't need an ambulance!" Damien insisted.

Jerry glared at Harley.

Harley sneered at Jerry.

Tim wrung his hands.

And Damien prayed for some sort of natural disaster to occur and end his misery. Unfortunately, his prayer went unanswered.

As Jerry and Harley helped him stand, he felt like the goddamned rope in a game of tug-of-war. Harley clucked, dusting him off like he was two years old. He caught her wrist before she reached the front of his jeans.

"Stop it. I told you I'm fine. I did not fall, and there's no need for an incident report. No one will be fired. Thank you." Giving Jerry and Tim a dismissive wave, Damien yanked Harley's hand, maneuvering her into the elevator.

"What happened?" Her ragged breathing filled the small space.

He forced himself to look straight ahead, not at the rise and fall of *Bite Me*. "Nothing."

At her snort of indignation, he glanced over.

"Don't placate me. It's obvious something happened. You were on the ground, soaked in sweat, and you're still pale." Spontaneously, she hugged him and quickly stepped back, wrinkling her nose.

"Did you just sniff me?" He gave her his darkest look.

"Maybe. I mean, I didn't mean to. You stink of sweat, by the way. Did you fall? You fell, didn't you? If you refuse to go to the hospital, at the very least you should be checked out by a doctor." She had her finger on the *open door* button, and he pulled her back to his chest, his arm wrapped around her collarbone.

Through clenched teeth he warned, "Press that button, and I will put your little ass out on the street." His cheek twitched with the effort it took to hold his temper.

Her tempting *little ass* grazed his crotch. He let go and stepped back, irritated with himself for losing control. Angrily he punched the button for his floor.

Instead of slapping him for manhandling her, she blinked and turned to look at her butt in the reflection of the elevator. "You think my bum's little?" She gave it a smack and grinned. "That's one of the nicest things you've ever said to me."

He rolled his eyes and counted to ten in Romani, the language of his mother's family, wanting very much to smack her ass himself. "You need to go back to the garage with your driver's license and complete the paperwork."

"I will. You're sure you're okay?" she asked, looking him over with a slight frown. She stood so close he could see the varying shades of blue in her eyes and smell her peach lotion.

"Yes. I'm fine. I think I just overdid it a little," he confessed.

He waited for her to exit the elevator first but moved ahead of her into the hallway. As he unlocked the door and walked into his living area, he let out a deep breath, relieved to be back in his comfort zone and out of the enclosed space with *Bite Me*.

"Okay, I'll start lunch." She smiled and left, leaving him alone.

He blew out a deep breath, annoyed with himself for having not one but two panic attacks today. How the hell was he going to go back to work?

Harley poked her head out from the kitchen. "Is Caesar salad with grilled chicken okay to eat?"

"That'll be fine. Thanks."

"Why don't you go get a hot shower? I'll get lunch ready, and after we eat you can take a nap."

"I'm not eighty years old. I don't want a nap."

Ugh, no, asshole, you're whining like a five-year-old.

"You just got out of the hospital, and you're still on antibiotics. You need to take it easy. If you're a good boy, I'll give you a massage later. Or we can do yoga. It will help you relax."

"A massage?"

"Part of the perks of me taking care of you—I'm a licensed massage therapist, remember?"

"I'd forgotten." He couldn't resist teasing her. "Was this before, after, or in the middle of cosmetology school and bartending?"

"After, smartass."

"Before or after you told your father you wanted to be a tattoo artist?"

She huffed. "Before."

"Before or after you broke your finger pole dancing—"

"Stop! That was an exercise class—and after. See? It's all better." She flipped him off and crossed her arms.

He laughed. "No massage, and definitely no yoga. But I will grab a quick shower."

Harley heard the shower start and leaned against the counter, covering her face with her hands. *He's okay.* She took a shuddering breath. Seeing him on the garage floor had scared her silly. Rationally, she knew the man who shot him was dead, but that didn't alleviate her unreasonable fear of losing him. That was why she was here, after all—not so much to take care of him, but to ease her own worry.

Chapter
Four

The next morning Damien tucked a towel around his waist and walked into his bedroom. He jumped when he found Harley lounging on his freshly made bed. He'd avoided her after lunch yesterday by faking a nap and retiring early after dinner. He wasn't used to having someone living with him. Unnerved and unsure what to do, he crossed his arms.

"What the hell are you doing in here? We need to set up some boundaries. My bedroom is off limits."

"Is that a hard limit or a soft limit?"

Speechless, his eyebrows rose.

"Oh, get your knickers out of a wad. I came to see if you needed help shaving or anything. And I brought you your coffee."

"You *honestly* think I would trust *you* with a razor? Have you lost your mind?" He marched to his dresser and pulled out a pair of black boxers.

"*Honestly*, do you own anything that isn't black, gray, or white?"

"A few ties, why?"

"Monochromatism is boring." She stood on his bed and jumped like a six-year-old on a trampoline. "This bed is awesome!"

"Get down before you break your foolish neck. You need to look up the meaning of the word *monochromatism*. I'm not color blind; I just happen to like black, white, and gray." He stormed into his closet and shut the door, slipping into his boxers and a pair of black pants. Grabbing a starched white shirt, he walked back into the bedroom, shrugging into it. No longer jumping on the bed, Harley now lay on it, looking entirely too enticing as she smiled. He buttoned his shirt as if suiting up in armor.

"Geez, you're grumpy. Maybe you should write a book. You could call it *Fifty Shades of Black Humor*. By the way, I'm a licensed cosmetologist. I'm perfectly capable of giving you a shave and a haircut—not that I think you need either. Your hair looks sexy longer, and with the beard stubble, you could be some girl's pirate fantasy." She wiggled her eyebrows and grinned.

He crossed his arms and glared.

"So, what's the real story with you and Lauren?" She smoothed a wrinkle from the duvet.

Lauren? Lauren, who? Your ex, idiot.

"She broke things off the day after Christmas."

"I'm sorry." Harley looked anything *but* sorry.

He grabbed a black-and-gray striped tie. "I'm not. She wanted marriage. I just wanted—"

"An occasional shag?" She waggled her eyebrows and grinned. "Claire said Lauren was throwing out hints just before Christmas that there would be a wedding in June, which is so cliché."

"Shag, knickers, bum? You're an American, Harley."

"Yes, but me Dad is from England and Mamma is Norwegian, *ja?*" Harley replied with a convincing mix of her parents' accents. "You didn't answer me."

"No, nor will I. It isn't any of your business, and you shouldn't listen to idle gossip. However, let the record reflect that I will *never* marry." He straightened the knot on his tie.

Her shoulders relaxed, and she bit her lip. Was that a smug look on her face? The look vanished, and he made a mental note to schedule an eye appointment.

"Sexy beast, where are you going?"

"Sassy wench."

What the fuck just came out of my mouth?

She blushed. Her fair skin always turned a beautiful shade of red when angered or embarrassed. It would start at her chest and move toward her neck, infusing her cheeks. When he and Angel were kids, they'd tormented her just to watch her blush.

What the hell was wrong with him? Maybe he should call Renata and find out when she'd be back home.

"To work, inquisitive imp."

She snorted. "Inquisitive? Bonus for the alliteration, but who uses words like that in everyday conversation?"

He grinned, proud of himself. "Thank you. And that would be people who read more than tabloid trash and illiterate text messages."

"You're not going to work. You just got out of the hospital. I'm supposed to be here to spoil you and take care of you, remember?" She eyed him like a mama bear watching her cub.

The thought of her spoiling him and taking care of him was both disturbing and comforting at the same time. It had been a long time since anyone took care of him. Not that he needed or wanted it. Grabbing his coat and briefcase, he left, declining her offer of breakfast. The fat remark still lingered.

A few minutes later, Damien stepped out of the elevator, thumbing through his texts, and promptly ran into a little girl, tripping them both.

She screamed bloody murder, and his shoulder throbbed from hitting the floor. He reached out to help the kid up, vaguely recognizing her as living in the building.

"Stranger danger! Stranger danger!" the girl shouted.

Her mother spun around. It was Mr. Gavosovich's daughter.

"What happened?" she demanded.

Wheezing like an asthmatic, he slowly stood. He couldn't seem to catch his breath. "S-Sorry," he managed to gasp.

The mother picked up her child and hurried onto the elevator. People stared at him as he straightened his tie and dusted off his pants. Dammit, he was filthy. And exhausted…He made his way to the wall and leaned against it, still trying to catch his breath. The thought of work now seemed daunting. They'd written him off for the rest of the week. Maybe he should adhere to doctor's orders.

The elevator dinged open, and Harley stepped off, carrying her yoga mat. Thankfully, she didn't see him. Worthy of James Bond, he darted behind her and slid into the elevator to return to the safety of his home. After calling the office and letting his father know he was fine but still not up to coming in today, he arranged to have some files sent over for review. Slipping on a pair of pajama pants, he sank into bed. He'd needed to come up with a plausible excuse before Harley returned.

Instead, his mind dwelled on the shooting, trying to remember anything after leaving the courtroom, but all he succeeded in doing was triggering a migraine. Closing his eyes, he tried to keep the growing fear at bay. *There's something terribly wrong with me.*

After attending her yoga class and picking up the yarn for Tim's baby blanket, Harley hurried home. She'd tried calling and texting to see if Damien wanted anything special for dinner, but he hadn't answered. Trying his office number, she was told he wouldn't be back until next week. What had made him change his mind? Or had something horrible happened?

He wasn't in the living area nor his office. In the kitchen sink she found a plate and half empty cup of coffee. Mr. Neatnik would never leave dishes in the sink.

Something's not right. I should've been here!

Skidding to a stop in front of his closed bedroom door, she hesitated. Should she knock and risk waking him up? Or just peek in and check on him? Cracking the door open, she tiptoed to the side of the bed.

"Go away."

"Are you okay?" She felt of his forehead.

He rolled away from her. "Stop it. I'm fine. Just leave me alone."

"Did you take your antibiotic? If I'd known you were going to be home, I'd have left something for lunch…"

"I'm not a child. Yes, I took my damn antibiotic."

"What happened?"

"Goddammit, just go home. I'm fine."

"You're not fine, and I'm not going home!"

She slammed the door behind her and then paced for an hour, worrying.

Later, he refused to eat dinner and only reluctantly ate a piece of toast to take his medication. Harley debated on whether to call his father but decided that would only piss him off further. Plus, no one knew she was staying here. Eating her lonely supper, she camped out in the living area and crocheted Tim's pink baby blanket, listening for any sounds that might come from Damien's room, but hearing none. By eleven, she couldn't keep her eyes open and curled up on the couch...

"Hey, Harley, you okay?"

Startled awake, she sat up, her heart pounding, her recurring nightmare still fresh in her mind. Sin sat on the edge of the couch, his hair tousled and his five o'clock shadow heavy. He was frowning, but not in a mad way, more like a worried way.

She blinked. "What time is it?"

"Two in the morning. Bad dream?" He smoothed her hair.

Choked by the memories, she nodded, and the tears leaked down her hot cheeks.

"Hey, it's okay. It was just a dream." Drawing her into his arms, he held her, stroking her hair.

She shook her head. This nightmare held tinges of reality, and it would never be okay. Only one other person would understand. But she took the comfort Damien offered, enjoying the smell of his skin, the feel of the dark springy hair on his chest, and the lulling sound of his voice as he offered her sweet assurances. But before it became awkward, she pulled away.

"Did you need something?" she asked.

"I was hungry," he admitted. "I snuck a bowl of ice cream." He nodded at the bowl on the end table. Picking it up he offered, "Want a bite?"

She gazed at the rare smile on his lips and wondered if they'd taste like the coffee ice cream. For a moment she held her breath as he stared back, looking at her as if he wanted to kiss her. But the look vanished, and he pulled away, as if he'd read her thoughts.

"No, thank you. I'll just go on to bed." She tucked the pink baby blanket away with a sigh, unable to look him in the eye.

"Good night." He disappeared into his bedroom.

Chapter
Five

Three days later, Damien decided he couldn't take being cooped up in his home one minute longer. He'd tried every day of his forced convalescence to review the files his father had sent by courier, but the headache always began after about an hour.

Aside from arguing with Harley, he had nothing to do, and he was going stir-crazy. Reading was out—the headaches didn't care if it was for work or pleasure. It was Friday, and he seriously wondered if he'd be able to return to work on Monday. Or ever.

What if he couldn't do his job? Would he end up having to hire a shyster lawyer to file a disability claim? His father would be less than pleased.

Harley had left after lunch for God knows where, probably to shop for more organic crap. The pastry shop around the corner seemed to be calling his name. Fresh air could only do him some good; maybe he'd go for a run, too.

He felt better as he changed into sweats, but as he stepped out of the elevator, panic set in. Sweat poured down his back, and his heart jackhammered as if he'd already completed a five-mile run.

Mr. Gavosovich, the crazy man who lived below him, wandered by in his bathrobe, talking to himself. Maybe he should book a double room at the asylum for both of them. Defeated, he returned to the safety of his home. He wondered where Harley was, and then berated himself for becoming too dependent.

A few restless hours later, Harley surprised him with take-out pizza for dinner. He missed junk food and devoured three slices, thinking he'd have to hit the treadmill soon. He passed on the healthy brownies she offered. Hummus disguised as chocolate sounded disgusting. After eating and ignoring her pointed looks and questions about his day, he made his way to the couch and collapsed, stretching out and closing his eyes. He was exhausted; moping around all day was tiring business.

He heard Harley humming to herself in the kitchen as she did the dishes. Part of him wished she'd go away; the other part was grateful for the company, no matter how annoying she was. Life didn't seem so damn terrifying with her here.

She walked out of the kitchen and frowned. Today's T-shirt read *Namastay In Bed*. The thought of her in bed was disconcerting.

She perched beside him and picked up his yellow legal pad and pen.

"So tell me, Freakout Freddy, when did you start having these feelings of being out of control?"

He frowned, wondering if she'd just read his mind. "What?"

Waggling her brow, she said, "I'm the psychiatrist, you're the patient. Jerry told me you came downstairs this afternoon but changed your mind. He said you looked sick. We're going to talk about feelings. You know, those things most humans have. I'll start. I feel sad because you're unable to snap out of this funk."

He glared and rolled onto his side, his back to her. "Just leave me alone."

"Sin, I'm teasing but not teasing. If you won't talk to a psychiatrist, talk to me. I'm your friend. Or we could do some yoga? It will relax you."

She rubbed his arm, but he shrugged it away.

"No. Just leave me alone. Go to your room."

She laughed. "Okay, *Daddy*. What if I don't want to? You gonna spank me?"

The thought is tempting… Scrubbing his face with the heel of his hand, he took a moment before responding. She wasn't intentionally arousing him, she was just being Harley. He needed to gain control of his baser needs.

"Sorry. I'm bored, my head hurts, and I can't concentrate. I'm brain damaged or something. Maybe I'll just go to bed and try to sleep off whatever the hell this is."

"Hiding and pretending to sleep isn't the answer. You conked the heck out of your skull, and your brain is so big in that fat head of yours, it's going to take time to heal. Just relax and give yourself a minute. I could entertain you, if you'd let me…"

He raised one eyebrow and grinned for the first time today. "What did you have in mind, Gypsy Rose Lee?"

As children, his mother had caught them watching the old movie *Gypsy*, which in hindsight was pretty innocuous. However, when she'd realized Harley was practicing stripping for him, she'd called in Harley's mother as well.

Harley laughed. "Oh my God. I don't think I was able to sit down for a week after our moms caught us. A game? A movie?"

"No games. You cheat, and I can't concentrate."

"Cheat? Me?"

"Yes, you. I used to make precise notes about how much Monopoly money everyone had, the number of houses and hotels, and where we were on the board. You cheated. Every. Time."

She rolled her eyes. "Of course you did, Anal Andy." Cocking her head to the side, she smiled. "I know just the thing. I'll be right back. May I go into your closet?"

"Why?"

"I need props. I promise I'll put everything back in its proper place. Or better yet, you can do it, and it will give you something to do."

Intrigued, he nodded.

When Harley returned, he realized too late his mistake. She'd knotted her T-shirt under her breasts and rolled her yoga pants down to expose the prettiest goddamned dancer-toned abdomen he'd ever seen. He wanted to lick those hipbones… Tucked into her waistband, she had his silk ties, which swooshed back and forth as she walked over to his sound system. After she plugged her phone in, the exotic sound of Middle Eastern dance music filled the room.

"I don't have any zills, but I'll do the best I can. I used to take a tribal belly dancing class. Let's see if I can remember the moves."

The part of his brain that dealt with self-preservation screamed, *Please don't.* His dick screamed, *Shut the hell up.*

She danced around the room, her hips circling slowly in time with the music, her arms and hands accenting the moves. His silk ties swayed as her hips undulated. She was so captivating, if watching meant going blind, he'd risk his eyesight. Her eyes closed as she absorbed the music, her movements controlled and graceful.

It was the longest six minutes of his life. When she finished, her breasts rose and fell from her efforts as she awaited his reaction. As the silence grew awkward, her arms folded across her chest and her face fell.

Say something, dumbass!

"Be sure to fold the ties and put them back where you found them." He fled to his bathroom and locked the door.

"Come on. It'll do you good to get some fresh air. A walk will help you build your strength." The next morning, Harley put the last of their breakfast dishes in the dishwasher.

"Maybe you're right. I still can't seem to concentrate without getting a headache." *Or thinking about that damn dance.* After Harley's performance last night, Damien had tried and failed once again to review the work files.

"That's normal. That's what the doctor told you on Wednesday at your follow-up appointment." She snickered and bit her lip, her blue eyes dancing.

He glared. "What's so damn funny? It's abnormal."

"I'm going to start calling you Abby Normal. You know, like in that funny old movie *Young Frankenstein* we watched the other night."

He chuckled. "Don't expect me to tap dance to 'Puttin' on the Ritz.' I can't dance for shit. I'll go change shoes and grab a hoodie."

A few minutes later, the elevator stopped at the floor below on their way down, and Mr. Gavosovich stepped on, wearing a fake nose and glasses. Holding his hand was the little girl Damien had collided with a few days ago. She was dressed in a princess costume and holding a Raggedy Ann doll.

"Shaney, where's your mom?" Harley asked.

"We're on the lam," Mr. Gavosovich replied.

"I see. But even escapees need a coat. You don't want Shaney to get sick, do you?" Harley took out her phone and sent a quick text.

Damien wondered how she knew so much about his neighbors and who she was texting.

The elevator door opened, and Jerry met them.

"Thanks, Harley," the normally gruff man greeted them as they got off. "Miranda's on her way down. They snuck out while she was in the shower."

"Not a problem." She smiled and knelt next to the little girl. "Shaney, you and your grandpa need to come see me for a tea party. I'll fix your doll's dress where it's ripped. Okay?"

"Thank you, Harley." She looked over when the next elevator dinged, and the frantic mother ran out in a robe, her hair wrapped in a towel.

"Oh my God, I'm so sorry. Come on Dad, Shaney. You two nearly gave me a heart attack!" She bustled her family back into the elevator.

"That man needs to be in a nursing home," Damien commented as they stepped outside. The sun was shining, but the air was bracing, and he picked up the pace.

Harley frowned. "Why? He'd die of loneliness. He just gets a little confused. Everyone in the building knows to look out for him and Shaney. Miranda's doing the best she can as a single mom."

"How do you know so much about this?" He'd lived here eight months and barely knew faces, much less the names of his neighbors.

She shrugged. "I don't know. I just do." She waved at Tim, who was walking toward them.

"You're late today!"

"Good reason!" He grinned and handed her and Damien each a pink bubble gum cigar. "Julie was born yesterday morning. She was seven pounds and eight ounces. I'd show you pictures, but I'm late enough!"

Harley laughed and hugged him. "Congrats!"

Belatedly, Damien offered his own congratulations before Tim hurried off. Again, he realized how little he knew about the goings on in his building. How was Tim going to afford a kid and go to school?

"Let's head to the park over there." Harley pointed. "And get out of these fumes."

Damien nodded. The traffic was lighter than a weekday but still busy and loud. His heart pounded more than it should've for a mere walk. And the sounds seemed amplified. Crossing the street, he reached for Harley's hand.

She looked up at him with wide eyes. Her nose was red, her braid shimmered in the sunlight, and her wide smile lessened his anxiety. Or was it just getting out of the hustle and bustle?

"Stay close to me." He eyed the park benches with their derelicts and homeless. He preferred his treadmill — less risk.

He let go of her hand and they slowed their pace, taking refuge in the middle of downtown. Two older men were playing chess and laughing. A mother jogged by pushing a stroller. On a park bench farther down the path, a man sat slouched over. Beside him was a shopping cart full of what Damien assumed were his belongings.

Harley broke away, jogging toward the unsavory character.

"Harley!" *What the hell? Dammit, is she trying to get us killed?*

He ran after her, but an escaped dog darted in front of him, his leash trailing behind.

"Grab him!" yelled the man chasing the dog.

Damien caught the leash and handed it to the guy. Horrified, he then saw Harley handing the dirty stranger a plastic bag.

He darted toward her, listening for sirens.

"Your brownies are the best, Harley," the guy said through a mouthful as Damien ran up. He definitely looked under the influence.

"Aw, thanks, Carl."

Brownies? In a plastic bag? What the fuck? Damien took her hand and hurried her back toward a more populated area of the park. Glancing behind them, he was relieved to see that the guy remained on the bench, looking through the bag.

"What the hell are you doing?" Damien didn't pull the punch on his anger. "For fuck's sake, Harley, there are probably cameras set up all over this place."

"So? It was just a brownie."

A police siren wailed.

"Shit! Let's go! This is just fuckin' great…" He grabbed her hand, jogging toward the street, his heart pounding with each step.

"What is your problem?" Just before they reached the park exit, she shrugged out of his grasp and stopped.

"Fine. You go to jail. I'm not. And I'm not paying for your legal defense, either. You better hope it was less than an ounce—that's only a misdemeanor, not a felony."

She grinned. "I'm not selling it; I'm giving it away." Digging in her purse, she pulled out a brownie, took a bite, and offered it to him. "Yum. Want some? It might help you chill the fuck out."

"Put that away," he hissed, looking around for the cops.

He'd once found Angel shooting heroin. This wasn't quite as bad, but still…

Laughing, she took another bite. "Oh my God, the sky is so blue. And I'm starving—let's go eat junk food. Crunchy, salty junk food." She spun around in a circle, laughing and giggling.

"Harley, stop!"

She threw herself into his arms, and he stumbled, catching her.

"Come fly with me." Grabbing his face, she kissed him.

Her lips still tasted like cotton candy…so sweet, so soft. Despite himself, he kissed her back, memories flooding his mind as her tongue teased his. She pulled away, her eyes wide and slightly dilated. Her shallow breath puffed in the cold air. Grinning, she shoved a piece of brownie in his mouth. The moment was over. He spat it out.

Grabbing her arm, he started marching her toward home. "There's help for this…"

She laughed the entire way. "I don't want help. I'm addicted to them. You should try one—"

"I can't believe this. Shut up, Harley. No wonder you're always so goddamned cheerful…"

When they arrived back home, he quickly propelled her toward the elevator.

The doors opened to reveal Mr. Gavosovich, dressed in a suit and tie. He smiled. "Going up?"

"Yes, please. I want to get high," Harley sputtered through her laughter.

"Where's Miranda?" Damien asked sharply, glaring at Harley.

"At home. I'm working today. I'm operating the elevator."

"Good job!" Harley dug in her purse. "Would you like a brownie, Mr. Gavosovich?"

Damien's mouth dropped. "No!"

"Why, thank you. I love your brownies, Harley."

Damien grabbed it out of his hand as the elevator dinged for their floor.

"Sorry, Mr. Gavosovich. Damien has a thing for my brownies, too. I'll bring you some later."

Damien shoved her into the penthouse and began pacing. "All right, the way I see it, there are two options. You can go get treatment on your own, or I'm calling your parents."

She opened her purse, removed three plastic bags, and tossed them at him.

"Go ahead, call them."

He looked at the bags, which held more than brownies. "What is this?"

"I make care packages and give them to the homeless. Your mom used to give me all her travel shampoos and toothpastes. Your dad still does, and I supplement them with other stuff. This morning I added the brownies I made that you didn't want, dumbass."

"That homeless guy called you by name."

She shrugged. "I see him every day when I go for my run. Carl's always there. Everyone knows that."

Everyone knows that? He didn't know that. "What all is in here?"

"A toothbrush, toothpaste, shampoo, soap, coupons for free meals at fast food places, a suicide hotline number, and a note to cheer them up. Oh, and a condom."

"So, these are normal brownies?"

She giggled. "Yup, aside from being organic and made from hummus. But I had you going."

He looked again at the bag. "Why a condom?" he croaked.

"Duh. Even homeless people need to be safe."

He pinched the bridge of his nose, unable to argue with her logic.

"You got me. You and your pranks."

"I know! It was a good one."

"These care packages are actually a good idea. I'm sure it's appreciated. But please, be careful."

"I don't do it to be appreciated. I do it because kindness is important. And I *am* careful."

Damien looked at her. Despite having a brother who'd been homeless and attending fundraisers to help those in need, he couldn't remember actually doing anything hands-on to assist those less fortunate.

Harley headed toward her bedroom. Shame kept him silent, but his respect for her grew. He'd known this woman practically all his life, but she'd surprised him — it was as if he didn't really *know* her at all.

And then there was that kiss…

Chapter
Six

"Damn, you're hard, Sin."

"Oh, fuck, that feels great. Don't stop."

"My hand's tired."

"Harder, Harley. Jesus, don't stop! I thought you were a professional. What do you mean your hand is tired?"

"I've been doing this for over a year, but the repetitive motion makes my hand cramp. You're going to give me carpal tunnel syndrome."

The bedroom door slammed open, and Harley jumped. She rocked back on her legs and stopped massaging Damien's shoulders.

He lifted his head and promptly buried his face back in his pillow. "Shit."

After her prank in the park yesterday, Damien had been wound up tighter than a top. Knowing he was worried about returning to work tomorrow, she'd offered the massage to help relax him, and he'd finally accepted.

The irate look on Lauren Cuthbert's face was priceless. Too bad she couldn't snap a picture to share with Claire. They couldn't stand Damien's ex-girlfriend, and the feeling was mutual.

Lauren's ice-cold glare affirmed it. "I didn't realize you weren't alone."

Harley returned to massaging the knot in his shoulder.

"Damien, I'm so sorry. You know I've been in Paris with Mother, but of course I've kept up with how you're doing through Daddy. I can take care of you now that I'm back..." Lauren patted her hair with a manicured hand.

Harley couldn't remember a time the woman had looked anything but perfect. She'd bet a dollar her bottle-brown hair even stayed in place during sex. Lauren's dark eyes were venomous when they locked with hers.

"No need, Harley's doing a fine—ahhhh, yesssss, right there, damn that feels good—job. Is it anorexia week already?"

"Don't be an ass. You know it's called fashion week, and not yet. I'm not going this year because of that benefit for those dirty people in the park." Her collagen-enhanced lips pursed.

"I believe they're homeless, Lauren." Damien raised his head. "I say, bird, did you stop by for a shag, yeah?" His Austin Powers voice made Harley giggle.

"A *what?*" she shrieked. "Are you high? You know, with your brother's history, you might need to lay off the pain pills. Besides, you know I don't discuss things like that in front of...*you know*."

Harley glared at her. *Say it, bitch. I'm the hired help.*

Lauren looked like she'd just chomped down on a lemon.

"Gor blimey, govenah, do I need to leave so you and your crumpet can rumpy-pumpy?" Harley asked in her best Eliza Doolittle voice.

"Oh, geezus." Damien buried his laughter in his pillow.

Harley worked the knots out of his tense muscles, enjoying getting under Lauren's skin as she massaged Damien's.

"She really crosses the line of impertinence. I would never allow an employee to speak to me like that." Lauren slammed her purse down on the dresser and stared daggers.

Anger flooded her cheeks. Lauren had always looked down on her because her parents worked for the Sinclair family. And although she and her brothers had attended the same schools as Angel and Damien, there were some, like Lauren, who always made it clear they thought she was *less than* because of her parents' socioeconomic status.

"Sheath the claws, Lauren. That was uncalled for. It was just a joke, and besides, she isn't my employee."

"Oh? What is she then?" Her tone implied she thought she knew and didn't approve.

"She's my friend."

Harley's heart soared. She lowered her eyes so the witch wouldn't see her gloating.

"Having a side of Jarlsberg with your enchilada, darling?" Lauren's cattiness knew no boundaries.

Damien sighed and sat up. "Harley, would you please give us a moment?"

Reluctantly, she left the room, but she stopped in the hall to eavesdrop. No way would she miss this.

Leave it to Lauren to show up just when things were surprisingly good with Damien. They'd been rocking along like, well…an old married couple—watching movies and shows from when they were kids. She enjoyed taking care of him and loved living here. But tomorrow he was returning to work, so more than likely he'd make her go home. And now with Lauren back…

Her old insecurities flared. Would Damien go back to that bitch? They'd dated on and off since high school…*Please God, no.*

The door slammed shut. Harley eased closer to listen.

"Stop being a bitch. She's my friend, a *good* friend, who came to help me." Damien hadn't raised his voice, but the delivery was succinct.

"Damien, I know we've had a rough patch. But you know I love you—"

Was that fear tinging her voice? Harley crossed her fingers.

"You need to stop, Lauren. We're not together anymore. You left the day after Christmas when you didn't get the damn engagement ring you expected. Face it, what we had has been over for a very long time. I've told you repeatedly, I don't want to get married."

Harley pressed a hand to her mouth to keep from shouting with glee. She pictured Lauren getting mad, but then remembered her plastic face would never show any emotion.

"I see. Well, if you prefer the company of women like *her*, go for it. It wouldn't be the first time you've strayed, but you always come back…" Lauren's voice quivered and dropped off.

Harley almost felt sorry for her. *Almost.* She never understood why Damien had dated her to begin with.

"We're done. Goodbye, Lauren. Leave with some dignity and a shared respect between us. I hope you find what you're looking for—"

The sound of a slap interrupted him.

"You bastard! You can't do this to me!"

"I haven't done anything to you. Don't worry, you can hold your head high at the country club. You broke up with me, remember? Now go snare some other unsuspecting sap."

Harley quickly darted to the living area and sat on the couch. She picked up some boring law journal and pretended to read as she waited for her arch nemesis to leave.

Lauren stormed out of the bedroom, her eyes bright. On her way to the door, she did an abrupt turn and walked back over to Harley. She shook with anger.

"I'll be back. Don't get too comfortable here," she hissed before leaving.

The door slammed in her wake, and a moment later Damien wandered into the living area. He picked up his phone. "Jerry, Lauren Cuthbert is no longer on my approved list for entrance." He hung up.

"That was a bit harsh, Sin."

"Eavesdropping, were you?"

"Of course."

"If you use the information, it becomes a crime."

"Thanks for the law lesson, Percy Prosecutor."

Harley followed him back into his bedroom, and he re-positioned himself on the bed.

"As for my dealings with Lauren, they're none of your business. I'm not a particularly a warm and fuzzy kind of person. You know that. As you heard, I'm a bastard."

She resumed massaging his neck and shoulder. That was the image he liked to portray, but she knew better. He'd once held her when she cried over a dead goldfish. And more recently when she had a nightmare…There was only one time he'd been a bastard toward her, but that was long ago, and she'd let it go. Life's too short to hold on to bitterness.

"I'm sorry. I mean, Lauren must've meant something to you at one time; you dated for years."

And the tears I've shed because of that would fill the Atlantic Ocean.

"Never exclusively, and I'm not sorry."

His shoulders began to shake, and Harley rubbed his back in soothing circles. It must have affected him more than he wanted to admit.

"Everything will be okay, Sin…" She paused when she realized he wasn't crying or upset in the least. He was laughing.

"*Rumpy-pumpy?* Did you really ask Lauren Cuthbert if she was here for a rumpy-pumpy?" Sitting up again, he howled until tears ran down his face. "Oh damn, I needed that. I haven't laughed this hard in ages." He wiped his eyes, still chuckling.

Harley giggled. This was the Damien she loved.

"Lie down so I can finish your massage, and then I'll give you a haircut and shave."

His dark, enigmatic eyes seemed to peer into all her secrets. Swallowing nervously, all rational thoughts fled as she stared at his lips. Heat worked its way up from her chest to her cheeks before zipping straight down south. She spun around, afraid he'd see the depth of her feelings on her face.

"It's Sunday. I think maybe I'll leave the hair and skip shaving for today. I rather fancy being a pirate." He lay back down.

"Aye, aye, sir."

Harley stared at the back of his head for a moment and resisted the urge to run her fingers through his dark hair. How she longed to feel his coarse beard stubble on her neck. Taking a deep breath to steady herself, she slowly massaged his tension away until he was sound asleep.

Tenderly, she covered him with the duvet, resisting the urge to kiss his cheek. He stirred, but relaxed into a deeper, exhausted sleep. Harley slipped from the room and danced with pure abandonment toward the kitchen. Damien had defended her to Lauren! She hugged herself and did a pirouette. She paused in her celebration. He'd said he hadn't dated Lauren *exclusively*. She wondered who else he'd dated… He'd never brought anyone but Lauren to meet his family. Her mother would have mentioned it.

The dancing stopped as she pondered this sobering bit of information.

Disoriented, Damien awoke with a start. He'd dreamed about Harley and had the boner to prove it. *Goddammit, what brought that on?* That hadn't happened in ages… *That kiss in the park, that's what brought it on.* He needed to regain some control.

Checking his phone for the time, he saw a text from Renata. She was home from Brazil.

He staggered to the bathroom where he swallowed some ibuprofen for his never-ending headache and threw water on his face. Shrugging into his T-shirt, he wandered into the kitchen where he found Harley chopping vegetables and singing along with the music she had playing. He chuckled when she added some graceful, but suggestive dance moves.

She turned around, and her face flushed. "Sorry, did I wake you? I thought an egg white omelet would taste good for supper." She bit her lip, clearly amused by something.

"That's fine," he replied, waving aside her apology. "What's so funny?" He sat down at the table and rubbed his brow.

"You have sleep creases on your face and a bad case of bedhead. You must've slept hard." She turned the music down and resumed chopping vegetables.

"You didn't have to turn it down." He rubbed his face, wishing the god-awful headache would ease.

"No, it's okay." She looked over at him with a frown. "Need something for your headache?" Harley poured the egg into the pan and started the toast. She'd obviously just showered as her hair was still in a wet braid. Her fresh, clean face was a direct contrast to Lauren's.

"I'm fine." His eyes tracked *Bite me* as she bounced about his kitchen. She needed to get rid of that T-shirt. He tore his gaze from her breasts.

"Isn't that perjury?" she asked, giggling.

"Perjury?"

"You're not fine. You have no secrets from me; I know you," she commented with her back turned to him.

"Okay, you're right, I'm not fine. My head hurts. How did you know?"

Harley added the vegetables to the omelet, thankfully oblivious to his train of thought.

"Didn't I ever tell you about that stint I did as a carnie fortune teller?"

"You did what?"

"Daddy says I was born with the gift of second sight. His Irish mother had it, too. Anyway, it was about six years ago. Remember how I always wanted to run away with the circus?"

"Um, yeah. We both did. You wanted to tame the lions, and I wanted to work the trapeze…" He stared at her, but her face was serious.

"Well, I didn't join the circus, but I worked the carnival circuit for about four months. Byron finally tracked me down. It's terrible having a brother who has access to records. Anyway, I'm good at reading people and knowing their inner secrets."

"You're shitting me, right?"

"Totally." She laughed. "But admit it, for a split second I had you going!"

"No, I knew it was bullshit." Dammit, he'd halfway believed her, but he'd die before he admitted it.

"Liar. It wouldn't take a detective or a fortune teller to figure out your head was hurting. You're pale, you have circles under your eyes, and you're rubbing your head, dumbass."

He grunted. "There you have it. The defense rests. You've proven probable guilt. What's my punishment?"

She smiled. "I'll think of something suitable."

"Your turn. Tell me your secrets."

She paused a moment before folding the omelet in the pan and glancing over her shoulder. "Secrets? Me?" She gave a nervous laugh. "A woman without secrets is boring."

"You could never be boring."

Jesus H. Christ, asshole—shut the hell up before she thinks you're coming on to her!

"Thanks, I think." Her laughter filled the kitchen, and she scooped the omelet onto the plate, splitting it in two for them to share. Toast and sliced tomatoes completed the simple meal. She poured him a cup of decaf coffee and herself a cup of tea, then flipped the music to classical and placed his food in front of him.

"Your mom loved this piece. Do you still play the violin? You haven't since I've been here."

"Not since Mom died." He hadn't had the heart to play; music had been such a huge part of his mother's life.

Eating together like this reminded him of when they were children and her mother would feed them in the kitchen. He'd always preferred eating with the happy laugher and banter of the Taylors. In the dining room with his parents, children were expected to be silent unless spoken to.

"I have some fresh blueberries and an angel food cake for dessert."

Damien grimaced. "I don't eat blue food."

"Still? Not even blueberries?"

"No."

"That's weird. Blue cheese?"

"Disgusting."

"Blue corn chips?"

"Nope."

"Blue M&Ms or Skittles?"

"Nope, and there are no blue Skittles."

"Shut up. There are no blue Skittles?"

"Nope. Not in the original. Everyone knows that."

"I didn't know that. I don't believe you."

Damien shook his head. "Seriously? We're going to argue about Skittles?"

Harley laughed, and he found himself smiling in return. She had a big, infectious laugh. She always had. It would start with an uplift at the corners of her mouth and spill out as if she was unable to contain it.

"We're not arguing; we're having a lively discussion," she said. "You know, I credit myself with your success as a lawyer. Think about all those years you practiced arguing with me. I can't believe you still won't eat blue food. I still love blueberry Icees—they turn your teeth blue. How about sports drinks. Can they be blue?"

"No. Blue is not a color that should be found in food—only in beautiful eyes."

He stared at his plate, horrified. *Holy shit? Did I really just say that out loud?*

"Aww, sometimes you can be a very sweet man." Harley smiled, leaned over, and kissed him on the cheek.

Her soft lips and the flush of Harley red on her cheeks came close to undoing his resolve.

"I am not a sweet man, nor have I ever been a sweet man. I'm a bastard through and through. Don't ever forget it."

I need to call Renata.

He pushed his now-empty plate away. Harley, Renata…He didn't need to complicate his life. He needed to focus on getting back to work.

"I'm going to let the ibuprofen do its job and try to get a little work done. I'm returning to the office tomorrow."

"Okay. I still think you should let your doctor know about these headaches…"

"You're not my mother. Just lay off," he snapped.

Hurt flashed across her face.

"Sorry, it's this headache. Good night." Giving her what he hoped was a reassuring smile, he returned to his bedroom, where he blissfully sank into bed and closed his eyes.

He couldn't think when his head ached like this, much less try to review cases. Maybe he could sleep it off.

But sleep eluded him as a vision of bewitching blue eyes, soft pink lips, and Harley red blushes teased his thoughts. Blowing out an exasperated breath, he punched the pillow and rolled over. This was ridiculous. She was just a friend. Like a sister, really.

Liar.

He rarely allowed himself the luxury of wondering *what if*…But he did so now.

Their first kiss had been at the fair with her parents and brothers when she was seven and he was nine. Terrified on the rollercoaster, she'd white-knuckled the safety bar with her eyes squeezed shut. Mad because her brothers had paired up, leaving him stuck riding with Harley, he'd teased her unmercifully, reducing her to tears.

When he realized he'd gone too far, he'd leaned over and given her a quick, chaste kiss. Her lips had tasted like cotton candy. She'd shoved him away, wiping her mouth, but she'd stopped crying. Of course once they'd disembarked, she'd kicked him in the nuts and brought him to his knees.

And then there was his freshman year in college. He'd come home for spring break and been amazed by the changes in his little shadow. He'd found her running around in short shorts and tank tops with her glorious, pale blond hair and wide blue eyes. The flirting began, and with hormones raging, things escalated fast. For a solid week, they couldn't keep their hands off each other. To this day, the smell of summer peaches reminded him of Harley and those few days of uninhibited passion.

The day before he was to fly back to Harvard, they'd snuck into the pool house, only to be caught by his father. He'd later told Harley his father hadn't seen that it was her — a lie to keep her from feeling more embarrassed than she already was.

But his father had seen, and he'd given him a blistering lecture on the responsibility of being a Sinclair heir and how *"being involved with the help was unacceptable."* Young and impetuous, he'd told his father to go to hell and stood to leave. His mother, who had been sitting quietly, watching the heated exchange, then wrapped up the argument with one sentence: *"If you don't stop this insanity with Harley Taylor, I will fire her parents."*

It had felt like he'd been knifed in the gut. But knowing his parents and their aristocratic sensibilities, he'd believed her. Elise and John Taylor had been like second parents to him and Angel. They not only handled the day to day operations of running a large household, they'd been warm and loving and considered — at least by him and Angel — to be family. He'd loved them and couldn't risk their jobs.

He'd left the room silently and returned to college, angry with himself for hurting Harley and hating his parents.

At nineteen, he'd caved to his mother's ultimatum, but as he grew older, he'd come to acknowledge that his parents had been right; hormones had hijacked his rational thinking. Getting involved with this free-spirited girl with the amazing eyes would've been reckless. They were total opposites; things wouldn't have ended well. And of course they would've ended. Happy relationships were fairy tales…

He rolled over again and thought about taking one of his prescription painkillers, not for the pain, but to lull himself to sleep. The door opened, and Harley tiptoed into the room.

"What are you doing in here?" He sounded harsher than he intended.

"I heard you tossing and turning. Are you okay? Do you need anything?"

"No, I'm fine. Go to sleep."

"It's only eight o'clock." Leaning over, she stroked his cheek, and he fought the urge to rest his face in her hand. By the dim light from the crack in the door, he peered up at her. He closed his eyes again.

"Thank you," he mumbled, giving in to her tender ministrations. The bed dipped, and she sat beside him. Her soft, cool fingertips massaged his forehead as she softly hummed the gypsy lullaby his mother had sung when they were children.

His last coherent thought was how right it felt to have Harley in his bed.

As she slipped out, Harley left a note for Damien in case he woke up before she returned. She left the wrapped baby blanket at the security office for Tim and went to wait for Claire.

After a few minutes, Claire pulled up in her bright blue vintage Miata and waved. Harley hopped in and gave her best friend a hug.

"Where to?" Claire asked as she pulled away from the curb.

"I don't care, I just...I kissed Damien," she blurted.

Claire's lips thinned as she sped through a yellow light. "Aw shit. I told you this whole taking care of him idea was a mistake. What did the dumbass do?"

"Nothing. I mean, he was pissy because I'd just pranked him, but... Well, he kissed me back, briefly. That's something, isn't it? And he's totally over Lauren. I heard that with my own ears."

Claire sighed. "Lauren and Damien go through this once a year or so. She starts hinting at marriage, and he pulls away. But you realize they're probably going to marry in the long run, right? I mean, her father is part of the same firm. And after what he did to you, how can you even think of starting up with him again?"

"We were just kids..." Harley defended.

Claire pulled into a parking lot. "I can tell this is going to take alcohol. Come on. If we get too drunk, I'll call Charlie to come get us."

She'd chosen a quiet neighborhood restaurant and bar, and on Sunday evening, it contained very few customers. Claire ordered them both a glass of wine.

Her gray eyes bore into Harley. "This needs to stop. I've been telling you this for how long? Damien hasn't shown you the least amount of interest since we were kids. You can't continue with this..." She shrugged and flipped her long, dark hair over her shoulder. "Whatever you want to call it, unrequited love thing. I'm not saying this to be mean; I'm saying it because I love you. Have you spoken to Mark lately? Does he know?"

Harley ran a finger up and down the stem of her wine glass. "No, not since Christmas." Mark MacGregor was Claire's adopted brother and someone who knew her better than most. "Damien's a touchy subject with Mark…"

"I know. Never mind. I just thought he could talk some sense into you."

Harley took a deep breath. "How do you talk sense when dealing with love?"

There. She'd said it out loud.

"Love? Are you sure? I mean, he's a hot guy, and you've been sharing space. Sure it's not just lust? I could totally see him wanting sex, but he's too cold and impersonal to ever want a meaningful relationship. I mean, look at his history with Lauren. I hate her, but damn, I know she wants that ring and the Sinclair name. And she's put up with his shit for years. He's never been that into her. Or anybody. What makes you think he'd change for you?"

"He's not that way. I don't think anyone really knows him. He's funny and can be really sweet. And he's fiercely protective…" Harley looked away. "We're meant to be, like it's written in the stars or something. I just feel it, and I always have."

"Shit." Claire sighed. "That bad, huh?" She raised one eyebrow.

"'Fraid so."

Claire swirled her wine, taking her time before answering. "Then double down, girlfriend. You have to be willing to risk the heartache. I'll be here to celebrate if you succeed or pick up the pieces."

Harley smiled. "Thanks, Claire Bear."

"That's what girlfriends do, Harley Harlot."

They clinked glasses.

Chapter
Seven

Harley woke up Monday morning to find the coffee made and half the pot already consumed. Damien was up earlier than usual. After making herself a cup of tea, she went to investigate the whirring sound coming from his bedroom.

When she walked in, she found him running fast enough to break a sweat on the treadmill. He was a beautiful sight to behold. His dark, damp hair fell on his brow, and her fingers itched to run through the unruly waves. He seemed unaware of her presence, so she allowed herself the luxury of staring. He wore a pair of gym shorts and nothing else. Had she really told him he was fat? There wasn't anything fat about him. He was still one of the most gorgeous men she'd ever known. The gleaming sweat highlighted his muscles.

A cup of coffee sat in the cup holder as he watched the news. She snickered when she realized he had the news on with the closed captioning and was plugged into his came-over-on-the-ark music player at the same time. Maybe he was better if he was multi-tasking like this. She still hoped he'd just do a half day at work. He needed to see someone about these headaches.

"What?" he snapped.

She jumped.

Panting, he pulled the earbud out as he waited for her response, not missing a step on the treadmill. The faint pounding beat of The Rolling Stones made her grin.

"Do you ever listen to anything from this century? The Rolling Stones? How boring."

The annoyed look he flashed was the same he'd given her since they were kids. He glanced down at the treadmill. "They're the best band, *ever*. One more mile. Please have breakfast ready in thirty minutes—poached egg, wheat toast, and orange juice." He replaced the earbud and picked up his pace.

"You're overdoing it," she shouted.

He ignored her. She'd just been dismissed.

Harley shrugged at his stupidity and left to start breakfast for his majesty.

Fuck, I'm out of shape.

As soon as Harley left the room, Damien slowed to a jog for a few seconds before quitting altogether. Male pride had pushed him to run faster when she'd entered the room. Being in the hospital, followed by lying around the penthouse not doing a damn thing, had left him hard pressed to do three miles. There was no excuse for this except his lack of discipline.

Damien detested weakness, especially in himself.

He turned off the treadmill, television, and his music. Softly groaning, he collapsed on the side of the bed to catch his breath. It was a full two minutes before he managed to stand on wobbly legs. Easing into the hot shower, he let the water pulsate and soothe his overworked muscles.

A second after he'd wrapped a towel around his waist, Harley walked into the bathroom after a quick knock. *Doesn't she understand boundaries?* Irritated, he stared at her in the mirror, not saying a word. It was a technique he used with clients on the witness stand. Silence made people nervous. Oblivious to his lawyer superpowers, she flashed him a bright smile.

"Breakfast is ready."

"What part of *my bedroom is off limits* don't you understand?"

"Off limits when? You let me give you a massage in here. I clean, put away your laundry, and make your bed. You didn't throw me out when I soothed your aching hard head. Plus, to be precise, this is your bathroom." She smirked. "The defense rests."

Dammit, she has a point. I need to set down basic rules and stick to them.

Blowing her bangs out of her eyes, she crossed her arms over her chest. Wearing yoga pants and an oversized Harvard sweatshirt he'd given her years ago, she still gave off an aura of blatant sexuality. If she didn't get out of the damn bathroom soon, his towel would tent, and that would be humiliating.

Note to self: Call Renata today.

"Your services won't be needed any longer. I'm going in to the office today. You can stay one more day to get your things packed. Until then, my bedroom is off limits. Period."

"Yes, *sir*." Her tone of voice was anything but respectful when she left, slamming the door.

He was pretty damn sure she'd muttered "wanker" as she stormed away.

Damien joined her in the kitchen ten minutes later, wearing charcoal gray pants, a starched white shirt, and a maroon tie—to prove he wore color, dammit. He sat, and she refreshed his cup of coffee as he began to eat his perfectly poached egg and toast.

"Sit. Aren't you eating?" A cursory glance revealed the stubborn set of her mouth and the angry spark in her eyes. *Good.* Maybe if he'd pissed her off, she'd leave.

"Should I sit in a chair, or at your feet and gaze adoringly up at you? You're pushing it to think you can jump into a full day at work. Why don't you try a half day?"

"Pack your bags," he ordered.

"Excuse me?"

He looked up at her sharp intake of breath. Hurt splintered across her face as if he'd struck her. He regretted the delivery but refused to back down.

"It's time you went home. I'm fine."

"You're not fine, but *fine*. I'll be gone before you get home, you ungrateful ass."

She threw a dishtowel on the counter and stormed out of the room. Damien wished he hadn't been such a jerk, but in the long run, this turn of events was for the best. His thoughts regarding her were much too complicated and growing dangerously out of control.

On the way to work, Damien stopped by the barbershop where he'd been getting his hair cut since he was in elementary school. He surprised himself—and Samson—when he asked the aged barber for just a trim, leaving it longer than it had been since high school. He left feeling a hundred percent better and tipped Samson well, promising to return in a couple of weeks.

He needed to send a check to Harley as well. He had no idea how much his father was paying her, but she deserved a bonus. *Or am I paying off my guilt?* He shoved the thought away.

The barber shop was around the corner from his law office, and he walked at a brisk pace. It felt good to be on his way to doing something useful. For the first time since the shooting, he felt alive, almost as if he was in tune with the pulse of the city. And dare he think it? *Normal.*

Walking in the office, he was surprised when the usually reserved Mrs. Allen jumped up and gave him a hug, dabbing her eyes behind her glasses with a tissue. She'd been the receptionist since he was a kid visiting his father's office. Efficient, calm, cool, and collected, this demonstrative side of her was unforeseen, and a little unnerving. Her gray head bobbed as she smiled, telling him how much the office had missed him—what he was sure was a white lie. Damien was well aware of his reputation as a perfectionist. It's why he was a successful lawyer, and why he'd been through three legal assistants and two paralegals in his short career.

With a wan smile, he nodded and accepted greetings from various staff members. Several wanted to discuss cases; a few simply wanted to gossip. Thankfully, Lauren's father was in court, as was his father. After a half hour of small talk, he sought cover behind his closed office door. He loosened his tie, which seemed to be choking him, and took several deep breaths.

Pull your shit together!

His heart quit racing, and he readjusted his tie and shrugged out of his coat, hanging it neatly in the closet. Sitting at his desk, he glanced around and sighed. Like his home, it was sleek, modern, and austere, decorated in gray and white. But the plants were now dead. Morosely, he wondered if the staff had let them go, thinking he'd die and never come back.

Mrs. Allen interrupted his maudlin thoughts by presenting him with a lengthy list of pressing issues that needed to be handled.

Two hours later, his head pounded, and he'd accomplished only a fraction of the things on the list from hell. But he needed a break and decided to wait on his dad at the courthouse. Maybe he'd want to grab a quick cup of coffee.

Harley had been right, dammit. Coming back to work today was pushing it. He'd talk to his father and see if he could adjust his schedule.

Guilt pricked his conscience for even acknowledging this weakness. His father and law partners had picked up his slack, handling all of the cases while he'd been off. Dad had said he relished the work, but he'd always been a workaholic. His father hadn't even been by to see him since he'd gotten home. Leaving the office, he walked briskly around the corner to the courthouse, trying to look like he had his shit together. Appearance was everything.

Halfway up the steps, he looked up at the place where it had happened. Static, disjointed images of the shooting flashed like a grainy newsreel through his memory. Ice-cold fear wrapped around him, freezing him in his tracks. It took him three tries to loosen his tie, and he cursed under his breath as sweat dotted his brow. The coppery taste of panic filled his mouth.

I'm having a heart attack. Or my pneumonia's back.

It was the only reasonable explanation for the tightness in his chest, shortness of breath, and pounding heart. Dammit, he hadn't died on the courthouse steps a few weeks ago; he refused to do so now.

Hyperaware of his surroundings, he scanned the area, searching for danger. Every movement and sound seemed magnified. He closed his eyes and sank to the edge of the step.

Breathing's supposed to be automatic, isn't it?

White stars danced in front of his closed eyelids as he reminded himself to inhale and exhale. A dull roaring noise muffled the sounds of the bustling city around him, and a welcoming darkness offered relief. Forcing his eyes open, he tried to pretend he was all right. He pulled out his cell and called home, praying Harley was there, angered and panicked by the uncontrollable trembling of his hand.

No answer. He tried her cell, and she picked up on the second ring.

"Where are you?" he managed to croak.

"I'm headed home after my yoga class, o divine dickhead, per your instructions. Jerry is ecstatic."

"I'll double your salary if you'll reconsider and come back." His offer was met with silence. "Hello? Harley?"

"I'm here. What's wrong? Why did you change your mind?"

"Look, can we talk about it later? And uh, could you swing by the courthouse and get me? *Now?*" He clenched his shaking hand in his coat pocket and prayed he gave the appearance of consulting on a case to the people nodding at him as they walked by. He didn't want to look like a blathering, paranoid idiot, even if he was.

Fake it until you make it…

"I'll be there as fast as I can with this traffic." She hung up.

Refusing to look back up the steps, he watched the throng of people passing back and forth in front of him as if nothing was wrong—as if his perfect, logical world wasn't disintegrating before their curious side glances. For a brief moment, he considered calling Harley back to instruct her to pick him up at the office, but he wasn't sure he'd be able to stand, much less walk without collapsing. Taking deep breaths, he sat up straight, smoothed his tie, and wiped the sweat from his forehead. He looked at his phone and logged into some social media account Harley had installed for him. For the life of him he couldn't figure out why people wanted to look at pictures of cats.

"Damien?"

Hearing his father call his name, he pocketed his phone and turned, feeling the relief of a lost child. His dad descended the steps in haste, his brow furrowed. Known for his commanding presence, his father appeared to have aged ten years since the shooting and Mom's death. His hair was grayer, the lines around his eyes deeper, and his shoulders were slightly stooped, as if the weight of everything that had happened was too heavy to endure.

Damien vowed to resume having Sunday dinner with his father. Maybe he'd even suggest they take a quick trip to see Angel and Maggie's bed and breakfast. With him and Maggie running interference between Dad and Angel, it might work, and even do some good in repairing his father and brother's relationship.

"Are you okay, son? Brad Cuthbert came in and told me you were on the steps and looked ill."

Great, so much for my attempt to be inconspicuous.

"Uh, yeah…" He attempted a smile but was pretty sure he hadn't pulled it off, judging by the concern on his father's face.

He stood and gave him a hug, trying to divert his attention while keeping a covert eye out for Harley.

His dad dove into a rundown of some of their current cases. "Why don't you come have Sunday lunch with me," he concluded. "I'll have Elise cook a roast."

"Okay, yes, I'd like that."

Harley pulled up in the painted van with music blaring so loud it could be heard through the rolled-up windows. His father frowned, his eyes darting between the vehicle from hell and Damien.

Suck it up; admit defeat. "Thanks for sending Harley over to take care of me. I appreciate it, Dad."

His father raised one eyebrow. "I didn't send her. What exactly is she doing to 'take care' of you? Be careful, son. Remember the boundaries. We don't want any sexual harassment cases. Plus, I can't imagine Lauren will be thrilled. Is Harley driving into town every day?"

"Lauren and I aren't together. She broke it off after Christmas."

"I see. That explains Brad's attitude lately…" His father again glanced over at Harley and back at him.

His parents had pushed him and Lauren together since high school. With the skill of a talented lawyer, Damien avoided commenting on where Harley lived at present to circumvent the lecture.

"So, you didn't hire Harley to come take care of me?" he asked.

"No." His father shot another questioning look toward Harley, who seemed to sink lower into her seat.

The car behind her leaned on the horn.

"Ah, well, it must have been Elise's suggestion. I appreciate the help, regardless. Look, I think coming back full time this quickly was a mistake. What if I work from home for a few more days?"

"Sure. I'll see that a courier gets you what you need. If you have any questions, give me a ring."

They descended the steps, and his father opened the passenger door of the van.

Harley turned down the music and offered him a faint, nervous smile and wave. "Hi, Mr. S."

"Thank you for taking care of Damien, Harley." His dad stared intently at her.

"Yes, s-sir," she replied.

Damien didn't like the look that passed between them. It made him feel like a teenager again.

His father straightened and patted him on the back. "Be careful, son. Remember the rules." He paused and whispered, "Tread carefully. She's like family."

What? As if things between him and Harley weren't muddled enough, now his father was calling her family? Damien threw his briefcase to the floorboard. Relieved to be going home, he buckled his seatbelt and looked over at Harley, who stared straight ahead.

"Thanks for picking me up."

"What about your car?"

"I'll send Tim to get it. I suspect he takes it for a joy ride every now and then, anyway. I check the mileage."

Harley rolled her eyes. "Of course you do."

She turned the music back up to rock-concert level and pulled into traffic, ignoring the blare of the car she cut off.

Closing his eyes, he rested his aching head against his fist and didn't complain at all.

"I guess I'll just drop you off…"

"You can stay," he mumbled without opening his eyes.

"What?"

"You heard me. You can stay."

Silence.

He cleared his throat. "I'm sorry. Please, stay?"

"Okay. I've got a yoga class right now, so I'll let you out at the front door and be back later."

He grunted an affirmation.

Harley parked her van and cut the engine. *What made Damien change his mind?* Claire would kick her ass when she found out she'd gone back. When he called, she'd just finished packing her van, ready to leave after teaching class. Jerry had gladly stricken her from the approved list.

With a few minutes before class, she decided to break the news and get it over with. Nervously she traced a spray-painted heart on her dash as she waited for Claire to pick up.

"*Harley Harlot.*"

"Hey, Claire Bear."

"*What's up? I got your text—about time you were done catering to that ungrateful ass. I tried to warn you.*"

"He just asked me to come back."

"*Please tell me you said no.*"

Harley kept silent.

Claire sighed. "*Oh shit, here we go again…I wish you'd call Mark. He might be able to talk some sense in to you.*"

"I will…" *Eventually.*

"*All right. This is your decision. I'm here for you, blah, blah, blah, insert more supportive friend bullshit. I hate to cut this short, but I've got to get back to work. Let's go out, soon, okay?*"

"'Kay. Love you."

"*Back atcha, bitch.*"

A night out on the town was definitely needed. Teaching this yoga class would give her a little cash.

She stopped by the security office and asked Tim if he'd take her things upstairs.

"Sure thing. Hey, thanks for the baby blanket! I'm glad you're… staying?"

"For now. Poor Jerry."

They both laughed.

She turned around, bumping someone with her yoga mat. "Jerry!" She hugged his neck. "Never mind! You can put me back on the list!"

Jerry's look of annoyance made her day. She flipped her braid over her shoulder and made her way to the gym on the ground floor of Damien's building. As she entered, several of the residents called out their greetings.

"Who's ready for yoga?" Harley asked.

"I am!" Mr. Gavosovich answered. He was wearing his bathing suit and a sweatshirt today.

"You need to actually do the moves to get the benefit," Harley teased. "Remember, if you can't do the floor exercises, just do them in your chair. Everything is at your own comfort level." She unfurled her mat.

There were six in the class, five women and Mr. Gavosovich. He and Mrs. Little remained in their chairs while the others were already waiting on their mats.

"He just wants to look at your butt. It isn't like the old goat could do anything about it," Mrs. Little retorted with a cackle.

"Nothing wrong with window shopping as long as you don't handle the merchandise," he replied.

Harley just laughed. He was from a different era, harmless, and unlikely to change. She'd discovered the class the first week she was at Damien's and offered to fill in for the teacher who was off on maternity leave as of last weekend. So far, she'd taught it twice. The students were mainly the retired people who lived here.

She doubted Damien was aware of all the amenities offered in his building. He lived in his own self-imposed bubble on the top floor.

She led them through an hour of stretching and breathing, and then after the class came the best part: hearing the stories of these remarkable people. Sure, some of them, like Mr. Gavosovich, repeated the same stories, but seeing their faces light up as they talked was worth it. However, today she cut the visiting short to check on Damien. Promising to spend more time after the next class, she gave each of her students a hug and left.

Chapter Eight

Heading upstairs, Harley's anxiety grew as she pondered what Mr. Sinclair might have whispered to Damien when she picked him up. Mr. S must've known she'd lied…And what had made Damien change his mind about having her leave?

Quietly, so as not to disturb him, she let herself into the penthouse. He'd left his briefcase by the front door, which was very unlike Mr. Everything-Has-a-Place. She picked it up and placed it on his desk, mindful not to get fingerprints on the glass desktop.

The door to his bedroom was closed. She wanted to check on him, but hesitated, remembering it was "off limits."

Harley took her yoga mat to her room and found her duffel and craft bag on her bed. After a quick shower, she decided she'd unpack later, still unsure how long she'd be staying.

When Damien had left for work, she'd gone online and put applications in at various gyms, restaurants, and hair salons around town. She didn't relish the thought of moving back home, but she'd need to save some money before moving out.

Heading back to the kitchen, she decided to surprise Damien with a snack he'd appreciate—and her mother would find repugnant.

Five minutes later, she knocked on the door to his bedroom with a tray.

"Come in." His voice sounded weary.

She entered and found him in bed, lying on his back with an arm thrown over his eyes. Drawn shades made the room dim and depressing. The covers pushed low on his abdomen revealed his sculpted, naked chest.

"I didn't know if you'd had anything to eat. I brought you a snack."

"I'm not hungry, but thank you." He put his arm down and opened his eyes. His smile made her heart do a funny little flip-flop. "Is that a cinnamon toaster tart?"

She placed the tray on his bedside table. "I figured you'd had a rough day, so you needed comfort food. Wanna talk about what happened?" Without thinking, she ran her fingers through his hair. "You've had a haircut. It looks nice, not too short."

He caught her hand in his and interlaced their fingers. Fear tinged his dark eyes. "What's wrong with me?"

She sat on the bed beside him. "What do you mean? What happened?"

When he moved over to make room, her concern grew. *What happened to "off limits"?* She lay down on top of the covers on her side, propping her head on her hand. It reminded her of when they were kids and would eat popcorn and watch scary movies. Although he'd teased her endlessly, he'd also let her curl up at his side and hide her eyes in his shirt.

"At the weirdest, unexpected times, I find I can't stand being around people. My heart starts racing, my head pounds, and I break out in a cold sweat. I've lost my ability to think anymore. I'm hyperaware of everything around me. I'm fucking going crazy. It's like I don't know who I am. Am I Damien Sinclair, heir to my family's legacy? Demon Sinclair, cutthroat, asshole lawyer? Or just some crazy idiot scared of his own fucking shadow?"

"You need to speak to your doctor."

"I don't want to." He turned onto his side, facing her.

Everything about this man tugged her heart. His smell, the deep rumble of his voice, those dark eyes that seemed to see straight through her…

"If I do, the problem becomes even more real," he quietly admitted.

"I'm not a professional, but it sounds like some anxiety, or post-traumatic stress. It isn't anything to be ashamed of."

"How can I function as a lawyer if I can't even get up the damn courthouse steps?" He sighed and closed his eyes.

"You need to cut yourself some slack. Your mother died, and a few weeks later, you were shot. Give yourself some time. You've never stopped thinking about work, whether you can get there or not. You're too hard on yourself and much too regimented. Live in the moment; be spontaneous. Take some time to relax." She stroked his cheek before moving to leave, but his arm snaked out and held her.

"Don't leave me. Please?" It started as an order but ended as a soft plea.

"I won't." She meant it. Rolling over with her back to him, she settled down on the pillow.

He didn't realize it, but she'd go to hell and back for him. Harley closed her eyes, enjoying the warmth and weight of his arm wrapped around her as he spooned her from behind. She'd just lie here for a little while until he fell asleep.

The familiar, comforting scent of summer peaches and a soft breast in his hand made him smile. He must be dreaming, he mused. Or he'd died and gone to heaven. Either way, it was enjoyable.

Damien cracked open an eye and spit blond hair out of his mouth. *Harley!* He snatched his hand away from her T-shirt as if burned. *Shit!*

She stirred like a sleepy kitten, rolling onto her back. Today's shirt read *Bad Influence*. Turning toward him, Harley opened her eyes, and he did his damnedest to keep his eyes on her face.

"Hello." She gave him a sleepy, innocent smile.

But her breathy voice made him think of sex. Shit, everything about her lately made him think of sex. It didn't help when she stretched and *Bad Influence* emphasized her hard nipples.

"Hey you. What happened to off limits?" he grumbled, reaching across her to pick up his cold toaster tart.

"You invited *me*, Admiral Alzheimer."

He smiled and took a bite of the tart. "Nice one."

"Thank you. I aim to please."

"That's what he said," Damien replied.

She giggled. His eyes scanned her pouty lips, and he shifted away.

He took another bite of his toaster tart. "What time is it?"

With her mouth, Harley took the last bite of tart from his fingers. Her eyes darkened, and her lips seemed to linger a second longer than necessary. His already sex-deprived cock stood up and took notice. He rolled onto his stomach.

Dammit, what the hell is wrong with me?

A sharp intake of breath hissed through her teeth, and she croaked, "It's four in the afternoon."

"What?" His brain had turned to mush.

"You asked me the time."

Turning, she shifted to put a safe distance between them. The Harley red blush on her neck and cheeks made him suspect she was aware of whatever the hell was going on between them, too. A myriad of unspoken emotions parleyed back and forth as they gazed at one another.

Memories of her sex-flushed face in the pool house years ago taunted him. He needed to get his mind off of the past.

"Harley?"

"Yes?"

"What happened to you on New Year's Eve?"

"Nothing."

He stared and waited.

"It was an accident."

"Bullshit. If you'd told me who did it, I would've done more than provided you a ride home. The bastard who did that to you would've been prosecuted and thrown in jail."

She rolled onto her back and stared at the ceiling. "I made a poor judgment call."

He stayed still, waiting for her to continue.

She sighed. "You'll think I'm certifiable, and justifiably so."

"You've always been nuts, and lately I seem to be riding the crazy train, too. We make a good team," he encouraged. He reached out and pulled her toward him, wanting to give her comfort. "Tell me. I'm not going to judge or prosecute. I'm your friend. No matter what happened, I'm here for you."

She eyed him for a moment, seeming to be making up her mind. "I just wanted to live life on the edge, to try something out of my comfort zone. You know what I mean?"

What? She's the most spontaneous person I know.

Damien knew he could simply nod, and she'd continue. But something compelled him to be completely honest with her.

"No, not really. This surprises me. You're the kid who always colored outside of the lines. Me, on the other hand…"

Harley giggled. "Black. You only colored in black and gray, and neatly, in the lines. Some psychologist would have a field day analyzing you."

Damien shrugged. "What can I say? I've always liked things black and white."

"But lawyers are notorious for shading the truth in the gray area."

"True, but we remain within the constraints of black and white. No freestyling. That's part of my problem. My comfort zone was compromised by the shooting. Now I don't feel at ease anywhere."

She rested her head on his shoulder. "That's totally understandable, Sin. You were shot and nearly killed in a place where you were used to being in control. Give yourself time." Easing up, she rested her cheek on her fist and gazed down at him. With her other hand, she pushed the hair off his forehead.

Damien closed his eyes to avoid watching the rise and fall of *Bad Influence* and gave in to the pleasant feeling of her fingers in his hair. "Tell me what happened, Harley," he murmured.

"I, uh, went to this special kind of club with a friend." Her voice caught, and she lay back down and stared at the ceiling.

"I thought Claire was with Charlie." He'd always liked Harley's best friend—Claire's brother, Mark, not so much.

"She was. It was, uh, someone else."

Damien opened his eyes.

"But I didn't like the place, and my friend did. She'd hooked up with this guy, so I decided to leave."

Damien raised his head and propped it on his fist as she continued.

"While I was waiting outside, this guy came up behind me." She paused as if struggling for the words. "He grabbed me, surprising me. He kept saying he'd give me what I wanted. When I tried to get away, he hit me."

"What?" Damien reeled in his fury for Harley's sake. He needed to stay calm and be rational. He kissed her hand, an overwhelming need to protect her coursing through his veins. In his mind, he was already filing the necessary paperwork to put this guy away forever.

"Someone must've heard me scream, because he stopped and ran away. They offered to get me an ambulance, but I was too ashamed. There was no way I could let my parents know where I'd been. I refused, and someone from the club took me to the ER."

"Why the hell weren't the police called? Did he—?" Damien's anger now simmered close to boiling, but he kept his voice soft and level.

"No, no, I was lucky…Nothing that bad happened. The police weren't called because no one wanted the publicity. Especially me." She pulled away from him and turned to her side. Her knees pulled up to her chest, and her shoulders shook.

"Publicity be damned! What club was it? Where was the damn security? What kind of dive bar were you in? Why didn't anyone stop him? This isn't making any sense, Harley. Why didn't whoever the hell drove you to the ER stay with you? Why didn't you tell me this shit that night? I would've helped you." He leaned over and stroked her shoulder, but she kept her face hidden.

"You'd just been shot and were in the hospital. What could you have done? The guy who took me to the hospital was afraid he'd get in trouble, so he dropped me off at the door. I was grateful for that much," she choked out, her head buried in her pillows.

"Grateful for being dropped off like garbage on the curb? What the fuck?"

"Just leave it alone. It won't happen again. I've learned what happens to silly girls with overactive imaginations who read too many stupid erotic romance novels."

"Sweetheart, it wasn't your fault some asshole hurt you. Which club was it? And what does a romance novel have to do with this?"

Something wasn't right with her story. He mentally ticked off a list of things he'd need to pursue so he could make a case. No way in hell would he let this drop. He should've done something when it happened. Dad would've helped.

"No! I don't want my parents finding out, or my brothers. Just drop it. I told you more than I should've." Her shoulders shuddered.

"Okay…Okay, I'm sorry." He rubbed her shoulder and gentled his tone. "Finish the story. You can tell me anything…"

Harley turned, but kept her hands over her red face. She took a deep breath. "I read these books…I was curious." She took a deep breath and whispered, "It was a BDSM club."

If she'd said it was at a club inhabited by space aliens, he wouldn't have been any more shocked. He hauled her up to a sitting position and shook her. "What the hell were you looking for in a club like that?"

"Gotcha." Two blue eyes stared at him from behind her fingers, and her laughter rang out and echoed in the room.

"What?"

"Gotcha!" she howled again.

"Sonofabitch!" He shoved her away; angry he'd once again fallen for one of her stupid stories.

"God, you're so easy to punk. You really believed me." She collapsed, holding her stomach.

"I did not. Okay maybe for a minute." He ran a hand through his hair. "Goddammit, you had a black eye. What really happened?"

Her face fell, and she crossed her arms as if shielding herself. "I met a guy through a dating app. Of course I didn't let him pick me up; I arranged to meet him at the bar. Like I told you, who wants to be alone on New Year's Eve? But alcohol changed the guy into a douchebag octopus. I wanted to go home, so I left. As I walked outside to flag a cab, some guy tried to grab my purse. I held on, and in the process my heel caught in the sidewalk. He ran off, but I wobbled like a newborn giraffe and hit the ground. As I fell, my purse hit my face, giving me a black eye.

"Some stranger helped me up and wanted to call the police, but I was embarrassed for being so foolish. A cab pulled up, and I talked the stranger out of calling the police by telling him I'd go get checked out at the ER. The nice guy made sure I gave the driver the address of the hospital closest to us, which happened to be where you were. The ride over was kind of a blur. I was pretty shaken, and too late I realized I wouldn't have enough money to change my mind and go home. Subconsciously, I don't think I really wanted to go home alone…You know the rest."

Her laughter gone, she hung her head and a real tear slipped down her soft, pink cheek.

"I know you say nothing was stolen, but you were hurt," he said. "You should've reported it to the police. And at the very least, you should've told me all this that night."

"I didn't want to admit to being stupid and hear the lecture from my parents and Byron. I'm not totally ignorant; I know no one thinks I'm able to take care of myself…"

"But your parents had to have seen your black eye the next day."

She shrugged. "I told them I tripped, which was kind of true."

"Getting mugged is serious. How have you been handling it?" He traced the pattern of her long braid.

"Truthfully?"

He nodded, concerned and curious. Maybe if she was handling her trauma better than he was handling his, he could learn from her how to get his life back to normal.

"I'm here." She sighed and looked away. Her cheeks bloomed with color.

"Here?"

When she looked him in the face, a rare vulnerability settled around her eyes.

"I-I don't want to be alone. I need you…Never mind…"

He pulled her back toward him, under the covers this time, and wrapped his arms around her. A need to protect and comfort her negated her silly fabricated story and any of his self-imposed boundaries. He'd let her stay as long as she needed. He didn't say a word as she fell asleep, rather enjoying the feel of her in his arms.

"I've got you, Harley," he whispered into her hair.

She sighed in her sleep and snuggled in tighter, her face relaxing.

As a kid, whenever he spent the night with her brothers, she would beg him to check under her bed to make sure there were no demons hiding there. At age nine, he'd told her to quit acting like a girl, but he'd secretly been thrilled he could put her fears to rest. He'd always felt protective of her. And now she was in his bed. And he *liked* her acting like a girl—a little too much.

However, it was damn hard to feel protective of her when he was, in fact, damn hard.

Harley opened her eyes and realized she'd fallen asleep in Sin's bed. *Oh great.* She'd just planned to spin a story and punk him, not tell Mr. Fear-of-Commitment she *needed* him.

She scampered to use his bathroom, praying he wasn't around to gripe about the off-limits rule. Rinsing her hot face with cool water, she wished it was as easy to wash away her embarrassment. She sighed.

"Sleep well?"

Harley jumped and screamed at the sound of his voice.

"Easy. I didn't mean to scare you." He grinned. "Although, you deserve it for that ridiculous story."

Barefoot and dressed in a pair of black jeans and a long-sleeved black T-shirt, Damien stood behind her. Unable to look him in the face, she stared at the floor. *Even his feet are sexy. And long.* She blushed, remembering he proved the old adage true, despite her teasing about his bits.

"I'll be in the kitchen." He turned and left.

She followed him and found pasta boiling on the stove. He stirred it and checked his watch.

"I'm sorry. You must think I'm ridiculous." She moved to take over stirring the boiling pasta, but he shook his head.

"Stop. If anyone knows the emotional upheaval of being attacked and the strange and curious places it manifests, I do. Sit. I'll cook. You do the dishes."

"B-But this is my job."

"Not tonight. Your benevolent boss is giving you the night off." He winked at her, and she released the nervous breath she'd been holding. She hopped up on the counter next to the stove and glanced down at the pasta.

"Do you know what you're doing? How long has it been boiling?"

"Three minutes. And no, I haven't got a clue, but your mother does."

Rut-roh. Harley mentally started packing her bags.

"I had an interesting conversation with her today, after she gave me the instructions for her olive oil, basil, and tomato pasta recipe." His eyes bore into hers.

I should've known this was too easy.

"Let me make sure I have my facts straight. Neither my father nor your mother asked you to come here to take care of me. And neither of them knows you're staying here." He all but purred as he methodically stirred the pasta.

"No and no."

"You lied to me."

She stared at her pink toenails. "Yes, I lied. *Mea culpa.* I'm guilty. Punish me."

The words flew out of her mouth before she could stop them. *Great.* Considering her recent tall tale about the BDSM club, he'd probably nail her to the cross—metaphorically speaking, not an actual St. Andrew's cross. Mr. Stick-Up-His-Ass probably wouldn't know what that was—not that she'd ever really seen one either.

"Your confession is duly noted. The question remains, why? Why did you tell me they sent you here?"

He drained the pasta, and the steam rose. One lock of his hair curled on his forehead.

She looked at the floor, unsure what to say.

"Because I knew you wouldn't let stay me if I simply offered."

Harley watched him toss the olive oil, garlic, tomato, and basil with the pasta. There was something sexy about a man cooking. It smelled divine, and she smiled, knowing her mother would indeed be proud of him. Mamma loved and worried about Damien and Angel as much as she did her own children.

"I don't need anyone to take care of me." Damien took a clean fork and sampled the pasta before adding salt and freshly ground pepper. His lips shone with the olive oil, and Harley wanted to taste them so badly she gripped the counter to keep from doing so.

"You needed me to pick your butt up at the courthouse earlier." As soon as it came out of her mouth, she regretted it.

Color flushed his chiseled cheeks, and he looked away, his jaw tightening.

"I'm sorry, Sin. That was a low blow. I was happy to do it. I just, well, I think you *do* need me. I know I need you."

"Why do you need me?"

The tension in the room was as taut as the strings on his violin. Harley squirmed. Damien had a way of focusing his attention on people and drawing out unwanted confessions. However, his ability to listen and read people applied to everyone *but* her. For some reason, he wore blinders and didn't see—or chose to ignore—the way she'd always felt about him. Honestly, she didn't know whether to be relieved or insulted.

She offered him a half-truth. "Because I don't want to live with my parents at age twenty-nine. Because I want to feel safe. I make myself run in the park every day and give out my packets to the homeless because I don't want to give in to the fear. But I haven't truly felt safe since I was mugged—unless I'm with you. I always have. And because I cried after you were shot, scared you were dying. Because I miss your mother and her music, and I know you do, too. Because goddammit, I c-care about you."

Damien looked puzzled. "You miss my mother? She didn't exactly treat you well."

"She wasn't unkind, just direct and to the point. I liked that about her. When I was little, she used to let me play dress-up in her closet and wear some of her jewelry. She liked braiding my hair and told me she'd always wanted a daughter. And when my dog, Shakespeare, died, she held my hand and stayed with me as my dad buried him in the backyard. And she taught me about music and how to play the piano."

Harley shrugged. "I mean, sure, Mrs. S always believed in everyone having their place, and she could be abrupt, but the nice things she did for me over the years outweighed her snootiness. She overheard me talking about the prom with my mom and took me shopping for my prom dress..." Harley bit her lip, not wanting to get into what happened after the prom.

"My mother did all that?" Damien stared at her for a moment.

Harley nodded, her heart hammering a staccato rhythm as her fate lay in his hands.

He shrugged, looking surprised. "I guess she had her moments."

"Just before she died, she told me she was sorry and thanked me."

"What was she apologizing for?"

"I'm not really sure, probably for yelling at me about those protein drinks she didn't like. She just held my hand and said, 'I'm sorry,' and told me to keep an eye on you. She was worried about you and Angel."

"Perhaps…" He started serving their dinner. "Now, because I care about *you*, I'm glad you're here. Sit. Let's eat and see if I made *your* mother proud."

That's it? Have I really been given a reprieve?

It was like getting a Christmas gift. Her father had once told her love was an action. Maybe she was reading too much into this, but he hadn't sent her packing, *and* he'd cooked her a meal…

Chapter
Nine

For the rest of the week and through the weekend, Damien had worked from home, each day a little better in terms of his ability to concentrate without the debilitating headache. This morning his dad had called and canceled Sunday lunch due to a cold, but Damien had felt confident enough to tell him he'd be back to the office tomorrow. Harley kept things running smoothly, to the point that he wasn't really aware of her comings and goings. He supposed she'd learned it from her parents, who had been in service all of her life.

Tonight, after they'd watched an old movie together, she'd retired to her room. Damien now sat in the dark, staring out the window, drinking his scotch, and thinking. Their parents hadn't sent her. She'd lied to him. But the truth was, he liked having her here. It was *comfortable*. She kept his place immaculate, ran his errands, and was a damn good cook, even if it was healthy food. Her sense of humor cheered him up, and she put up with his OCD tendencies. She'd even laughed at the shirt-folding board he'd ordered for her and wrapped like a present.

Harley Blake Taylor was unlike any other woman he'd ever encountered.

The first lecture he'd ever received regarding Harley had come after his father overheard an argument he'd had with her friend Claire's adopted brother, Mark MacGregor. He and Mark had been in high school. He'd been a senior and Mark—having flunked a grade—a junior. The fucker had been flirting with Harley, and he hadn't liked it. Mark was troubled and, more importantly, a player. He'd warned Mark to stay away, feeling protective. Looking back, he realized he'd been jealous and possessive.

Dad's lecture had been succinct:

"Don't cross the line with the help. Ever."

"Think with the head on your shoulders, not the one between your legs."

"You're a Sinclair and have responsibilities to the family, and those who work for us."

"Appearances matter."

"Failure is not an option."

Of course, it was mild compared to what he'd heard after being caught literally with his pants down.

After college and law school, he and Harley had only crossed paths on the rare occasions when she came home to visit her parents while he was visiting his. When thrown together, they'd been cordial, or teasing, but they'd never scratched the surface of their relationship, or discussed the past. As a matter of fact, the only time he could remember being alone with her was when she'd sat quietly with him after Mom died. And he'd been involved with Lauren...

He stopped, realizing he had no idea if Harley had dated anyone seriously after Mark MacGregor. Surely she had. Some man would be lucky to have her. She was beautiful, funny, and sweet...

Which made her dangerous for a self-proclaimed bachelor. Maybe that's why whenever she returned to the Sinclair home, his father would hit the high points of his lecture again. But the day she'd picked him up at the courthouse, Dad had softened his approach, calling Harley *family*.

Did Mom's death change his perspective?

At nineteen, parental pressure had repressed his feelings. Regret and anger had kept him away when his mother informed him Harley was dating Mark and they were serious.

He swirled his scotch.

But now she was back. And old feelings had resurfaced. This was becoming a problem. As much as he wanted her to stay, he needed to send her home before things got out of hand. He'd seen the way she looked at him, and he didn't want to offer false hope. Harley wanted the happily ever after, and he didn't believe in fairy-tale endings. *I'm a divorce lawyer, for crying out loud.* Not to mention, he'd grown up with the façade of his parents "happy" marriage, which had been anything *but* happy at times.

He walked to the window and leaned his forehead against the cool glass, gazing over the city, taking in the lights of the moving traffic. Living on the top floor with soundproof glass, it was eerily quiet. The silence magnified his loneliness.

He turned, hearing a soft rustle behind him. *Am I dreaming?* A walking, living sex goddess floated toward him.

Illuminated by the moonlight, the flowing, white diaphanous gown hugged and enhanced her lush figure. His fingers itched to take it off. Harley's hair was loose and spilled around her shoulders like a flaxen waterfall. An overwhelming urge to wrap that hair around his fist and pull her to him surged through every fiber in his body.

"I'm sorry. I didn't know you were still awake." Her soft, breathy voice teased his senses. Even in the pale light he could see the color rising from her chest to her cheeks.

"I think I slept too much this afternoon," he offered, unwilling to admit that thoughts of her were the cause of his insomnia.

"I could make you some hot cocoa."

He held up his empty glass. "I could pour you a tumbler of scotch."

Her musical laugh reeled him in closer. "Even better."

Harley gazed out the window. "Your view is spectacular, but someday I want to go visit Angel and Maggie. He says there are millions of stars to be seen in the country. I can't even imagine. We've always lived where lights and trees block them. When I get there, I'll count them all."

"You can't count the stars." His voice sounded gruff even to his own ears.

"How do you know unless you try?"

He shook his head and smiled at her whimsical answer. Knowing her, she'd give it a shot.

Damien poured their drinks. Handing her the glass, his fingers grazed hers, and the sexual energy between them charged the air like an electrical storm.

Disturbed, he pulled away. "Go see him. He and Maggie have plenty of room at their bed and breakfast."

"Come with me?" She reached out and held his hand, her luminous eyes full of hope and desire.

He took a breath. The moment had come. "Harley, you know we can't cross this line." Staring at her beautiful face, so open and honest, he wondered just where the damn line was.

"Why not? We're both consenting adults."

The line blurred even more.

"Please?"

"It wouldn't be ethical. I'm your employer."

"Um, well, no. Technically, you're not."

"But I offered to double my father's salary."

"Double times nothing equals zero. Nobody has paid me. I came because I care about you. I always have..." She placed her drink on the coffee table and moved back to him, wrapping her arms around his waist. "And one plus one can become one if done properly."

She looked into his eyes, undisguised longing dancing across her features. Her almost sheer gown left little to the imagination, and when her hard nipples pressed into his chest, it was almost his undoing. He stepped back to regain his equilibrium.

"Or one plus one could also equal three, which would be disastrous."

Pain flickered in her eyes. He immediately regretted taking his frustration out on her. She pulled away and crossed her arms.

"I'm on birth control. I'm an adult. I know what I want."

The confession disturbed him and threw him off course.

Run!

His conscience screamed as his mind reeled, and his body reacted to her very nearness. The woman gazing at him did indeed appear to know what she wanted, and it terrified him because he knew on some level he wanted the same. He loved the way she smelled of peaches, the way her neck and cheeks blushed Harley red. Her sense of humor matched his, and she could be incredibly sweet. But he didn't like the way these things made him feel out of control.

"Sin —" Her warm breath seeped into his cold, withdrawn heart.

"Harley, no. I can't. I won't." Turning away from her, he put more distance between them, looking out at the clear night sky and wishing he could escape the storm brewing inside his home. He'd never give anyone that much control over his heart.

He tried to temper his words with kindness while laying out the facts. "After our discussion the other night, I'm not entirely convinced you do know what you want, or what you need. It's time to grow up. As you stated, you're twenty-nine. Yet you flit through life working one job after another. You don't stick to anything you start. And this business of putting yourself in danger without thinking…"

And, because I don't know what the hell to think about my feelings toward of you.

"Whatever. I'm not desperate. I can satisfy my needs in other ways, or with other people," she snapped.

The words fell into the chasm between them, suspended like a rickety bridge across a canyon of turbulent emotions. He didn't dare breathe for fear the bridge would collapse and he'd drown. Didn't she understand that sex complicated things? They'd already been through this once.

Throwing back her drink, Harley gasped at the burn, and tears filled her eyes.

Were they from the liquor, or his rejection? *Way to go, asshole.* He'd done precisely what he'd hoped to avoid. He'd hurt her. She exited the room, leaving behind the scent of peaches and the unsettling feeling of loss.

Damien followed her into the kitchen. Ignoring him, she rinsed her glass and put it in the dishwasher. She moved to leave the room, but he caught her by her chin and raised her face up to his.

"I'm trying to be realistic and define our relationship. I thought you were being paid. I'll rectify that immediately. And we can't muddle the boundaries."

"It isn't about the stupid money. And I don't believe you. This isn't about the so-called boundaries, either. The problem is, you don't want to lose control. This wasn't *your* idea. If it had been, you probably would've had me on my back with my legs spread in no time."

Her crudeness shocked him speechless, something that never happened. He was, after all, a lawyer who could talk for hours about nothing.

"If you ever decide you want to 'muddle the boundaries,' let me know. Maybe it won't be too late. Now, if you don't mind, remove your hand from my face. I'm tired and want to go to bed, *Mr. Sinclair.* I need to be rested so I can perform my duties as your maid and cook tomorrow. Since you don't want what was offered as a *gift*, payment for my *services* will be required. And don't expect anything beyond what my mother would do for you. Despite what you may think, I'm not a whore." She crossed her arms and glared at him with a look so cold the room temperature seemed to drop fifteen degrees.

"Good God, Harley, I'd never think that…" Guilt kept him silent for a moment. Pride kept him from apologizing. "First of all, you came here under false pretenses. I assumed you were being compensated for your work. As I said, I'll pay you to cook, clean, do laundry, and run errands for me. I don't want you to go, but I also don't want to hurt you. I'm trying to be fair and honest here. That's why we can't cross the line. *Ever.* I'll be your employer and remain your friend. Trust me—friendship is more valuable than a quick toss in the sack. I don't want to ruin that with you because you mean too much to me. Do you understand?"

He brushed a strand of her silken hair off her face. She nodded, looking at the floor.

"Look at me," he whispered roughly.

Twisting her fingers together, she slowly raised her head. Sorrow was quickly replaced by a look of indifference.

Not wanting to hurt her further, Damien gentled his voice. "Understand?"

She tossed her chin in the air. "Yes, *sir.* I understand. Thank you so much for clarifying my situation for me, *sir.* May I be excused, *sir?* I have a long and interesting day ahead of me scrubbing your damn toilets."

Her sarcastic submissiveness relieved him. Harley's fiery spirit was her essence—he truly didn't want to see it dampened. "Poached egg, wheat toast, orange juice, and coffee at seven. See you in the morning."

"As you request, o mighty master." She curtsied and turned to leave. He caught her by the arm.

"And topping from the bottom is not acceptable if that's the lifestyle you choose. It's BDSM 101."

Harley's mouth opened and shut, her eyes wide. Giving him an almost imperceptible nod, she turned and fled the room with deferential meekness—that is, until she slammed her bedroom door.

Harley crawled in bed and finally let the tears flow. Over the years she'd compartmentalized her feelings for Damien into a nice, neat little spot she rarely visited. They'd both been incredibly young and, in her case, incredibly stupid. Eventually, she'd even grown up enough to forgive him.

But sometimes, when alone at night, she'd recall every detail of that fateful spring break—the heady feeling when he'd responded to her flirting, stolen kisses that had led to roaming hands and shedding of clothes. Their first time had been awkward and thrilling. He'd been gentle, considerate, and loving. She'd been scared, excited, and *in love*.

Even now, she could recall the feel of his hands and lips on her body. The smell of his cologne, the taste of chlorine on his damp skin, the sound of his voice when he'd whispered her name. Even when his father had walked in on them the last time they'd been together, he'd hidden her from view, protecting her.

But then he'd returned to school, never giving her a second thought—crushing her dreams and leaving her devastated. Anger and her own insecurities had kept her from reaching out to ask why. Her parents had put up with her moping for a while, but they'd finally sat her down and lovingly, but firmly reminded her of the class differences between their families, and the unlikeliness of summer infatuations ever being anything more. A few weeks later, Damien's mother had let it drop that he and Lauren were serious. To compensate for her broken heart, she'd gone and done things she regretted.

She pushed those memories aside. They were too painful to dwell on right now.

Maybe Claire was right. She should give up, admit defeat. Damien would never see her as girlfriend material. In the last twelve years, he'd never apologized or given any indication he was remorseful for the way he'd left things. At the time, Claire had bluntly told her she might have been nothing more than a notch on his belt.

But she'd never given credence to that. It wasn't Damien's style. And she had to believe something so beautiful as her first time had meant something to him, too. She'd forgiven him long ago, but nearly losing him to a bullet had reminded her life is short, stirring the feelings she'd repressed for so long.

Rolling on her back, she stared at the ceiling. Should she just wave the white flag and go home? Twenty-nine, single, and living with her parents. Great. All she needed was a dozen cats to complete the depressing picture of her future.

No! That couldn't be the end of it. She'd seen the way he looked at her when he thought she wasn't aware...And he was sick, whether he acknowledged it or not. She'd been reading online about post-traumatic stress and survivor's guilt, and she had no doubt those were a lot of his problem. He needed help. And until he got it, he needed her.

And anyway, admitting defeat wasn't in her nature...

Chapter Ten

Harley dragged herself out of bed and staggered to the kitchen after a restless night. Next to the coffee pot she found a legal document outlining her salary, work hours, and benefits, including a highlighted clause spelling out sexual harassment—he was ever the lawyer. With a yawn, she started the coffee, glanced at the clock, and scowled when she realized it was already six-thirty. She'd have to hustle. His Lordship would be upset if breakfast was late. The whirring sound of the treadmill stopped, and she heard his shower start. That meant she had twenty minutes, tops.

She'd just finished plating his breakfast when he walked into the kitchen, dressed in black slacks, a starched white shirt, and her favorite black-and-gray patterned tie. His hair was damp but combed, and he was freshly shaven. Harley placed his breakfast in front of him and took a deep breath.

God, I love how he smells.

"I swear to God, did you just sniff me again?" he asked with a baffled look.

"No, I, uh, just, uh, er, allergies." She faked a sniffle, grabbed the coffee, and poured him a cup. "I agree to your terms but would like back pay."

"That's a given. I'll write a check before I leave for work. Where's your breakfast?"

He opened the paper and appeared to be reading, but Harley caught him stealing glances at her. Wearing yoga pants and a sports bra, she did a ballet stretch, in front of him, on purpose. He shifted in his chair, looking uncomfortable.

Take that, friend…

"I didn't figure the help should eat with you. Wouldn't that be crossing the boundary?" She didn't hide her sarcasm. Handing him his coffee, she sipped her hot tea.

A flush of anger crossed his face. "Don't be ridiculous. Sit down and eat some damn breakfast. It's the most important meal of the day."

"I'll eat a protein bar on my way to class." She busied herself with wiping down the kitchen counter to keep from staring at him. He was too handsome for his own good, and too damn stubborn to acknowledge the chemistry between them.

She'd decided last night it was time to change the game plan and teach Ollie Oblivion a lesson. He wanted to be friends? *Fine.* Friends it would be, but she'd darn well make sure she drove him crazy in the process.

"What class? Now what are you studying? Nuclear physics?"

"It isn't that type of class, and I don't appreciate your condescending attitude. It's a self-defense class. Not that it's any of your business, *sir*."

Damien placed his fork down and motioned her to sit. With a huff, she sank into the chair with her arms crossed and glared at him. Her anger diminished when she realized he wasn't looking at her face. Sexual harassment clause, huh? She squeezed her breasts together a little more, making sure to show her cleavage.

"I'm glad you're taking the class. As a matter of fact, I feel quite remiss no one ever thought to have you take one before. All women should—I think it should be mandatory in junior high school."

"Thank you. I never want to feel that helpless again." She glanced away. "I want to be a strong woman, despite my stupid mistake and what you must think of me."

"I never said you were stupid. Despite what you think, I *do* care. Yes, you should've been more cautious, but hindsight is always twenty-twenty. As you've said to me, don't be so hard on yourself. You *are* a strong, capable woman." He took a sip of his coffee and wiped his mouth with his napkin.

I'll show you strong. You're going to suffer until you realize you want me the way I want you.

"So are we good? Friends?"

She stood. "Sure. I have to go. Just leave the dishes; I'll do them when I get home."

"Go kick some ass."

Harley gave him a thumbs up. Once out of his sight, she shrugged against the wall in the hallway. His scent, that crazy lopsided smile, and his concern...She couldn't squelch the hope that still bloomed in her heart.

Chapter
Eleven

Not again, dammit. Glutton for punishment—that's the most accurate description. Or dumbass. Yes, that's simpler and more succinct.

A week and a half later, Damien stood on the courthouse steps, unable to move. He'd successfully worked four full days at the office, and next week he was due in court, so he'd thought it wise to see how he'd do. Turned out not very well.

He stared at the steps with his pulse jack-hammering in his throat. Loosening his tie, he wheezed in air through his constricted windpipe. He sounded like a defunct bagpipe. Stars danced in front of his eyes, and despite the cold, sweat beaded his forehead. Angry and embarrassed, he turned away, praying no one had noticed his inability to walk up a few damn steps. Faking it, he nodded at acquaintances walking by.

What the hell is my problem?

This irrational fear had turned him into a scared rabbit, and he wasn't having it. There wasn't anything he couldn't overcome through sheer determination. Spinning around, he marched up three steps… But he couldn't go any farther.

He bent over and promptly threw up his breakfast. *Fuck.* A passerby handed him some tissue, and he sank to the step, closing his eyes, feeling like a fool. He hadn't thrown up in public since he was eight years old and ate too much junk food at the circus.

As soon as he could stand without passing out, he hurried down the steps, away from the courthouse. He stepped into his favorite bakery around the corner and went straight to the bathroom. Looking in the mirror he groaned, disgusted by the pale, drawn face before him. After cleaning up as best as he could, he ordered his usual and sat down to collect his thoughts.

How the hell was he supposed to go back to work if he couldn't even enter the courthouse? *Thank God for trust funds*, he thought, rubbing his eyes with the heels of his hands.

His father would be furious. Weakness was not acceptable in Sinclair men, and hard work was expected. A Sinclair did not live off a trust fund. A Sinclair contributed *more* to the trust fund. That was part of his father's problem with Angel, even though his brother was using his money fund philanthropically...

Damien pulled out his phone and sent a quick text. Before he could put it away, it rang.

"Angel, you didn't have to call, you could have texted a reply." Damien swept his gaze around the shop.

His brother chuckled on the other end. "*Shit, you're just lucky I had the damn thing on me. The only reason I have minutes is because of Maggie. Whazzup? Everything okay? I spoke to Taylor yesterday. He said you hadn't been home since being released from the hospital.*"

It was no surprise that Angel had spoken to Harley's father, and not Dad. For the first time in his life, Damien understood the pressure of being a failure to Sebastian Sinclair. No wonder his brother had chosen to leave home.

"Physically, I'm fine. But I swear to God, I'm losing it mentally. I can't even make it up the steps to the courthouse."

He closed his eyes and pinched the bridge of his nose. *Why did I call Angel to spill my guts?*

It wasn't like they'd been close in recent years. Vastly different views on life had put a wedge in their relationship. But his younger brother had changed; Angel wasn't as restless since he'd fallen in love with Maggie Robertson. Their mom's brief illness and death had brought them closer. He was even working with Angel as a board member on his new project to help abused kids, a residential treatment facility named The Phoenix Rising. And right now, he needed to feel a connection to someone besides Harley.

His resolve to keep her at arm's length had been sorely tested this morning with her lithe, toned body prancing around in a sports bra and yoga pants.

"*That's great*," Angel said. "*You can give up being a shark and do something meaningful with your life.*"

Maggie fussed in the background. "*Angel, you have it on speaker; Damien might not want his conversation broadcast.*"

"She's right, dickhead. As for doing something meaningful with my life, unfortunately I'm not artistic enough to paint graffiti on the underpass of the loop. You know, enlightening those who trudge to real jobs about the beauty of property defacement." Damien goaded his younger brother out of habit. At one time, Angel had been a well-known presence among graffiti artists.

Angel laughed, and Damien wished he were here to talk to in person. He needed someone to vent to. All of his friends were bloodthirsty lawyers. They'd be like sharks circling a wounded seal.

"*Oops, sorry. I didn't realize the damn thing was on speaker. It's true you'd never be king in the underground—especially since you can't draw for shit. But there has to be something you could do besides dealing in the misery of others. Actually, I was going to call you later this week. I have another idea I want to run by you.*"

Maggie's soothing voice came on the line. "*Damien, are you okay?*"

"Yes...No...I don't know, but I'll be fine."

"*You don't sound fine. Come visit. You've never been to our home. It's peaceful here and would be a good place to heal. You need time to recuperate after everything you've been through. I'll even make sure to have toaster tarts on hand, although my scones are to die for.*"

Her invitation tempted him. Maggie's kind, nurturing spirit had helped heal his brother from unspeakable pain. Angel had once told him his soul had connected with Maggie's the moment they met. At the time, Damien had snorted with derision. He didn't believe in love at first sight or soul mates.

But if he were honest with himself, right now he was jealous of Angel's happiness and peace. He longed for that kind of connection, but feared it as well. He refused to end up like his father.

"Harley said you can see the stars there," he murmured reflectively.

"*You can,*" Maggie affirmed. "*It's positively magical. We'd love to have you.*"

"*You and Harley finally hooking up?*" his brother shouted in the background. "*It's about damn time.*"

"*Angel, quit shouting in my ear,*" Maggie fussed. "*Come see us, Damien. This is our down season; I have plenty of room.*"

Someone accidentally bumped into him, and he jumped. The noise in the bakery rose as more people poured into the shop. His heart rate once again picked up to an uncomfortable rate, and he found it hard to catch his breath. He grabbed his coat and left, still on his phone.

"Hey, Maggie? I think I'd like that. Would you have two rooms? Harley's wanted to come stargaze." *We'll go just as friends, of course.*

"*Sure, just let me know when you'll be arriving.*"

"*Are you sure you want* two *rooms?*" Angel asked. "*We could pretend all the rooms but one are closed. You know, for remodeling or something.*"

"*Angel, stop. I'm not lying to Harley,*" Maggie chided.

"Thanks. And Angel? Mind your own damn business. Keep him in line, Maggie. I'll call and let you know when."

She laughed. "*It's a tough job, but I can handle it. And don't worry; I can even put you in two rooms at opposite ends of the house.*"

They hung up, and Damien sent his father and Mrs. Allen a brief text saying he'd be working from home. Thankfully it was Friday. Or as Harley called it, Poet's Day: piss off early, tomorrow's Saturday.

Hell, he didn't want to deal with life at the moment, much less his responsibilities to the firm. The thought of sitting in silence looking at the stars was pretty damn appealing, especially with Harley by his side.

What the fuck?

Two rooms at opposite ends of the house would, without a doubt, be for the best.

Harley threw open the front door, thoroughly hyped up. She'd passed her self-defense class with flying colors. To celebrate, she'd gone shopping and bought a new T-shirt, one with *BITCH—Babe In Total Control of Herself* scrawled across the chest. Never again would she be at the mercy of some asshole mugger. In the midst of her excited Herkie cheerleader jump, the hair lifted on the back of her neck.

Someone was behind her.

Her heart nearly exploded in her chest, but her training kicked in. With a sharp jab, she elbowed the person behind her, jumped away, and screamed, "Fire!"

"What the hell?" Damien gasped, doubled over in pain.

"Bloody bugger, Sin. Why are you here? You scared the crap out of me!" She held a hand to her chest.

"Why wouldn't I be here? I live here, remember? Holy fuck. That hurt like hell." He staggered to the couch and collapsed with an aggrieved grin. "But well done."

"Why aren't you at work? I'm so sorry. Let me see." She tugged at his shirt, brushing his hands away, and looked at the red spot on his side. She refrained from running her hands through his chest hair.

Things had been strained for a few days after the night she'd practically propositioned him, but they'd since settled back into an easy, comfortable relationship. Last Sunday Damien had even joined her for a tea party with Mr. Gavosovich and Shaney. His headaches weren't as bad, and he'd worked four full days this week, though it was unclear what had happened today.

With a gentle touch, she assessed the damage. When he inhaled sharply, she looked up. His dark eyes were darker than usual.

"Want me to kiss it and make it better?" she asked, only half kidding, waggling her brow.

"W-What? No!" He scooted away from her as if she were contagious.

She giggled. "Gotcha. I'm really sorry. Do you think I cracked your rib?" She rubbed the spot again with her fingertips, but he brushed her away.

"No, I'm fine."

"I'll get you an ice pack, just in case." She hurried to the kitchen, grabbed a bag of frozen corn, and held it to her heated cheeks, attempting to cool down. Dammit, touching him had left her more worked up than he was. Wrapping the frozen corn in a dishtowel, she hurried back to the living area. Damien had pulled his T-shirt back down over his bruised ribs.

He stretched out on the sofa and opened his book, laying it across the crotch of his jeans. Harley bit her lip to keep from giggling. How she'd love to peek under that book. Maybe she wasn't the only one affected after all. Classical music played softly in the background, and a glass of iced tea with a half-eaten burger sat on the glass coffee table next to his violin. Had he been playing?

He brushed the ice pack away. "I don't need that."

She shrugged. "What do you want for dinner? I'm going out tonight."

Damien raised his dark, stormy eyes to hers and scowled. "Oh? Where are you going, and who's going with you? Please tell me you're not going alone."

"I've got a part time job at a strip club."

"What?"

"Gotcha. Look, intrusive inquisitor, I'm not crackers. I'm going with friends to a club, and I don't have to check in with you. You're not my father."

"I'll take you."

Her mouth dropped open. She shut it, instantly suspicious. "*You'll* take me?" She paused, trying to decide on her next move. "Why would you want to take me? You're my boss and we're *just friends*, remember?"

"You just stated you were going with friends," he noted with a condescending smirk.

When will I learn? Never argue with a lawyer. "Fine, I'm calling for a ride at eight. You can share it with me or meet us there. I may or may not be coming home." She tossed her braid over her shoulder and watched with satisfaction as Damien pulled at his scowling lower lip.

To her surprise, he smiled and actually looked excited.

"I'll get us a ride, and I want to take you someplace first for a bite to eat. As friends, of course."

"Of course. Dutch, right? I mean, since we're friends. What time should I be ready?"

"I don't mind paying."

"Friends go Dutch."

"Fine, Dutch, if you insist." He picked his book back up and hid behind it.

"Okay. Just make sure it's in my budget. My boss is a tightwad. I'm off to do some serious pampering and soak in a tub of bubbles."

She walked away to keep from laughing out loud when he moved the open book back to his lap as a tortured sigh escaped his lips.

Harley had baited him on purpose. She knew it, he knew it—and dammit, he wasn't used to losing. He was sick and tired of her *gotchas*. She was going to learn that payback could be a bitch. He stood in his closet, debating what to wear. Black or gray? Hell, he didn't even know what kind of club they were going to after his *surprise entertainment and dinner*. He was lucky he'd been able to arrange it. He pulled on a pair of clean black jeans and headed down the hallway to knock on Harley's bedroom door.

She cracked it open and peeked up. Taking in her appearance, he grinned. Her hair sat on top of her head in rollers with torturous-looking pin things sticking out in all directions. She looked like some sort of alien from a B-movie. Her makeup was heavier than usual, and she had on only one fake eyelash. Dropping his gaze lower, he noted her silky blue robe, the exact color of her eyes. The damn thing was parted just enough to see the swell of her full breasts. He clenched his fist on the doorjamb.

"What are you wearing tonight?" he asked, his eyes reluctantly moving from her tits to her eyes.

"Nothing. Didn't I mention it was a clothes-optional event?"

"What?" *Was she on to him?*

"Gotcha. Clothes, dumbass." She smirked, raking her eyes over his bare chest.

He sucked in his gut. The scale this morning had said he was back to his pre-hospitalization weight. "What kind of clothes? I don't even know where we're going."

"It's a dance club—casual. For God's sake, don't wear a suit. I'm wearing a skirt. Where are we eating first?"

"A skirt? Are you insane? You're not wearing a skirt. And dinner is a surprise." *Oh. Hell. No.* He knew what guys tried with girls in skirts. He'd done it too many times.

"Excuse me?" She stared daggers at him.

He watched her breasts rise as she huffed with annoyance.

"You're wearing jeans." He used his won't-take-no-for-an-answer voice.

"I can wear whatever I bloody well want. You seem to be under the misguided impression that you're my father. Even my parents no longer tell me how to dress."

Leaning against the door, he crossed his arms. "What were you wearing the night you were attacked?"

Outrage flooded her face, and she gasped. "You think because I had on a skirt I deserved to be attacked?"

"*Of course not.* I'm saying maybe it would have been easier to get away if you'd been in jeans and running shoes."

"Rape culture is precisely why I didn't go to the police. I'll wear whatever the hell I want." She slammed the door in his face.

"That was totally unfair!" he shouted at the door. "You act like I'm a misogynist. I'm not! I fuckin' love women."

The door flew open. "No, you love to fuck women. There's a difference!" The door slammed once again.

Damien scrubbed his face with his hand. Dammit, he didn't mean it the way she took it. He wanted to protect her. Why couldn't she see that? Strictly as a friend, of course.

Liar.

Seeing her injured had affected him on some unexplored, deep level of his soul. It made him want to kill whoever had done that to her.

Maybe going with her tonight wasn't a good idea. More than likely he'd end up in a fight if some asshole put his hands on her.

Damien stormed back to his room and put on a starched white shirt. He rolled up the sleeves and opted not to shave—he'd show her he could do casual. In the bathroom, he finger-combed his hair and wondered why the hell he hadn't cut it.

Because Harley likes it longer, you pussy-whipped fool.

He gave the mirror one last glower before heading to the living area to wait. Next week he'd see Samson for his usual shorter haircut, maybe even a buzz. With his hands on his hips, he stared out the window at the city lights. Why the hell had he agreed to go to a dance club?

He didn't dance.

He didn't like dance music.

He didn't like crowds.

He liked Harley.

Fuck me. I'm screwed.

He paced like a caged panther, thinking about everything that could go wrong at the club. But if he didn't go, he couldn't surprise her beforehand…He smiled. It would be totally worth it to see the look on her face.

"Ready?"

Damien spun around and inwardly groaned. He was in trouble. *Deep trouble.* As in sinking-fast-in-quicksand-type trouble. His eyes traveled her body not once but twice. Goddamn. She looked stunning.

"Satisfied? No skirt, Mr. Misogyny."

The song about no satisfaction ran through his mind. Her hair was a mass of shiny loose curls all the way to her ass. Her makeup accented her normally fresh face, and extra-long eyelashes framed the bright blue eyes now glaring at him.

She wore jeans, but now he wondered if a skirt would've been better. They were low riding, curve fitting, and so tight he wasn't sure how she'd managed to zip them. Her top was a neon pink, long-sleeved cropped sweater. It showed no cleavage but clung tightly to her braless breasts and was cut low in the back. Her hard nipples, the expanse of toned, bare abdomen, and chiseled hipbones would have every male in the club sniffing around her like a horny mongrel. It was going to be a long, difficult night.

"Didn't you forget something?" He attempted, belatedly, to temper the question with a smile.

Harley looked in her purse with a frown and then up at him. "ID, phone, money, condoms. I don't think so, why?"

"A bra, perhaps?" *Condoms?* He ground his teeth.

"I never wear one unless I'm going to church or something." She threw her shoulders back a bit and smiled.

He found himself speechless, which she seemed to interpret as confusion.

"I don't need it." She circled her breasts with her finger. "The girls are perky."

He pinched the bridge of his nose. "Of course." He looked down and frowned. "And how the hell do you plan to keep from breaking your neck in those shoes?"

Harley looked down at the four-inch stilettos. "What? Stop it. You're not my father." She ran a hand through her loose blond curls and patted his arm. "You look great. Did you call for a ride?"

"No, I called Taylor to bring the Rolls."

She sputtered, "W-What? You called *my father* to take us clubbing? Are you nutters?" She threw her purse down on the couch, and the contents spilled everywhere.

"Gotcha." He smirked.

"Bloody hell." She angrily gathered her things.

He scowled as he realized that in addition to her phone, ID, and money, there were *six* condoms, a toothbrush, and a scrap of a thong—*that wouldn't leave anything to the imagination*—being stuffed back into her purse.

"Planning an interesting evening?" It was damn near impossible to keep the jealousy out of his voice.

She glared at him, blowing her bangs with exasperation as she finished zipping her purse. "Why, yes. It's my night off, after all. And we're just employer-employee friends. You're treating me like your kid sister. Although with our history, that's kinda gross. Are you with me, or have you changed your mind?"

"Oh, I'm in. Let's go." He grabbed his black leather jacket and a black hoodie from the hall closet, offering it to her. It would at least cover her up some. Shaking her head, she headed out the front door. *Dammit.*

She might not realize it, but she'd just acquired a bodyguard for the entire evening. A moment ago, he'd considered bailing after his little surprise. But now? He'd be damned if she was going to use those condoms anywhere but right here at home.

What? Wait, that's not what I meant...Liar.

Chapter
Twelve

Damien gave the limo driver the address.

"A limo?" Harley asked. "Isn't this a little over the top? Where are we going?"

She took in his appearance and wished it were to get a room and be alone. He looked sexy as hell.

"Some place with a view. I think you'll like it."

"Oh, snap. Look, I know we said Dutch, but I also told you I'm broke. I can't afford some ritzy restaurant like that blue dome place that turns. Besides, don't people get sick with it going 'round and 'round?"

"No, it turns very slowly. It isn't like a carnival ride; you wouldn't toss your cookies. But that's not where we're going. This is someplace *special*. And the meal is on me. Consider it part of your back pay."

Harley frowned and looked out the window as they drove past mansions in an upscale, yet familiar neighborhood.

"Are we going home?" she demanded. "You cheapskate. Did you make Mamma cook?"

"No."

They pulled up to a massive gate, and Damien rolled down his window to push the intercom.

"*ID*," said the voice from the speaker.

"Silver-Tongued Devil," Damien replied.

Harley giggled. The driveway was even longer than the one to his father's house. And at the end of it stood a huge Victorian mansion.

When they stepped out of the limo, she looked around, feeling underdressed and nervous.

"Whose home is this?" she asked.

"It's not." Placing a hand on her lower back, he gently urged her up the steps.

She shivered, more from the feel of his warm hand than the cold night air. "What is it?"

"A private club."

"In this neighborhood? How come I've never heard of it?"

"Duh, because it's private? And exclusive."

There were only a few cars parked next to their limo, and unease slipped through her bones.

Damien smiled down at her. "I wanted to do something nice for you. You know how you keep referencing that BDSM stuff?" He motioned expansively toward the front door. "Here you can fulfill your wildest dreams, in a safe place."

If he'd told her they were standing at the doorway to hell, she wouldn't have been any more surprised.

She blinked and stared at the front door. "I, uh…What?"

"Oh, don't worry. The Masters and Mistresses are well qualified. Everything is safe, sane, and consensual." He smiled. "You weren't far off the mark when you said clothing optional. Only here, it isn't an option. You'll need to strip." He looked down. "They might let you keep the shoes."

"And you?" she squeaked.

"Public scening isn't my thing. I'll be at the bar, watching. Don't worry; you'll be fine! You have your safe words, right?" He tugged her toward the door. "Let me guess—green, yellow, and red?"

"Watching? You're going to watch me?" she whispered.

He paused, frowning. "Would that be awkward? Look, if you want, I'll introduce you to the owner and leave. They can call me when you're done."

He rang the doorbell.

"Sin—"

The door opened, revealing the biggest man she'd ever seen. He was dressed entirely in black and stood well over six feet five, with biceps the size of tree trunks. He tapped his massive palm with a crop.

"Ah, the Silver-Tongued Devil has arrived. And this must be our special guest. Welcome, Ms. Taylor. You'll have a bit of paperwork to complete first. Just the usual: a nondisclosure and a list of your soft and hard limits. Sub, correct?" He stepped aside and motioned them in. "You may undress in the room to the left."

From another room came the sharp sound of a whip and a woman screaming.

Harley jumped back and looked up at Damien. He raised his brows, questioning.

In her life, she'd made plenty of dumb mistakes. This wasn't going to be one. "I, um, thank you, but no. I'll just wait out here and call for a ride."

"You'll be perfectly safe, and no one will do anything you don't want," the host purred.

She shook her head, backing up and out the door. She would've stumbled down the front steps if Damien hadn't caught her.

"Not no. But hell, no. RED! RED! RED!"

The huge man shrugged, and the front door closed. Her knees felt weak, and she buried her face in Damien's chest. Gulping air, she gripped his shirt.

"You okay? I just wanted to give you a night to remember..." His chest started shaking, and his snort turned into a rumble under her ear.

She frowned. *What's going on?*

"Gotcha," he whispered, followed by outright chortling.

It took a few seconds for his words to sink in. Then she shoved him.

"What?" she screeched.

He laughed so hard he doubled over and had to wipe his eyes. "Oh my God. I wish I'd gotten this on video!"

"It's not funny!" She wasn't sure yet if she was mad, hurt, or impressed by his prank.

"Hell to the yeah it is." He held his knees as he laughed even harder.

"What is this place?" She smacked his arm. "Quit laughing."

He quit but didn't wipe the shit-eating grin off his face. "It's a friend of mine's home. I gotcha good! You'll have a hard time topping that one." He started guffawing again. "Get it? Hard time? Topping?"

She marched back to the limo. "You're definitely paying for dinner after that."

The chauffeur held the car door open for her. She slid in with Damien following.

He nudged her shoulder, still snickering. "Come on, admit it. That was the best prank *ever.*"

She tried to keep from smiling but failed. It had been a great prank. And she loved seeing him having fun and laughing, even at her expense. And she kind of deserved it after the ones she'd pulled on him lately.

"Fine. You're the prince of pranks. Where are we eating? I don't want to drink on an empty stomach."

She laughed outright when he had the limo stop at a hamburger joint. Her mother still fussed about Damien's love of junk food. And these steamed mini cheeseburgers were one of his favorites.

As they drove to club, she decided this might turn out to be a fun night. Damien was more relaxed than she'd seen him in months, more like he used to be, back before her dreams were trashed after the pool house incident.

Surely history wasn't going to repeat itself.

"No drinking unless it's from a bottle and you see it opened," Damien shouted into her ear above the pulsing sound of the dance music.

"Quit trying to control every damn aspect of your life and *mine,*" she shouted back. "Relax and have fun. You just want to drink a bottled beer because you're cheap. Be spontaneous." She shoved herself against his chest, enjoying how his pupils dilated at the contact. With a smug smile, she watched as he tried to look anywhere but at her breasts, which she knew were outlined to their best advantage in her cropped sweater.

"I'm not cheap. I'm fiscally responsible…" His voice trailed off and his look darkened at whatever was behind her.

She turned at the tap on her shoulder.

"Oh my God," she screamed, throwing her arms around Mark MacGregor's neck. With a wide, easy grin, he lifted her into a huge bear hug. She ran her fingers through his wavy, auburn hair, wondering what had happened to his usual ponytail. He kissed her soundly on the lips. His shirtsleeves were rolled up to reveal strong forearms, and he had on his freakin' kilt, which made him look like some hot-as-hell Highlander. The tattoo on his right wrist read *Alba an Àigh*. She'd been with him when he had the tattoo on his left arm done, and it was her favorite. The corner of a new tattoo was visible where his shirt was unbuttoned. His blue eyes danced with amusement.

"Do I pass inspection?" He put her back on her feet and stared down at her, clearly pleased with her reaction.

She smiled at him. Her life had been painfully intertwined with his ever since Damien had disappeared after that fateful spring break. They would be bound together forever, one way or another. Despite their somewhat turbulent, painful past, she adored him. He knew her better than most, and was always there for her when needed.

"Look at you! Yes, of course! Claire didn't tell me you were in town. I've missed you. You almost look conservative with shorter hair," she teased, jumping up and down.

Mark being here could play right into her hands. He was handsome and fun, and by the look on Damien's face, perfect for tonight's purpose—to make Damien take notice of her as a woman, *not* as a friend.

"Wow, baby. You look fantastic. Claire didn't know I was coming until I showed up on her doorstep. I wanted to surprise Dad for his birthday, and we both know Claire can't keep a secret. She's around somewhere getting us beer. I cut my hair when I got the new day job. I'm here for a week. I'll catch you up when we can talk."

He gave Damien a curt nod of acknowledgment.

Damien looked as if he was ready to punch Mark in the face. Maybe now he'd wake up and smell the proverbial coffee—she being his hot shot of espresso. She flagged a waitress and ordered a drink before turning her attention back to Mark and Damien.

"Damien, aren't you going to say hello to Mark?" She slipped her arm around Mark's waist. He shot her an amused, puzzled look but didn't move away.

He held out his hand to Damien. "It's been years. Heard from Angel lately?" His left hand toyed with one of her curls.

Damien scowled, scanning the swelling crowd as it became louder and more boisterous in the club.

When he didn't answer Mark, Harley tapped him on the arm. "Mark is Claire's brother, remember? Claire's parents adopted him, but he kept his surname." She waved to Claire as she made her way through the crowd holding two beers.

"I know who he is," Damien snapped, giving Mark a perfunctory handshake. "I'm fine. I spoke to Angel the other day. He's enjoying playing house with Maggie."

"Yeah, the last time I talked to him, he told me he'd settled down. I was surprised. He's the last guy I ever thought would want to get tied down. He's never been in one spot more than a few weeks," Mark replied, affably.

"Claire Bear!" Harley yelled.

Claire hugged her. "Hi, Harley Harlot. Hello, Damien. Next round is yours, Mark."

She handed Mark a beer, which he guzzled before handing the empty bottle back to her. "Come on, babe. Let's dance." Mark grabbed Harley's hand and pulled her to the crowded dance floor.

Damien kept his eyes on Two-Time MacGregor and Harley. A known player whose motto was never to date a girl more than twice, Mark used to stay in almost as much trouble as Angel.

"When did Mark get in?" he asked Claire.

As a kid, Claire had been a studious girl with coltish long legs and large, gray eyes hidden behind coke-bottle glasses. The glasses had long since been replaced with contacts, and Claire Lassiter was a stunning woman.

"This morning."

The noise in the dance club rose in direct correlation to his anxiety level. With the screeching banter from the DJ and shouts of happy, dancing drunks, talking was damn near impossible.

Damien narrowed his eyes when Mark smiled at Harley. His hands ran up and down the sides of her body, and they were dancing closer than necessary. The pulsating bass from the music got louder, beating in sync with the pounding now lodged behind his eyes. Damien felt an overwhelming urge to grab Harley and drag her back home. Ironically, the female singer sang about whips and chains exciting her.

"Are you fully recuperated from the shooting?" Claire shouted into his ear, smiling as she saw Charlie, who looked like a surfer-blond-haired god sauntering toward them from across the bar.

Without waiting for an answer, she handed Damien the two empty beer bottles and met Charlie on the dance floor. Damien shook his head, wondering how long it would be before Mark decked Charlie, who now looked like he was performing a tonsillectomy on Claire with his tongue. If he had a sister and anyone did that, he'd kill the sonofabitch.

Speaking of which, he turned his attention back to Harley, watching with growing annoyance as she danced down Mark's leg like she was working a goddamned pole in a strip club. The crowd got louder, the music pulsated harder, and his chest felt tighter. He did find it slightly humorous when Mark tapped Charlie on the shoulder and made a motion of slitting his throat. Claire shoved Mark away and flipped him off. Unfazed, Charlie kept his arms around Claire, grabbing her ass cheeks.

Damien jumped as a drunk stumbled against him, spilling his drink. He barely missed the beer baptism and sighed, wishing he were at home. Someone tapped his shoulder, and he spun around. A girl who looked underage slipped him her phone number on a napkin. He used it to mop his wet brow. His heart continued to pound in his ears as he watched everyone around him. Fed up, he made his way to the bar to drop off the empty bottles, and he ordered a shot of liquid courage, bottled beer be damned. Throwing it to the back of his dry throat, he immediately signaled for another.

He sensed her presence before he felt her hand on his back. When he turned, the faint smell of peaches tickled his nose. Harley peered up at him, looking worried. There was a faint sheen of sweat on her upper lip, and her breasts rose and fell with her dance-labored breathing. She held her hand out to him with an inviting smile. A slower song now played, and his anger melted like ice in July. Throwing back the contents of the last shot, he followed her onto the dance floor.

It was a mistake, but he couldn't have resisted her if he'd wanted to. She was like a trouser-snake charmer, and he followed her body like it was a *pungi*.

Damien pulled her into his arms, enjoying the feel of her soft breasts pressed against his chest. His favorite color, Harley red, crept up her long neck, sweeping across her cheeks. Wrapping his hand in her long tresses, he placed his other hand on the back of her bare waist. The feel of her warm skin and soft curves made him rock hard. Not giving a damn, he pulled her even closer. They moved together in sync, slowly and sensually. Her arms crept around his neck as he gazed into eyes hooded with desire. When her pink lips parted, inviting him to partake of their sweetness, a sense of coming home flooded him.

His pulse raced, but not with fear. His breathing was erratic, but not from anxiety. The music was loud, but all he heard was the soft sigh from her lips when he leaned down to capture them with his own. *Would they still taste like cotton candy?*

He wanted her.

He needed her...

He growled at the tap on his shoulder as Mark deftly cut in, placing his hands possessively on Harley's waist. Furious and frustrated, Damien shoved him, but Harley stood between the two men and shook her head, mouthing, "Later." Two bouncers eyed them with warning looks.

Damien weighed his options. His gut instinct was to beat the shit out of Mark, but he was nothing if not pragmatic. The asshole outweighed him by at least thirty pounds of muscle. Plus, he'd probably end up in jail, which would infuriate his father and make his kid brother laugh. The rational option would be to just leave. And he was a rational man.

Most of the time.

Not this time.

Mouth set in a grim line, he drew his fist back, but pulled the punch when Harley threw her head back laughing at something Mark said in her ear. It had the effect of an ice-cold shower.

Shit! He'd come close to jumping into dangerous waters. Instead of killing Mark, he should *thank* him. But for some reason, he didn't feel very thankful. Still, Harley was off limits for any number of reasons—not that he could recall any of them as he watched Mark's easy familiarity with her.

She continued the slow dance with Mark, but not nearly as close as she'd danced with him. Several times he caught her peeking at him, as if judging his reaction. Was this another *gotcha?* Was she doing this on purpose?

Damien shoved his way back toward the bar. Unable to breathe, his chest pain became almost unbearable. *Am I having a heart attack? Or is my heart being emotionally pulverized?* He had to get out of there.

A delicate hand stopped him, and he looked down to find blood red nails grasping his arm.

"*Boa noite,*" the voluptuous, black-haired beauty breathed into his ear.

The dark eyes of Renata Vicente searched his face. He smiled, relieved to see someone he knew and trusted.

"How did you know I'd be here?" he asked in her ear.

"It's the hottest dance club in the city. Lucky guess. Chris was called out of town after scaring your friend, so I'm free tonight. He enjoyed helping you with your prank, the sick *idiota*. He recorded the session we'd enjoyed just before you arrived. He said when your friend heard it, she ran out. I'm sorry I missed it. I was upstairs recuperating in a nice bath."

The anger and lust clouding his vision refocused. Damn if she wasn't just what he needed at this precise moment. They'd met when his father had represented her in a high-profile divorce case and won her a large alimony settlement three years ago. Wealthy, unattached, and sexually adventurous, Renata was uninterested in anything more than scratching the occasional itch when her lover, Chris, was out of town. They had an open relationship, and Damien used it to his advantage, and hers.

He glanced over at Harley, who was dancing and talking animatedly with that tattooed, skirt-wearing Moron MacGregor. His heart continued to race, and it had grown difficult to breathe. At this point he wasn't sure if this was his anxiety or a reaction to Harley being with Mark. Either way, Renata would be his ticket out of this confused state.

Damien's gaze caught Harley's, and he motioned he was out of here. Grabbing Renata's hand, he marched toward the door, intent on leaving before his heart exploded in his chest.

"What's the matter?" Mark asked.

"Damien just left with some dark-haired woman." Harley blinked away her tears and pressed her fake eyelash back in place.

She'd just finished catching Mark up on her current predicament with Damien, admitting she was still hopelessly in love with him. She'd also cued Mark in on her plan to make him notice her as a *woman*.

Talking to Mark had helped. He was always the voice of reason.

"The way I see it, you have two options," he shouted in her ear as the slow song ended and another, louder one started.

"They are?"

"Go after him or stay with me tonight."

She flashed him a wry smile. "I refuse to go after him. And I believe your second option has led to trouble in the past. I know another option."

"Yeah? Hit me with it."

"Let's get shit-faced. Where's Claire?"

Mark shrugged. "She left with Charlie a few minutes ago, probably to go back to his place for the night."

"Did she leave you the key to her place?"

"Yep, with strict instructions not to put the moves on you if you decide to stay over. But if you want to take advantage of me — hey, I promise not to tell, or protest." He threw an arm around her shoulders and walked her toward the bar.

Chapter
Thirteen

Someone shook his arm. Damien batted it away and groaned. His back was killing him.

A hand rubbed down his arm. "Did Harley come home?" a whispered voice asked.

He blinked and turned over to discover Renata perched on the edge of the couch, wearing the top to his pajamas.

"No, I don't think so," he mumbled, sitting up and rubbing his eyes. "You should've just gone home and left me alone with my misery."

Renata shook her head. "You weren't well when we left the club. I didn't want to leave you. You fell asleep out here…" Her warm brown eyes seemed full of sympathetic questions.

He rubbed his brow. "I'm sorry…"

She crossed her arms. "For?"

"For not manning up and telling you I was using you to make Harley jealous last night." He sighed. "I'm not proud of my behavior. We've always been honest with each other…"

She ran her fingers through his hair and cupped his cheek in her hand. "When you called me to set up the…prank, you called it?"

He nodded.

"You didn't ask me for anything else." She smiled. "I knew then this girl was someone special. Why do you think I came to the club? I wanted to see for myself what she was like."

"And?"

"My opinion isn't the important one here, is it? But since you asked, she's beautiful and full of life. You should go after her."

"Hard to do when you don't know where she is," he muttered.

"Why don't you go take a shower and we can discuss this further over breakfast?"

Guilt ate at him. He didn't deserve her kindness, much less breakfast.

"Renata…"

"Oh, you have it bad." She laughed, and although sadness lingered in her eyes, he also saw acceptance. "Do not worry, *meu amigo*. What we have had has served its purpose. We will always have our friendship. And I have Chris; he is my love."

He shook his head. "Friendship…That's where I went wrong with Harley. I tried to keep her at a safe distance. And now it may be too late. She wasn't with Claire when I texted. Of course with Mark's reputation, she won't be with him long…"

He'd blown his chance with Harley, and the thought of Mark using her made him livid.

"You will know nothing until you talk to her. Surprise her with that trip you were telling me about last night. To see your brother's new home." She kissed his forehead.

"You're a sweet woman, Renata."

"I know." She headed toward the kitchen, laughing. "That's why Chris lets me get away with so much. As you know, I like to top from the bottom."

He picked up his phone, only to see that Harley still hadn't responded to any of his texts or phone calls. *Where is she?* Worry made him angry.

And although it was early, he sent Angel a text asking if he could visit next weekend. He needed some peace and quiet to clear his head.

A slow, painful death by torture would be preferable to the insufferable pounding going on inside her head. Groaning, Harley rose and slapped the muscled back next to her.

"Move, Mark, I've got to use the bathroom."

"Oh, fuck." He moaned and rolled over.

Pressing a quick kiss to the heart tattoo that read *Jinxed* on his chest, she climbed over him. It took her a few minutes to find her purse and stagger to the bathroom. Ugh, her body was sticky from sweat and spilled tequila. A quick shower was tempting, but the thought of that much moving made her stomach spasm. She flinched at her reflection in the mirror as she washed her hands and face. It was worse than she'd expected. One fake eyelash was on her chin, and most of her mascara was on her cheeks.

After scrubbing her face, she patted it dry, careful not to jar her aching head. A reconnaissance mission through Claire's medicine cabinet turned up some ibuprofen, which she swallowed with a handful of water. The room swayed, and she hung onto the counter, praying they'd stay down. Taking the toothbrush from her purse, she rid her mouth of the awful taste of hangover hell, and then finger-combed her lank, dirty hair into a loose braid. After a quick change into the clean underwear she'd brought, she decided things were as good as they'd get for now.

Tiptoeing back into the bedroom, she glanced at the clock and panicked. *It's already seven?* Damien would be expecting his breakfast soon. She shook Mark, unable to keep the panic out of her voice. "Get up. You have to drive me home."

"That wasn't part of the deal. There's no way I can drive in this condition," he mumbled, raising his head. His glazed eyes were a patriotic red, white, and blue. He rolled over and sank back into his pillow. "I think I'm gonna be sick."

Harley ran to the bathroom. Returning, she placed a wet washcloth on the back of his neck and put the trashcan next to the bed.

"Poor baby." She stopped laughing when it intensified the pounding in her own head.

"I ordered you a ride. I'm glad you find my imminent death amusing. Just so you know, you're not in my will." He gagged, but thankfully didn't throw up. "You need to stay and take care of me. After all, this is your fault. I tried to stop at—fuck…How many shots did we do?"

Harley brought him a glass of water and the bottle of ibuprofen. "Way too many, as usual. I have to go."

He rolled over and accepted the water and pills. "Oh God, I'll never drink again." He looked worse than she felt.

"Hush. Lightning will strike you dead for lying. Will you be okay?"

When he merely moaned, she grabbed her phone, ignoring the texts, missed calls, and voicemails from Damien. She'd have to deal with him soon enough. Quickly she tapped out a text to Claire.

thanks 4 letting me crash. mark not well. ttyl, xoxoxo h

Shoving the phone back in her purse, she pulled out the six condoms, left them on the bedside table next to the meds, and gave Mark a kiss on the forehead.

"Gotta run. Love you and thanks."

He opened one eye and stared at her offerings. "I wouldn't have objected to using those condoms, ya know. Love you, too." He pulled her other fake eyelash off his cheek and shook it onto the floor.

"Neither one of us was in any condition last night to use the condoms. Besides, we don't do the benefits thing anymore, remember? Thanks for the ride. Don't miss the trashcan, or Claire will go nutters on you."

"I'm not that bad..." He groaned and clutched his stomach. "Ugh. Maybe I am."

Harley slipped on her heels and wanted to cry with frustration. *When did I break one? What is it with heels and me?*

Mark rolled over and hung his head off the bed, heaving into the trashcan. Guiltily, she hurried out the door, her stomach unable to take it. She'd never have made it as a nurse. Poor Mark. Claire was gonna be pissed if he didn't get his shit together and clean up before she got home.

The ride pulled up, and she climbed in the backseat, careful not to jar her aching head. He pulled out like an Indy 500 driver, and the car jerked forward. She closed her eyes, clutching her stomach to keep the motion sickness at bay. When they finally arrived, she gingerly exited the car and attempted to slide past Jerry without him noticing. Of course she had no such luck. She gave him her best go-to-hell look.

Raising her chin, she limped by on her one heel with as much dignity as she could muster. While *technically* not a walk of shame, it certainly resembled one. He raised a questioning eyebrow and smirked. Heat flooded her cheeks.

"Oy! Take a picture; it lasts longer, ya wanker!" She repeatedly mashed the button to close the elevator doors, fighting the urge to flip him off.

Like a thief, Harley eased in the front door of Damien's penthouse. Instantly, the smell of frying sausage assaulted her, sending her already queasy stomach into overdrive. Clenching her eyes shut, she held one hand over her nose and mouth as she clutched her rolling stomach, praying she wouldn't lose her ibuprofen breakfast.

"Good God, you look like shit."

"Thanks. You always say the sweetest things," she replied.

She opened her eyes and glared at Mr. Perfect in his black pajama pants. He stood sipping a cup of coffee. She wanted to slap the smug look off his face as he took in her drowned-rat appearance. His hair was still damp from a shower, but he hadn't shaved yet. Part of her longed to throw herself into his arms, smell the sweet spice of his skin, and have him hold her. The other part wanted to scratch his eyes out for leaving with that beautiful woman last night. Instead, she crossed her arms in front of her chest and glared.

"I'm fine. I came home to cook breakfast, but I guess you already started cooking—" Her mouth dropped when the woman from the club appeared wearing the top to Damien's pajamas. She had the longest, tannest legs she'd ever seen.

"Biscuits or toast?" she asked, making it sound like *beescuts* with her exotic accent. "Oh, hello. You must be Harley." She smiled as she tucked a strand of long, dark hair behind her ear.

It seemed grossly unfair. This dark goddess apparently rolled out of bed looking drop-dead gorgeous, while she, on the other hand, looked like a hung-over hot mess. Karma was such a bitch.

"What is *she* doing in my kitchen?" Harley spat, glaring at the exotic Barbie doll.

Immediately, the woman turned and went to Damien's bedroom, closing the door.

Harley's blood boiled. Apparently his room wasn't off limits to *her*.

Damien raised one eyebrow, and his lips pressed into a straight line. "Excuse me? Whose kitchen?"

Harley turned toward him, angry tears threatening to spill down her hot cheeks. She knew she wasn't being reasonable, but right now, she just didn't give a damn. "I hate you!"

"You hate *me?* So does that mean you love *Mark MacFucker?*"

She lunged at him, with nails bared like a snarling cat. Putting the coffee down, he dodged her attack and subdued her by wrapping his arms around her. With her back pressed into his chest, she dug her nails into his arm and sucked huge gulps of air. Rage infused every cell in her body, and she struggled against him, trying desperately to keep the tears and vomit at bay. All the hurt and pain from his past rejections came rushing back and fueled her anger like gasoline.

"Let go of me! I hate you! I hate that bitch, and I really hate the smell of sausage right now. I think I'm going to be sick." She slumped in his arms.

Please don't let me be sick. At least spare me that humiliation.

"What the hell is your problem? Good God, you stink of alcohol and cigarettes. Haven't you even showered? Where have you been all night? Do you have any idea how worried I've been? Did you even bother to check your phone?"

She gritted her teeth. "I said, let go of me. I was at Claire's. You were worried about *me?* Yeah, right. When did you have the time?" She struggled to break free. "Mark this on your calendar: *I admit it, you were right.* You once told me you were a bastard, and I didn't believe you. Well, now I do. You *are* a bastard through and through!"

As she shifted to use one of her newly learned self-defense moves on him, he anticipated it and let go. She stumbled and just stopped herself from falling. The firm set of his jaw and flash of irritation in his eyes served as a warning, but she chose to ignore it. Self-preservation dissipated, and she wished he'd hit her. That pain would be welcome compared to what she was suffering.

But he stood there watching her, the epitome of self-control.

Bile teased the back of her throat, and she ran to her bathroom and dry heaved over the toilet. When she could move, she collapsed on her bed, burying her face in her pillow. She held her rolling stomach while stifling her sobs with her pillow. Her heart felt like an empty, gaping hole.

But it wasn't just her heart. It was as if her very soul was gone. If only the emptiness meant she couldn't feel. But she could, and she felt stupid.

All of this was her own damn fault, and that was the worst part. *I did this to myself.*

Like a fool, she'd thrown herself at Damien and then tried to make him jealous. She had no claim to his heart. And by flirting with Mark, she'd succeeded in pushing him into another woman's arms.

Harley gripped the bedspread and willed her stomach to settle as she realized there was only one thing she could do. It was time to give up her stupid dreams and leave. Her mind became eerily calm, as if she existed in the eye of a hurricane. It was imperative she disappear before she drowned in her own self-pity—or worse, his.

Her emotions cooled as she put her plan into action. In less than fifteen minutes, she'd packed her things. As much as she hated the thought, she'd have to go home. She had nowhere else to go. Yet even living in a cardboard box under a bridge would be better than remaining at the scene of her greatest humiliation.

Claire...

She'd call Claire. As she finished packing her cosmetics, she dialed her friend's number, but it went straight to voicemail. She didn't have Charlie's number in her phone. Frustrated, she hung up.

A tear rolled down her face as she dialed the one person who'd always been there for her.

"Fuck, what?" Irritated and raspy, his voice was a beacon to her lost soul.

"Mark...I need you." She choked on her tears.

"Where are you? What's going on?" The sleepiness in Mark's voice dissipated, and she heard the familiar flick of his lighter. He exhaled and waited.

"It's over. I'll be there in a few."

"I can come get you and kick some ass if you want me to—"

"No, I'll be there. Wait on me?"

"Always. Are you sure you're okay to drive? Can I kick his ass later?"

"I can drive. I need to. It'll help clear my brain fog. And no, I don't want you to kick his ass. It's my own damn fault."

"Well, I love you, and I'll love you even more if you help me clean this place up before Claire gets home and kicks my ass."

"Will do."

She hung up, and her energy fizzled as fatigue and a sense of failure overcame her. Sinking to the side of the bed, she covered her face with her hands, taking a moment to pull herself together. Sniffing her clothes, she gagged at the stench of cigarette smoke, sweat, and stale alcohol. Dreading another encounter with that woman or Damien, she quickly showered. As she braided her wet hair, she gave herself a good hard look in the mirror. And she didn't like what she saw. The deciding moment was here. It was time for a change.

She'd never had a successful career, relationship, or handle on her emotions. At twenty-nine years old, she couldn't support herself, was too scared to live alone, and still had no idea of what she wanted to do with her life. It was time to grow up, be an adult, start over, and not look back at past failures. Grabbing the scissors from her cosmetics bag, she contemplated cutting her braid, but stopped. Although it would symbolize new beginnings, it was an impetuous act. The change had to come from within.

Pulling on clothes, she threw her broken heels in the garbage and slipped on her tennis shoes. With her head held high, she eased out of her room, pausing in the hallway when she heard that woman and Damien speaking in low tones.

Oh great.

Another face-to-face with that bitch had the potential to turn into an all-out catfight. Refusing to debase herself any further, she waited for the woman to leave. From her vantage point in the hallway, she could see them standing at the front door.

"*Boa sorte.* Are you sure you don't want me to talk to her?"

What? As if. Harley's fingers tightened on her purse and duffle bag. *No way.* She had nothing to say to that woman. She couldn't bear to hear her gloating.

"No, I'll handle her."

Handle me? In your dreams, wanker.

"Call me again, if you ever need me. You know I'm always here for you. *Até mais.*"

Harley rolled her eyes. *As if I don't feel sick enough already. Bloody damn tart.*

Brazilian Barbie reached up, cupped Damien's cheek, and kissed him on the lips. Jealousy shot through Harley. Digging her nails into her palms, she barely refrained from running and scratching the big brown eyes out of her perfect face.

"Thank you for last night. Goodbye, Renata."

Renata. Of course she'd have a beautiful name to go with her gorgeous body, sexy accent, and exotic looks.

Damien shut the door and leaned against it, rubbing the heels of his palms into his eyes.

I guess Renata didn't allow him to sleep much last night.

The thought was strangely sobering. He wasn't hers; he never had been. The man could sleep with whomever he wanted to. Harley took a deep breath and squared her shoulders before marching toward the front door.

Damien crossed his arms in front of his chest and watched her approach. He'd always given the allusion of a sleek, dark panther, and never more so than now.

That made her the antelope, the one he could destroy. Her only hope was to run.

Harley held her head high, but refused to look him in the face. She couldn't make eye contact. If she did, her resolve would weaken. And she'd be damned if she asked his forgiveness for being such a nitwit.

"Are you through with your temper tantrum?" His clipped voice didn't hide his annoyance.

Her anger sparked like a wire inserted into an electrical socket. For a second, she contemplated bashing his head with her rolled up yoga mat. Instead, she gripped her duffel bag with both hands to keep from slapping the condescending look off his face.

"Sorry, I didn't realize you wanted a little girl-on-girl action," she sneered. "Did you want me to wrestle her to the floor over you?"

Looking highly amused, he took his time answering. "Renata's bisexual. Girl-on-girl action would be right up her alley. She's also a masochist, so it would have been interesting to watch, I'm sure."

Dumbfounded, she stood still for a second and blinked. If she stood there one damn minute longer, she'd either kill him or herself.

"Get out of my way. I quit. Mark's waiting for me," she threw out, wishing it would hurt him as bad as she was hurting. Staring at his perfect, chiseled chest, the red, healing scar on his shoulder made her question her decision. She'd almost lost him…

Stop it, you fool. He was never yours to lose.

"If you quit without notice, I won't pay you one dime over what is owed, and there will be no reference for your next job."

Her eyes snapped up and locked with his as he volleyed the verbal ball squarely back into her court.

A reference? Like I care about a damn reference. She wanted to laugh but knew it would be tinged with hysteria.

"I don't want your money. It was never about the bloody money. *Ever.* Keep it, flush it, or stick it up your arse, for all I care."

She stood in front of him, so close she could feel his warm breath on her temple. Her mouth was as dry as sawdust, her tongue so thick she couldn't swallow. Without moving, she stared at his scar as she waited for him to get out of her way. If she didn't get out of there soon, she was afraid she'd collapse into a disgusting, pathetic, whimpering fool at his feet.

"If it wasn't about the money, what was it about, Harley?" His voice was as soft and smooth as the expensive scotch he drank. "Why are you so upset with me? You spent the night with your buddy, Mark MacFucker. Renata spent the night here. What's with the jealous-wife routine?"

His words stabbed the remaining piece of her heart and twisted with such ferocity she couldn't breathe.

He was right. Except she hadn't done anything with Mark last night. The blind fool, how could he not know her heart belonged to him? It always had. Even Mark knew it…How could such a brilliant man be so damn clueless? And now she'd used Mark to make him jealous, so Sin had every right to think whatever he was thinking…

But there was no stopping now. It was time for the grand-slam finish. Before she left, she would tell Damien Nicolai Sinclair exactly how she felt, once and for all. There was no way to contain it any longer; her feelings were ready to spew like Old Faithful. If she was burned in the process, so be it. It couldn't be any more painful than what she was going through at this very moment.

Once she let it out, she knew she'd be forced to move forward with her life. At age seventeen, she'd tried to move on and forget him with disastrous results. This time, she *would* succeed, or die trying. And how ironic that once again Mark would be the one to help her pick up the pieces.

Taking a deep breath, she prepared to rip out the last remnant of her barely beating heart. She'd leave it with Damien; she no longer had a need for it.

"I'm waiting."

She raised her eyes and stared at the man she'd loved forever. His eyes were dark, fathomless, and shuttered—completely closed off. She guessed the news reports had been right. Demon Sinclair didn't have a heart.

It took her two tries before she could get the words out of her mouth.

"Because I love you. *I've always loved you.* Every single goddamned day since you rescued me out of that tree when I was five years old, I've loved you. You were my everything. All I ever wanted was for you to give me a little of your time, your attention. But you never really knew I existed, did you? I've meant nothing more to you than an annoying little gnat that could easily be squashed or swatted away.

"In the process of trying to please you, I lost myself. I would've given you *everything,* but I was never good enough. *I wasn't worthy* of your consideration. I was just the daughter of 'the help.' You left me after one of the most important moments in my life, and still I forgave you—we were just kids, after all. But it's obvious you never gave a damn about me. I was a stupid, silly girl to think we ever stood a chance together. Someday I hope you find what you're looking for, because in spite of all of this, I want you to be happy and loved. It's all I ever wanted for you. I just wish it could've been with me."

She stopped to breathe. No longer smug, Damien now wore a gobsmacked expression. No doubt he was horrified that a twit like her had the audacity to think she'd be good enough for him. Opening his mouth to speak, he shut it again.

With a forceful shove, she pushed him out of the way and left without looking back. She vowed never to look back again. Holding her head high, she entered the elevator and hit the button to close the door on this painful chapter of her miserable life.

"Harley, wait!"

She closed her eyes, refusing to look as the doors slid closed.

Chapter
Fourteen

Damien parked his car beside Maggie and Angel's bed and breakfast and looked around. Although today was overcast, it was a beautiful place nestled in the woods with the lake behind it. He'd almost canceled coming, but after a week of work and emotional upheaval, he'd realized it might just be what he needed—a quiet, possibly boring place to reflect on the mess that was now his life. The front door opened, and Angel waved and jogged out, followed by Maggie and a black lab.

Damien opened the car door.

"Damn, Damien. Sweet ride. You always have the best taste in cars. Let me drive it, please?" Angel walked around the Jag, admiring it.

"No."

"Look, I got my license. Just a quick spin; you can ride shotgun." Angel ran a hand over the hood, stroking it like a beautiful woman.

"Not no, but *hell, no*. And quit; you're putting fingerprints on it."

"Stop arguing, you two. I'm so glad you came. We cleared space, so you can park your car in there." Maggie smiled and pointed to the barn that now served as a garage.

"But, Mags, he isn't sharing. It's a wet dream on wheels," Angel huffed with a grin. "At least let me pull it into the garage." The dog barked, wagging his tail, as if in agreement. "See, even Graffiti thinks you should let me drive it."

"Angel, there's no way in hell I'd let you behind the wheel of my Jag. The last time you drove my damn car, you totaled it." He threw his suitcase at him and got back into the car to move it.

"You sure hold a grudge. I was sixteen when I totaled that Mustang. Fine. But don't be surprised if I tag your car," Angel threatened with a good-natured grin.

Damien's eyes narrowed. "Touch my car with a goddamned paint can, and I'll sue your ass. I don't care if you are my brother. I saw what you did to Harley's van."

"Hey, she asked for it! *Sssssssst.*" Angel made a spray can motion with his index finger.

Scowling, Damien flipped him off and pulled in to the garage. For God's sake, he and Angel were grown men, but when they were together, the sibling rivalry never let up. He stepped outside, hit the button to close the electric garage door, and for the first time in days, he genuinely laughed. On the door Angel had spray-painted *Marry me, Maggie.*

Damien walked toward the house. Maggie's dark hair was pulled on top of her head, the gray streaks at the temple not quite contained in her messy ponytail. She was a beautiful, petite woman with amazing green eyes that gazed with adoration at Angel. Why, only God knew. Angel was as insufferable as ever. But damn if he wasn't glad to see his kid brother. He gave Maggie a hug and a kiss. She always smelled of warm vanilla. It was nice, but he missed the smell of summer peaches.

"You two need to talk. Angel, take Damien down to the dock and show him the lake." She took his suitcase from Angel—brushing aside both their protests about carrying the luggage—and headed toward the house.

Angel wolf-whistled at her backside as she sashayed toward the door. At the last minute, she turned with a bright smile and blew him a kiss.

"Damn, I never tire of that woman's ass. You got here early. Did it piss the old man off that you didn't put in a full fifteen-hour day?"

"No. I may have pulled the sick card for the umpteenth time. Have you talked Maggie into setting a date for the wedding?" Damien gave him a brotherly slap on the back. "Or did she finally wise up to your fallen-angel act?"

Maggie was divorced and had a son only a few years younger than Angel, but Damien had to concede, if there was such a thing as a love match made in heaven, it was Maggie and Angel.

"Now that you mention it, besides showing you the progress made on The Phoenix Rising, that's one of the reasons I wanted you to come visit."

Angel grinned like a besotted fool, and a small pang of jealousy dimmed his happiness for his brother. He quickly shoved it aside. This mess with Harley was his own damn fault.

"We're going to have a small ceremony here sometime in October. It's the down season and well…" He grinned. "It will be around our one-year anniversary. You're my brother, and Maggie thinks it's right…" He stared at the ground for a moment before looking him in the eye and blurted, "I wanted to ask you to be my best man."

Pleasantly surprised, Damien grinned and pulled him in for a hug, pounding his back. "Congrats. Of course I'll be here. So does she really want to marry you, or just want the garage door repainted?"

Angel laughed. "Honestly? Both."

Companionably, they walked toward the dock on the lake, with Graffiti following until he got side-tracked by a rabbit. Angel gave him an update on progress with The Phoenix Rising. Because he and the co-founder were both artists, art therapy would be a big part of the program. Angel promised to drive him over to see it tomorrow.

He nodded, but after a few minutes he was only half listening. His mind had slipped a million miles away, wondering about Harley, wishing he could turn back time. Regret washed over him as he marveled at his brother's changed perspective. If he hadn't been such an ass, perhaps he could've found something similar with Harley.

Wait, since when do I want that with Harley? With anyone?

Over the last week, he'd realized the difference Harley had made in his life. He enjoyed having her around—mostly—and begrudgingly, he could even admit she was good for him. He was, in a word, lonely.

If he could just have a do-over, maybe he'd find some of the peace his brother now seemed to have. But he'd never know. She'd refused to answer his calls or texts. He'd blown his chance.

"Yo, asshole. Are you listening to me? You look like shit. What's wrong?"

Damien rounded his gaze back to Angel. As always, his younger brother was his blond-haired, blue-eyed visual opposite. But for the first time in years, Angel also looked happy, at peace. The love he shared with Maggie was strong and secure, and Damien envied their happiness.

He leaned against the railing and looked out over the lake. The wind blew and whipped his coat, but the chill in the air paled in comparison to the cold, empty hole in his heart—a heart he hadn't realized existed until Harley had blown back in, and regrettably now out, of his life. Her presence had been like a damn tornado, leaving him a devastated mess.

Her admission that she loved him had stunned him speechless. He knew they shared a sizzling, sexual chemistry. It was, after all, the source of his frustration. *But love?* On the drive to Angel's, he'd pondered over and over why he'd made the biggest mistake of his life. Why hadn't he stopped her from leaving the penthouse?

The answer shamed him.

Fear.

Not an impulsive man, he examined all angles of a situation before making decisions. It's what made him a good lawyer. He wanted things laid out, plain and simple. He had an innate sense of right and wrong, and for too many years, thinking of Harley as anything but a friend had been wrong.

Black and white with varying shades of gray, that's how he viewed life.

But this weekend trip was to give him time to think and reassess away from the pressure of being Damien Sinclair, a man he no longer seemed to know. Although he'd made it into court this week without freaking out, his heart hadn't been in it. He felt lost.

He turned to look at his brother. "I've fucked up," he admitted, hanging his head.

"Wanna talk about it?" Angel leaned against the railing and waited.

The wind blew his unkempt blond hair, and he looked happy and content. Two things Damien hadn't felt in a very long time, if ever. *Except with Harley...*

"No...Yes." He looked at his brother, and the years of strife fell away. Maybe Angel would understand—at least the part of it he was ready to share. "I'm losing my mind." He paced, his coat whipping in the wind. "I don't know what the hell is wrong with me. It started after I got shot. I told you about it—I can't stand to be in crowds. I don't like noise, and I'm paranoid all the time. I can't think, I can't work, and I get excruciating headaches. Everything is chaotic. My well-controlled life has become a constant state of confusion, and *I can't stand it.*"

"Maybe you should cut yourself some slack. Learn to relax and let go a little," Angel offered with a nonchalant shrug. "It's perfectly understandable, considering what you've been through."

Damien slammed his fist on the dock railing. "I'm sick to death of hearing that. Why can't I get this under control? I've made myself go to the courthouse so many times, and this was the first damn week I actually got inside. I still felt ready to pass out. It's ridiculous and weak." He added softly, "And I hate myself for it."

"You need help—"

Frustrated, he ran a hand through his windblown hair. "That's just it. Needing help is unacceptable. I don't fucking want to *need* help."

"Nobody's perfect; you've been through a lot. Be patient with yourself."

"I *can't.*" His palms started sweating, and his shirt collar felt too tight.

"Why not?"

"Because…" He shook his head. Old insecurities held his tongue.

"What went down between you and Harley?" Angel's clear blue eyes bore straight through him.

The question startled him, and he felt himself teetering on the edge of the emotional abyss that had surrounded him since she came back into his life.

He pinched the bridge of his nose. "How the hell do you know about Harley?"

"She phoned, and I could tell she was upset."

"Where is she? What did she say?" Damien stopped pacing and gazed at the choppy gray water and dreary clouds overhead. His dark mood was in perfect sync with the cold, drab day.

"She said she didn't work for you anymore because things got 'complicated.' It doesn't take a rocket scientist to figure out that means something went wrong between you two. She's moving to New Orleans. Mark MacGregor's offered her a job as a waitress at The Highland Hangout, the bar he co-owns in the Garden District. She said she needed to get away from Atlanta."

Angel folded his arms. "What happened? I'm worried about her. She wasn't her usual chatty self."

"I need to stop her. I need to talk to her." Damien pulled out his phone.

"Put the phone away. What the hell do you think you're going to do? Physically restrain her? You can't stop her. You're not all-powerful. When will it sink through your thick skull that you can't control everything, especially people? In recovery, the hardest step is the first one. Acknowledging there's a power greater than you." Angel sighed and ran both hands through his hair. "I'm talking, but you're not fuckin' listening, are you?"

"I don't need to hear platitudes or religious recovery bullshit," Damien snarled.

Angel shrugged. "Fine. Go on the way you have been. And tell me, how's that been workin' for you lately?" He paused and smiled. "Letting go of your control won't be the end of the world. Believe it or not, the earth will still turn without Damien Sinclair being the puppet master. Those strands of control you're holding on to? They're frayed and tangled."

Angel grabbed his arm, but Damien shrugged out of it, angered by the truth.

"Can't you see how they're choking the life out of you? Cut the goddamned strings. You might be surprised at how freeing it is to just let go." Angel pushed away from the railing and started walking back toward the house.

At the edge of the dock, he turned and flashed a wide smile. "And as for Harley, you can talk to her in person later. That is, if she'll even give you the time of day. She should be here after dinner."

Damien's head snapped up, and he shoved his phone back in his pocket. Running after Angel, he smacked him on the back of his head. "What did you just say?"

"Ow!" Angel grinned but continued to walk backward up the hill. "A couple of days after you texted you were coming, Harley called. I invited her to stop by to see the stars before taking the job with Mark. It'll be your last chance to fix whatever the fuck happened. Make it right, Damien. Because if you hurt her, you'll not only deal with her brothers and Mark—you'll deal with me. She's loved you forever, although why is beyond me. You're an ass."

Damien didn't disagree but looked up at the overcast sky. "She won't see any stars tonight."

"Are you in control of the weather, too?" Angel shook his head and walked away.

The back door opened, and Maggie melted into Angel's arms. They kissed like they hadn't seen each other in ages, instead of thirty minutes.

Damien stared at the ground, thinking about everything Angel had said. A seed of hope took root. Love had been within his grasp, and like a fool, he'd pushed it away. He had to get her back—he had to make it happen. The sun broke through the clouds, and in that moment, everything became illuminated.

Shaken by the clarity and simplicity of his epiphany, he stopped and stood still, absorbed in the moment.

Monochromatic.

His life without Harley had been varying shades of black and white. He'd once corrected her for her misuse of the word *monochromatism.* He owed her an apology, because she'd been right all along. He'd been color blind to the life she offered. Her love had brought joy and color into his existence. She was his prism, displaying all the colors that had been missing from his dreary, monotonous world. The thought of being chained to the repetitiveness of his lackluster life for even one minute more was intolerable. He could no longer live in this black void.

He needed color.

He needed love.

He needed Harley red in his life.

Harley knocked on the front door of the old, white clapboard farmhouse that was now Maggie and Angel's bed and breakfast. Beside her, Mark wiped his feet as they waited, their breath swirling between them in the frigid air. Rubbing her arms, she shivered and glanced up at the stars overhead. Angel had offered to take her to the bluff where the stargazing was phenomenal.

Tonight would be her closure before starting her new life tomorrow.

Tonight she'd count the stars and her many blessings.

Tonight she'd put aside her regrets and losses.

Tomorrow she'd move forward and find happiness.

Her parents had been upset by her sudden plan to move, but somewhat reassured that Mark would be there to help her. They'd seemed comforted to know she wasn't moving off alone. They just didn't know how entangled she and Mark's lives actually were.

It was time to grow up. If she didn't, she'd stagnate and die. And she refused to give Damien Sinclair the satisfaction. She'd succeed if for no other reason than to spite him.

"You're right. It's beautiful here. I'd forgotten," Mark commented, looking up at the sky with her.

"You've been here before?"

"A lifetime ago," Mark replied softly, his face pensive.

"Oh my God, Mark. I'm sorry! I forgot Jinx was from this area. You should've said something; we could've skipped stopping here."

Mark didn't reply, taking a draw off his cigarette.

Harley hugged him tight. "You didn't have to come here with me, but I'm glad you did." She smiled and interlocked her cold fingers with his.

Mark shrugged. "I'm fine. That chapter of my life is closed. Pine Bluff isn't that far out of the way to get home. Besides, your Dad offered me a hundred bucks to make sure you arrived safe. Everyone knows you're a speed demon. Claire and Charlie will bring Velma next weekend."

"You took money from my Dad?" She gasped.

"No, of course not. I just wanted to get you going."

He grunted when she punched his arm.

The door opened, and Harley's resolve to be strong evaporated as Angel opened his arms for a hug. She buried her face in his blue flannel shirt. Where Damien smelled like autumn, warm and spicy, Angel smelled like spring, light and fresh. Four years younger than she was, he'd always been like another brother to her. He hugged her tight.

"Hey now, everything'll be okay. Come in out of the cold. Are y'all hungry? We can heat up some dinner for you. Maggie makes a wicked good stew, and there's plenty left over." He continued to hold her but held out a hand to Mark. "Good to see you again, Mark. Welcome."

"Hey, Angel. Long time, no see, man." Mark shook Angel's hand.

"I'm not hungry," she said. "Mark might be—he's always hungry." She wiped the unshed tears from her eyes and smiled at Angel. "Thanks for letting us crash here tonight. We'll push off early in the morning."

"You're welcome here any time. You know that. And stay the weekend if you'd like. We're empty until next weekend." He yanked her braid like he had when they were kids and grabbed her bag, motioning them into the warm, inviting living area. A fire crackled in the river rock fireplace, and the smell of home-baked bread permeated the air. Maggie greeted them, wearing a pair of jeans and a Tufts sweatshirt with splotches of flour on it. She gave Harley a hug and a kiss.

"I wasn't sure, uh, one bedroom or two?" Her eyes darted between Harley and Mark.

Mark raised his eyebrows and grinned. "I'm easy either way."

Harley shook her head. "You're too easy. You go through women like some people change underwear. Two, please."

Maggie directed Angel to take their things upstairs.

Mark gave a playful shrug. "You can't blame a guy for trying." Laughing at her sputtered outrage, he followed Angel.

"Do you want to go get settled? Or come with me for a cup of hot tea and something to eat?" Maggie asked.

She was the ultimate hostess, blessed with a warm personality that made everyone feel at home and at ease. Harley had liked her immediately when they first met.

"Tea would be nice. I'm sorry if I'm scattered. It's been a hard day. My parents weren't expecting the move. It was kind of sudden." She lowered her eyes and added softly, "Neither was I."

Maggie linked her arm through Harley's and guided her into the state-of-the-art kitchen that still managed to maintain the feel of a country farmhouse.

"I'm sure it was. Moving is scary and overwhelming. But this isn't your first time away from home, is it? And seven hours by car isn't that far. I've always wanted to visit New Orleans. How exciting the next month is going to be for you with getting settled into a new city and starting a new job, and with a very handsome young man." Maggie put the kettle on for tea.

Was she fishing for information? Or perhaps this was just normal conversation. Harley was too tired to figure it out.

"No, I've lived away from home several times. I, uh…Mark and I are just friends."

It was difficult to explain. Even she and Mark didn't fully understand their relationship. Guilt pricked her conscience. It wasn't fair. He deserved someone to love and care for him better than she ever had, or could. But because of their history, neither of them could let go completely…

Sadly, she realized Damien deserved better, too. Trying to make him jealous had been childish, and when she'd seen him with Renata, she'd acted irrationally. She should've been honest with him from the beginning about…everything. Instead, she'd acted like a spoiled brat who didn't get what she wanted.

Angel and Mark walked into the kitchen, the tension between them palpable.

"I'm going to walk down to the dock for a smoke, if you need me." Mark placed a chaste kiss on her forehead, but his look was thunderous.

Mark's agitation and Angel's uneasy demeanor made her nervous. Something wasn't right…

"Don't you want to go look at the stars with us? What's wrong, Mark?"

"Nothing." His jaw clenched. "You have my number. Call if you need me. I'll find you, *no matter what*. You know that, right?" He stared at her as if attempting to convey a secret message.

"Of course you'd find me. You have Harley GPS programmed internally," she joked, trying to ease his concern. She sucked at mind reading. It's a wonder Sin had believed her crazy carnie story.

Tomorrow, after a good night's sleep, she'd get it out of him on the drive to New Orleans. He shrugged into his black leather jacket and slammed out the back door.

Harley looked at Angel. "What thistle got up his arse? I thought you two got along."

Angel shrugged. "I don't know what you're talking about. We get along great. I've crashed with Mark many a night. Some of my best work was done outside his bar. He seems okay to me." He refused to meet her gaze.

Why is he lying to me?

Maggie offered her a piece of pound cake, but she declined.

"Harley, I don't want you getting upset…" Maggie scrubbed the already spotless counter and cast a nervous glance at Angel.

"Why would I get upset? What's going on here?" She pressed her fingertips into her eyes. She didn't think she could handle anything else right now.

The obvious tension between Maggie and Angel was their business, not hers. She wasn't up to deciphering the strange vibe zipping back and forth between everyone. All she wanted was to see the stars and have a few quiet moments to think.

Angel interrupted, flashing Maggie a strange look. "Nothing's wrong. Harley, why don't you run upstairs and get your coat? If you need gloves, Maggie can loan you a pair."

"Okay. I have gloves. I'll be right back." Feeling like a third wheel, she left.

When Harley returned, she had the distinct feeling Angel and Maggie had been arguing.

"Ready?" Angel asked with a wide smile.

"Don't you want to join us?" Harley asked Maggie, searching her face for a clue to the awkwardness that hung in the air like Spanish moss in a cemetery.

"No, thank you. I'll visit with Mark and keep the fire going. I'll have hot chocolate ready when you return…" She paused. "Um, Harley, remember to keep your heart open to all the possibilities—"

The ringing of the phone interrupted her. "Sleep Inn on the Lake," she answered with a worried smile and wave to Harley.

Wondering about the cryptic message, Harley waved back and followed Angel. A black shadow bounded toward them, tail wagging.

"No, Graffiti. Not this time." Angel chuckled and patted the dog's head. The lab ran back to the porch and pawed at the back door.

Harley giggled. "You always did want a dog. He's cute. I like the name."

Illuminated by the dim, dusk-to-dawn light on the boat dock, she saw Mark leaning against the railing, smoking. He looked lost in thought as he gazed out into the inky water.

"Hey, Angel, give me a minute. I think I need to go check on Mark."

"He's fine. Come on." He tugged her gloved hand.

The night air was cold, and she could see their breath by the porch light. He opened the passenger door to the truck, and it became clear what was going on. Damien sat in the driver's seat. Her heart stuttered, and she resisted Angel's push to get in.

"I changed my mind. I'm not interested in seeing the stars after all."

She turned to walk away, but Angel blocked her escape.

"No, please don't go. Just talk to him; hear him out. You both need this. If nothing else, it will give you some closure."

She hated when he used his persuasive voice. Very few could resist Angel's charismatic personality.

With a gentle push, he helped her into the truck. He gave Damien a pointed look. "If Harley wants to leave, you bring her home." He turned his attention back to her. "You have our phone number and Mark's. Cell service is sketchy, so if you're not back in a couple of hours, I'll find you." He shut the door and waved when Damien started the truck.

Harley refused to look at Damien and bit her lower lip to stop it from trembling. Over and over she reminded herself of her vow to never again humiliate herself in front of Damien Sinclair. He could rot in hell for all she cared.

Quit lying to yourself.

It was freezing cold in the truck, a welcome reminder to keep her cool. Damien turned the heat on, but didn't say a word. Super aware of his presence, she tried to concentrate on her surroundings, but it was no use. All she could think about was the fact that Damien was here.

Why?

Harley closed her eyes as the familiar scent of autumn surrounded her. Her resolve to remain cool and aloof splintered like a meteor shower.

Chapter
Fifteen

Damien didn't speak right away, escalating her anxiety. For the first time ever, she felt carsick.

He sighed. "I'm sorry for the deception. I'm sure you feel betrayed and angry. When I arrived, I didn't know you were going to be here, but I admit I took advantage of the situation after I learned you were coming. I coerced Angel in to letting me take you to see the stars. Maggie was totally against it, so please don't be mad at her."

He kept his voice low, but it was not without emotion. This was probably the tone he used when trying to persuade a jury. She could feel him looking over at her every so often as he drove. Keeping her eyes straight ahead, she fisted her gloved hands and blew her bangs out of her eyes, willing her racing heart to slow down. He could probably hear it ricocheting in her chest.

"Coerced? Seriously? Can't you talk like a normal human being?" Harley attempted to hide her nervousness with a snarky attitude.

"Oops, should I have tagged it as hash first?"

She refused to look at him, but swore she'd heard a smirk in his question.

"Don't be a douchebag, Damien. You don't do social media. It's 'beneath' you. And it's called a *hashtag*. Speaking of things you don't know, do you know how to get to the bluff?"

"Angel gave me directions, so there's a distinct possibility we'll get lost. Reception around here sucks, so using the GPS is out."

Harley sighed; he was right. Angel was terrible with directions.

"We'll be fine, unless you hear banjos playing. Then we're in trouble."

"Wonderful. Lost with you in Bumfuck, Alabama. My day just keeps getting better and better." She ignored his chuckle.

They drove in silence until Damien turned onto a dirt road. Harley glanced around nervously, realizing just how far they were from civilization. She checked her phone for a signal and glowered at the single bar of service.

"Why are you here, Sin?" *Dammit, why did I ask?*

"Somebody once told me the stargazing was spectacular."

Condescending ass. Crossing her arms in front of her chest, she bit the inside of her cheek as she stared out the window into nothingness.

"It's probably a good place to hide a body, too," she muttered.

"Murder hadn't crossed my mind." His low rumble of laughter infuriated her. "But you're right. I wonder how many bodies are at the bottom of that lake? And how many of them were jealous lovers committing crimes of passion?"

"Quit laughing at me. You're a dodgy dickhead!" Whipping around to face him, she pinched herself and vowed not to say another word. *Not. One. Damn. Word.*

"I'm sorry. I think you're adorable."

She snorted her response, but heat rose in her cheeks.

After he parked, he shot out of the truck and had her door open before she could object. Lit only by the overhead light of the cab, he looked incredibly tired. He cupped her cheek in his hand, but instead of looking up, she kept her gaze fixed on the loose button on his coat. Eyes were the windows to the soul, and she didn't want him to see her anguish. She'd revealed enough back in Atlanta.

"I wish I could take back the hurt I've caused you." His voice sounded gravelly.

Harley had difficulty swallowing around the lump of pent-up emotion jammed in her throat. She prayed the light in the truck didn't show her confusion as she stared holes into his chest. *I never got around to fixing that loose button...* He dropped his hand from her cheek and helped her out.

When he closed her door, they were submerged in total darkness, except for the stars shining above them. A dim flashlight provided the only guidance as they walked the uneven ground. She stumbled once, and Damien caught her to his chest.

"Easy now."

The feel of his broad, hard planes under her gloves was strangely comforting, yet devastating at the same time. He lowered the tailgate and opened a double sleeping bag. Before she could hop up by herself, he picked her up and sat her on the tailgate.

Leaning close, he whispered, "Just relax and enjoy the stars, my darling."

"I'm not your darling," she stuttered, doing her damnedest to ignore the kernel of hope his words kindled. *Stay strong. But...he... he smells so good...*

She held her breath, refusing to give in to the tantalizing pull of autumn in winter. He turned off the flashlight, leaving them in darkness. Without any lights to hamper the view, the stars looked like diamonds scattered across a black velvet sky.

Mesmerized by the beauty above her, she gasped. "It's prettier than a display case at Tiffany's."

Gazing into space made her feel infinitely small and yet part of something much bigger. The truck bed dipped as Damien hopped up and lay down beside her. Together they stared in silence at the innumerable stars.

"One, two, three..." She counted softly to get her mind off the man lying next to her.

"Are you seriously counting them?" He chuckled.

"Four, five, six, seven..."

"You missed one. Right over there." He pointed, and she elbowed him, annoyed.

Rolling on to his side, he propped his head on his fist. His warm breath teased her face. He was close...Close enough to kiss...

"Did you know the stars appear white, but they're actually different colors, based on the trace elements in their composition and surface temperature? It's the changes in temperature that affect the wavelength of light emitted by each star."

"How do you know that?" Confused, she turned and looked at his silhouette in the dark.

"Everyone knows that."

"Thanks for the science lesson, Dr. *Ass*-stronomer. When did you become interested in stargazing?"

"I'm not." He chuckled. "I looked it up online while I waited for you to get your sweet little *ass* in the truck. I didn't think 'Your beauty outshines the stars; come here often?' would work."

"*Rasshøl.*"

It probably would've worked, dammit.

He laughed. "Your mamma would wash that sassy mouth out with soap if she heard you."

He reached over, grasped her gloved hand, and gave it a slight squeeze.

Why, oh why do I let this wanker affect me like this?

Damien cleared his throat. "I'm a man who earns his living using words to sway people to my point of view. And yet, I find myself unsure what to say. All I can do is offer a sincere apology. I'm sorry, Harley. I was an idiot and blind to your feelings. My actions were cruel, insensitive, and childish. When I saw you with Mark at the club, it triggered all kinds of emotions, and I acted out of vindictiveness and frustration."

She sputtered to interrupt, but he placed his index finger on her lips. To her mortification, a tear tracked down her cheek. Gently, he wiped it away with his thumb.

"Please don't cry," he whispered.

For a moment, time seemed to stand still, and she held her breath, wishing she could see his face. He'd said the same thing to her all those years ago on the rollercoaster.

Slowly, he leaned in and slanted his mouth over hers, smiling against her lips at her half-hearted attempt to push him away. She stood no chance of resisting and kissed him back, hating herself for relenting so fast but unable to stop. Placing a gentle kiss to her forehead, he pulled away and again propped his head on his fist.

"Better than cotton candy," he murmured.

"W-What?" She tried to move away from him.

"Please, Harley, let me finish, and don't push me away. I'm not making excuses. I'm just trying to explain my actions—my very wrong, hurtful actions. We both know I don't deal well with emotions or touchy-feely stuff. While at the club, I had another goddamned panic attack. Renata appeared and offered to take me home. I was confused, not only by my anxiety, but also by my reaction to seeing you with Mark.

"I could say it was never my intention to hurt you, but I'd be lying. My male pride and jealousy led me to behave irresponsibly."

Harley blinked back her tears. She needed to be done crying over this man. "This is surreal. We have so much history between us…"

"I know I don't deserve your forgiveness. But I'm asking for it, begging even. I'm sorry, Harley, more than you'll ever know. I'm truly, truly sorry, and I want to make it up to you. Please forgive me and let me try to be the man you want and need."

Unable to speak, she wasn't even sure she'd heard him correctly. Damien Sinclair was apologizing? Was it just for the other night, or also for the pain he'd caused her when they were teenagers? She remained silent for a few minutes, trying to process her feelings.

What could she possibly say?

"Twice you've hurt me. What's that saying? Fool me once, shame on you. Fool me twice, shame on me. I don't want to be a fool. I may not be the smartest girl in the world, but I'm learning from my mistakes. We were a mistake."

"No, not mistakes. Missteps. Our lives have been…complicated by outside influences, immaturity…and my stupidity. But I want to start over. A clean slate, if you're willing."

She sat up, pulling her knees to her chest and wrapping her arms around them. Without saying a word, she stared into the black night. Was she ready to let go of her anger? It's what had driven her here. It was the catalyst for starting her new life. If she didn't have her anger, what was left?

My love for Damien…

"We've never talked about it," she said suddenly.

"Talked about what?"

"What happened when we were kids. I mean, if I hadn't been there—the one dumped—it would almost seem like it never happened…I was devastated."

He hung his head. "I know."

"You were jealous of Mark at the club?"

"Not just at the club." He sighed. "I've always been jealous of him where you're concerned. It's not a character trait I'm proud of."

"How ironic." Her small laugh sounded tinny.

As much as she wanted answers, she didn't know if she was up to it. She wasn't ready to explain her relationship with Mark. It was a complex mess with painful memories.

"What's your relationship with Renata? Is she the one you were nonexclusive with when you dated Lauren?"

"Yes. There were others, but mainly Renata. But not since before Christmas." Damien sat up and ran a hand through his hair. "Do you really want to get into this right now?"

"Are you objecting to the question, prosecutor? Let me clarify; when did you last have a notice of entry with her?"

He chuckled. "That's, uh, not the right legal term. And I'm not objecting, I'm asking for a stay of proceedings until we've had some sleep. But to put your mind at rest, I've not had intimate relations with Renata since before my mother died. Please, Harley. Will you accept my apology and we'll discuss this fully later?"

She closed her eyes, still unsure where their relationship was headed. Could her battered heart take any more?

"I don't know. I want to go home. Mark and I have an early start tomorrow morning." She hopped off the bed of the truck.

"No. Don't go. Not yet. I don't want you to move with Mark."

He'd used his prosecutorial bossy-as-hell voice. The one that had always given her a secret thrill. She had to get a grip before she fell under his spell and lost herself again.

"I'll call Angel to come get me." She pulled out her phone, but Damien jumped off the truck and grabbed it out of her hand.

"Give me my bloody phone."

"Not until we talk about your move. Are you and Moron Mac-Fucker *together?*" He tucked it in his pocket.

"You just asked for a stay of proceedings. That doesn't apply to me? And no, not like you're thinking. We're friends."

Damien pulled her close and smiled against her ear. "Stay with me." He backed her against the truck and whispered, "I don't want you to leave." His breath in her ear sent shivers of desire spiraling down her spine.

"I don't know if I want to stay." She gazed up at him defiantly, attributing her hardening nipples to the cold night air. She couldn't think with him this close. Lack of sleep, food, and emotional upheaval had her discombobulated. That had to be the reason her legs were shaking, her heart was racing, and she couldn't catch her breath…

He pushed her back onto the sleeping bag, leaving her legs to dangle off the tailgate. He smiled against her ear and leaned over her, caging her body with his.

She huffed and squirmed.

"I believe the witness has just perjured herself."

"I wasn't aware I was on the stand," she snapped.

He snuggled into her neck and repeated, "I want you, Harley Blake Taylor. Tell me my persuasive-lawyer superpowers are working."

She swallowed and stammered, "S-Stop it."

"Do you really want me to?" he asked huskily. "Please say no."

"Yes…Maybe…" She drew in a shuddering breath. "No."

What the hell is wrong with me? Where is my self-respect?

He paused to look at her. "You love me. I still can't believe it," he whispered.

"*I love you?*" she squeaked.

"I knew it. Say it again."

She could hear the smile in his voice. He stroked her jaw. Whisper kisses followed until he nipped her earlobe.

"You love me, Harley. You told me so last week just before you left. God, you were gorgeous, like a Viking princess. Tell me again."

She turned to face him and held his cheek with her gloved hand. "N-No. I don't."

Her lie sounded unconvincing even to her own ears. She sighed, knowing defeat was imminent.

He kissed her forehead. "Are you sure, my darling girl?" His words filled her empty soul, and her frozen, battered heart thawed a bit and stuttered to life.

"I refuse to answer on the grounds that anything I say could be used to incriminate me," she offered as one last rally before raising the white flag.

"I thought you weren't on the stand?"

His cold hand moved under her layers of clothing and began to rub circles on her stomach. She shivered, but her body burned with desire.

"What is this about, Damien?"

"I'm pretty damn sure I'm falling for you. Hard. Like, no damn safety net hard." He placed a gentle kiss on her lips. "And it scares the hell out of me."

"D-Damien." Her voice hitched, and she placed her hand over his. Her right hand lay fisted beside her face.

"Yes?" He stopped and rested his forehead on hers.

"For the love of toaster tarts, stop." What he'd said was too much to hope for.

"For the love of toaster tarts?" He laughed. "Why? Tell me what you need from me."

"Y-You can have me if you want, but please…I'm begging you… don't fuck with my heart. I can't take it again," she whispered, her voice catching.

"Oh, Harley, I promise not to fuck with your heart." He kissed her neck. "I'll be totally honest with you from here on out. Even if it means talking about goddamned feelings."

She paused, stunned. *Is he serious?*

"Let me just hold you. Okay? I don't want to mess this up. Honestly? I'm terrified," he murmured as he stroked her cheek.

Harley held her breath and waited…She swore she heard the thundering hooves of the four horsemen. It was the apocalypse. It had to be. Or maybe the world had quit spinning on its axis. A tidal wave had just swept up over the bluff. Some major, earth-shattering event had left her world topsy-turvy, her future as bright as the sun.

She cupped his face in her gloved hands. "Tell me something."

"Anything."

"Would you say falling for me is scarier than the courthouse steps?"

"Infinitely." He pulled her glove off and placed her hand on the pounding pulse in his neck to prove it before kissing the inside of her wrist. If she hadn't already been lying down, she was positive she'd collapse like an eighteenth-century woman with the vapors.

"S-Scarier than my driving?"

"I object to the question on grounds of irrelevancy."

"Shouldn't you be pleading the fifth?"

"No, you should. Your driving is criminal."

Harley giggled. "Sin?"

"Harley?" he murmured and licked the shell of her ear.

She shivered from cold and desire. "I'm f-freezing."

"I've read that if you get naked and share body heat, it works better to keep you warm." He teased her neck with kisses and his cold nose.

"Did you learn that online, too?" She pushed his hands away and laughed softly. "I'm pretty sure that's on the list that you, Angel, and my brothers gave me years ago called *Lines guys use to get in a girl's knickers.*"

"I'm quite sure neither Angel nor I said *knickers.*" He chuckled. "Scoot over and share the sleeping bag."

She moved up the truck bed, and he crawled in behind her. Zipping the sleeping bag, he pulled her close, their cold noses touching.

"Harley—"

She placed a finger over his lips and shifted so she was on top of him. The face she loved was hidden by the darkness, but her world was now bright.

"Don't say another word. Not tonight. I forgive you, but I'm too tired to think. We have a lot to talk about, but right now, I simply want to be with you and count the stars."

Grabbing the hand that had eased under her shirt, she brought it to her lips. The growl that emanated from deep in the back of his throat made her smile.

"And I don't want to have sex with you on the back of a pick-up truck freezing my bum off, you wanker."

His laughter started with a rumble deep in his chest and burst forth, carefree and happy. "You always say I'm not spontaneous. But okay, no boinking in the truck bed. So where did we leave off? Eight, nine, ten..."

She settled on his chest, her head tucked beneath his chin. "You know what I mean. I want to be in the moment. It's a beautiful, perfect night, one I'll remember forever." She inhaled deeply, the scent of autumn mixing with the cold night air.

"Did you just sniff me again?"

Listening to the steady beat of his heart, she smiled, but didn't answer. Maybe she shouldn't have given in so easily.

But after all, she'd loved him for more than twenty years.

And only hated him for a week...

Damien stroked her hair and for the first time in ages, he felt comfortable and at peace. They had on entirely too many clothes between them, but it didn't matter. A miracle had occurred. He'd been given a second chance. It was pitch black outside, and yet his life was suddenly polychromatic, full of color and joy.

Now what? Where did they go from here? He wrapped a loose tendril of her hair around his finger and smiled when she hummed in the back of her throat. He longed to hear that sound while he was buried deep inside her with his hands fisted in her hair...

"C-Can we go h-home, O cold conqueror?" She shivered, snuggling in even closer.

He laughed. "Where do you come up with these names?" He sat up, unzipped the sleeping bag, and helped her off the truck bed.

"I think w-we're too old to g-go parking in w-winter," she complained, dancing around and rubbing her arms to get warm.

Damien shoved the tailgate up, making sure everything was secure. "Wimp," he teased.

"I'll own it. Let's come back in May or June." Her teeth chattered.

"Did you just ask me out on a date, Ms. Taylor?" He opened the door for her and smiled. The dim light in the truck revealed her red nose and bright eyes.

"Maybe. Do you think we'll still be together?"

Kissing her forehead, he replied, "If I don't murder you before then."

"Better you murder me than me murder you. I look horrible in orange." She kissed his cheek, hopped in the truck, and slammed her door.

Damien chuckled, relieved things were moving forward. They'd only brushed the real issues, but she was right. Emotions were too raw, and they were both too tired. He slipped into the driver's seat and headed back to the Inn.

"I gave in too easily. I should have made you suffer longer. We still have a lot to talk about," she whispered, yawning.

"I know. It's complicated..."

"You don't have any idea about complicated." Leaning her head against her window, she closed her eyes.

Chapter
Sixteen

Damien paused on the landing outside of Harley's room. He'd carried her upstairs to bed last night and then left her alone, erring on the side of caution. The dark circles under her eyes had attested to her exhaustion, and he couldn't afford to make any more mistakes where she was concerned.

The door stood slightly ajar, and he had every intention of waking her up in a manner that would have her begging him to stay. Then they'd talk, and he'd take her home to Atlanta where she belonged. Just before barging in, he realized she wasn't alone.

"Move over, bed hog."

"Go away, Mark," Harley answered. Her voice sounded thick with sleep. A sound like a muffled slap had him reaching for the doorknob.

What the hell?

"Ow!" She giggled, and the bed squeaked.

Damien pulled his hand back and listened. He hated himself for eavesdropping, but there was no way in hell he'd leave now. *Super, something else I'll need to apologize for: stalking.*

"I can't believe you just slapped my bum. Go away." A loud yawn filtered out into the hallway.

"Not until we talk. I need to know you're okay. Christ on a cracker, your breath smells like camel ass."

"Camel ass? I don't want to know about your weird sexual preferences. I'm fine, and you don't have to worry about me." Again the bed creaked, followed by the sound of water running in the bathroom. A few minutes later, the bed squeaked again.

The sound of a loud, smacking kiss made Damien grit his teeth and want to ram his fist through a wall.

"Better?" Harley asked.

"Much better, and my sexual preferences have nothing to do with your breath. You love me, and I love you. You know I'll always worry about you."

More rustling of covers and bed creaks.

"I know. But I'm perfectly capable of taking care of myself."

Damien looked down to see if his heart was, by chance, rolling around on the floor. It felt like it had just been ripped from his chest. The beginning of a headache started pounding behind his eyes.

The covers rustled, and Mark snorted in response. "Uh-huh, *righhht*. What's the deal with Damien? I thought you were done with him for good. What gives? You still moving to New Orleans with me?"

Yeah, Harley. What gives? Why do you love Mark? Inquiring minds want to know.

"He says he's falling for me." Doubt tinged her voice.

Damien winced. He had to make her believe him…

He would…if he could get Mark out of her damn bed.

"You do know guys will say anything to get into your pants, right? It doesn't sound like much of a commitment to me."

The urge to throw Mark out the window grew stronger.

"Spoken from experience?" Something in her voice caught Damien off guard.

There was an awkward pause. "C'mon, Harley. That was a low blow, and you know it."

"I'm sorry. You're right. It was as much my fault as yours. Maybe more. Forgive me?"

The thought of Mark in Harley's pants made his blood pressure skyrocket. He gripped the doorknob, ready to throw the door open…

Angel shoved him away from the door. With his index finger to his lips, his brother pressed him down the hall into an empty bedroom. Once there, he shut the door behind them with a soft click. It was then Damien noticed the dog at Angel's feet.

"What the hell, Damien? Eavesdropping? Are you in junior high?" Angel whispered as he proceeded to make the bed with fresh linens.

"You let him in the house?" Damien pointed at the black Labrador who now settled for a nap where the sun shone through the window.

"Of course. Graffiti's family. Quit trying to change the subject."

"I'm about to throw that fucker Mark MacGregor out the window. Don't worry. I'll pay for the damages." Damien glared at him and paused, confused. "*You're* making a bed? Pull that corner tighter. And why is Mark in Harley's bed?"

Angel shook his head but pulled it tighter. "Yes, *I'm* making a bed. I've always made my bed when I've had one. I'm not as OCD as you are, but I am neat. Actually, I'm a better housekeeper than Maggie. She never puts her damn shoes away. It drives me fuckin' insane. And I have no idea why Mark's in Harley's bed. I assume since he's in her bed and you're *not*, things didn't go well last night?"

He tucked the covers and ran a hand over the comforter to get out all wrinkles. When he finished, he leaned against the dresser, crossing his arms. Damien straightened the pillows, stepping back and eyeing them to make sure they were even.

"It's fine, Damien. Leave 'em alone. And if you say one word to Maggie about her housekeeping, I'll tag your Jag: *Demon's pussy.*" He punctuated his threat with a spray can motion and sound.

Damien didn't doubt it. Angel was an asshole. Scowling, he ran a hand through his hair and sat on the bed, resting his elbows on his knees. He rubbed his pounding forehead. Would these headaches ever cease?

"I don't know what's going on. I thought Harley and I had made significant progress. Last night she gave every indication she'd forgiven me, and we could move on and explore this relationship. And then this morning, I find Mark where I want to be!"

"You realize you could be jumping to conclusions, right? Harley doesn't strike me as the type of girl to bed hop."

Damien looked up. "It isn't hard to jump. He's in her goddamned bed! And we both know his reputation." He stood up and moved toward the door. "I'm done here. Thank Maggie for her hospitality. I'm headed for home after I pack."

"Quitter," Angel goaded.

"What did you say?"

"You're a quitter. If you love her, fight for her."

He flinched, and Angel's eyes narrowed. "You do love her, don't you?"

Unable to say the words, he shrugged, suddenly wishing he hadn't come here.

"What's this really about, Damien?"

"What do you mean? It's about Mark and whatever his relationship is to Harley."

"What are you afraid of?"

Damien had a number of things pop in to his mind: *That love isn't real. That nothing this good can last. That Harley will leave me...That I can't actually do this...That I'll end up miserable and alone like Dad...*

He spun on his heels and left, storming down the hall. Throwing open Harley's door, he stepped in and slammed it shut with such force, the window rattled. She screamed and bolted upright, clutching her covers to her chest, her eyes wide.

"Oh my God, Sin! Have you gone nutters? You nearly gave me a bloody heart attack!"

Finding her alone, he relaxed and felt just a bit foolish. And yet, *Mark had been in her bed.* He needed answers.

"We need to talk." He locked the door and moved to her bedside before she could get up.

"I know. But now? What's wrong with you?" Her chest heaved with outrage in an oversized Tulane T-shirt.

Mark went to Tulane.

Fucking hell.

She rubbed her sleepy eyes. "Whatever has crawled up your arse, can't it wait until after I've had a cup of tea?"

He cradled her cheek and stared into her clear blue eyes. Desire and love flickered in their depths, and all thoughts of Mark dissipated. She was all that mattered.

Dammit, I do love her. I should tell her.

Fear kept him silent. He couldn't risk it. Not until she'd explained her relationship with Mark.

Instead he blurted, "I want you. I need you."

Disappointment flashed in her eyes. She straightened her covers. "I thought you wanted to t-talk."

On impulse, he pressed a kiss to her forehead. "I do. We need to."

Her skin flushed Harley red, and she pulled her bottom lip between her teeth. Up and down, her breasts rose and fell. A wild, kinetic energy sizzled between them, as if they'd been catapulted back in time to the raw desire of the pool house. If the world ended right now, he didn't think she'd notice, and he wouldn't give a damn as long as he was with her. She was as affected as he was, and they both knew it.

She held his cheek and whispered, "I've changed my mind. I don't feel like talking right now, do you?"

"Talking is way overrated," he agreed.

He lowered his lips to the pounding pulse in her neck. She gasped but didn't stop him. Nibbling, kissing, and licking—it wasn't enough. It was as if her skin fed his soul.

Her fingers clumsily unbuttoned his shirt. The bed creaked with their movements. She giggled, and he whispered *shh*. Their breathing was harsh, staccato. When she finally got his shirt unbuttoned, she used the two sides to pull him closer and kissed his bare chest. He held her face, his thumbs brushing her cheeks, his lips soon following. She purred in the back of her throat and inhaled.

"Silly girl, you're sniffing me, again."

"Mmm-hmm. You smell good enough to eat."

"Dear God in heaven." The mental picture her words invoked pushed him over the edge. He devoured her mouth, exploring with his tongue as his hands roamed her warm, supple body.

She peeled his shirt off and dug her fingernails into his biceps. A satisfied sigh escaped her lips when he nuzzled and kissed her neck.

"What's wrong, Sin? Why are you in here? What brought this on?" she gasped out between squeaks of surprise when he nipped her.

"You. You brought this on. Let me be perfectly clear. I want to fuck you. Then I want to make love to you. Got it?"

Harley gave him a saucy grin. "Why can't we make love first and then fuck?"

"Do you really have to argue every point?"

"I'm fucking a lawyer, what do you think?"

"Well, I am a fucking lawyer, so I'm pretty damn sure I'll win," he murmured, wanting to see her naked.

He shoved her T-shirt up and kneaded one breast, tweaking her hard nipple. "God, they're so perfect…Do you know how long I've wanted to do this again? I've fantasized about them forever…"

He gazed at her full breasts, the very ones that had teased and taunted him for weeks in tight T-shirts. He took one in his mouth, making her yelp and sigh at the same time.

Her breathing stilled. "We, uh, really need to talk."

"Mmm, in a minute…Busy…"

Her hands gripped his hair as she arched beneath him. His hand slid down her stomach, his thumb dipping into the definitions of her hipbone before making its way to the top of her silk thong. His fingers were halted in their descent by a grip on his hand.

"Please stop. I love you, Sin, but slow down. We can't risk making the same mistakes again. We're not horny teenagers anymore." Squirming out from underneath him, she moved him to his back before curling on top of him, resting her head over his heart.

She's right. I'm a wanker. His hard-as-a-rock dick agreed wholeheartedly.

"No, we're horny adults, but okay." *Let's start with your relationship with Mark MacGregor.*

She lifted her head and looked at him, her eyes hooded, her hair a tangled mess. God, how he wanted to wake up to this look every day.

He kissed her forehead and slid his hand down her back, cupping her delightful ass. It fit in his hand perfectly, just like he remembered.

"This is the best thing *ever*." Harley kissed the healed incision on his shoulder across to his heart.

"My scar?" She had to be the most whimsical person he'd ever known.

"No. Listening to your heart beat in your chest and not on that beeping monitor thing in the hospital." She took her time nibbling up his neck.

"Keep that up and I might die of a heart attack," he teased. Every sensory ending in his body was heightened to a new awareness of Harley. The sound of her lips on his skin, the feel of her fingers gently tugging his chest hair, her peach scent—he wanted to sink into her and never emerge, fully ready to drown.

"Don't talk about dying." Covering his mouth with her hand, she straddled him and kissed the ugly scar.

He took her hands in his and gazed at her. With her rocking against his hard cock, the blood had left his brain. He couldn't think.

"We all have to die sometime. It's a fact of life. But for right now, I'm not going anywhere. Not without you."

"Promise."

"I promise. Christ, most of the time I can't even walk up the damn courthouse steps alone, so I'm pretty sure I couldn't make it to heaven or hell by myself. Nor would I want to. Not without you."

"You've lost your perceived power, captain control. When will you realize control is a tenuous illusion? Or is it allusion, I never can remember."

"Illusion. Harley?"

"Sin?"

"Can we just fucking fornicate now and talk later?"

"Excellent alliteration," she whispered with a laugh. "But no."

"No?" Damien blew out a long, frustrated breath.

"We can't. Not here…"

"Why the hell not?"

"Because of Mark, Angel, and Maggie." She rolled her eyes like he was stupid.

"I locked the door, and they're not invited."

"*That* will *never* be an option." She scrambled off the bed, leaving him with the boner from hell. "We can't do it here. I'm a screamer; they'll hear us," she whispered.

Bending over, with her thong-covered ass in the air, she pulled up her jeans. He fell back, groaning at the visual torture.

"I may not die, but you're *killing* me." Damien sighed and sat up.

Now dressed, she crawled back on the bed and wrapped her legs around his waist, her arms around his neck. Foreheads touching, they didn't say a word for several minutes. His breathing synced with hers. She smiled, and he smiled in return. It was perhaps the most intimate moment of his life. And he never wanted it to end.

"Let's go home. We'll talk, and then I want to make love to you, slowly." He stroked her cheek and kissed her, adding, "For hours. No, make that forever."

"Sounds good to me. But we need to say thank you and goodbye to Maggie and Angel, maybe grab a to-go cup of tea and coffee. And I need to say goodbye to Mark and explain…" She hopped up.

Shit. He'd forgotten about him. "Oh yay, I can hardly wait. Yes, by all means, let's go talk to Marcas MacFucker." He sprang out of bed right behind her.

"Better, but his real name is already an alliteration, Willie Wanker."

Damien had her pressed to the bedroom door in a flash, his body caging hers, his hands holding her wrists captive above her head. He blew his warm breath into her ear, and her breathing hitched as he moved his erection against her backside.

"We're going home. At some point we'll talk, and at some point, we'll do something more interesting. But regardless, you will be in my car in less than an hour, or I'll drag you there by the hair. Understand?"

"Oh, brother. Is this where I'm supposed to say, *yes, master?*"

He smiled into her ear. "A simple *okay, Sin* will suffice. Though if that's the route you want to go, we'll negotiate terms later." He smacked her pert little ass.

"In your dreams, bossy balls." She shoved an elbow into his side and slipped out the door.

"Hey, I'm just trying to accommodate. You're the one who read those books."

Harley slammed back into the room and grabbed his balls before he could react. "Maybe I want *you* to be the submissive, Sin."

She kissed him hard on the mouth and was gone before he could take a relieved breath.

Chapter
Seventeen

Damien hurried down the hall, suitcase in hand, eager to get Harley home so they could work through their history. She deserved a full apology and a promise to do better. And then he wanted to…

A door opened, and Mark meandered out of his room dressed in jeans and a long-sleeved navy T-shirt. It took considerable effort not to just slam a fist in the fucker's face, but Damien brushed past him, determined to keep his cool. When they got back to Atlanta, he'd listen to Harley's explanation about her relationship with the notorious womanizer and come completely clean about his own past.

"Don't hurt her," Mark growled from behind him.

Damien stopped and counted to ten in Romani before turning to face him. "Our relationship is none of your damn business. However, we *are* in a relationship, so stay away from her. She's *mine*."

Mark held up his hands in surrender. "Trust me, *I know*. She always has been." He sighed. "But I'll always love her and care for her. Her brothers live too far away to protect her, but I can be on your doorstep in seven hours to kick your ass if I need to." Punctuating his words by pointing at Damien's chest he added, "So I'll say it again, *do not hurt her*."

"I don't plan on it, so stay out of it." Irritated, he glared at the audience now forming at the bottom of the stairs. Angel stood with his hands in his pockets, leaning against the wall. Maggie tugged on Angel's arm and whispered in his ear.

Harley ran out of her room, tying her robe, her hair still damp. "What's going on?"

"Looks like a pissing contest to me," Angel replied.

Damien decided right then and there he'd kick his brother's ass right after he kicked Mark's.

"Angel, I need *help* in the kitchen," Maggie insisted, tugging his arm.

"What? And miss this? No way in hell." Angel smirked.

"I'm leaving," Damien ground out. "Harley, get packed and get moving."

"Don't talk to her like that," Mark snapped.

Damien headed down the stairs with Mark and Harley following. The doorbell rang, waking Graffiti from his nap. He catapulted past everyone down the stairs, barking. Maggie answered the door, her cheerful voice hiding the tension in her home.

"Hello, Jinx! Angel told me your meeting was canceled, but won't you come in? My goodness, he wasn't lying about the size of your dog!" Maggie laughed. "Can I get you some coffee or tea?"

"Thank you. He did cancel, but I stopped by to firm up our decision on paint colors. The workmen want to get started on the inside later today. Angel said it was okay for Winston to visit…"

A fawn-colored English mastiff ran into the house ahead of his owner. It was the biggest goddamned dog Damien had ever seen. His tail swept across the floor like a windshield wiper, and his tongue hung out of his large mouth, giving him a ridiculous doggie grin. He barked once and jumped up the stairs past Damien, ignoring Graffiti's excited barking and lunging. His giant paws landed square on Mark's shoulders. The weight of the huge dog would have knocked a smaller man down. As it was, Mark staggered backward, but somehow managed to remain on his feet. However, the color blanched from his face as he endured the greeting.

"Hey, old buddy." Mark scratched the dog behind the ears as he gazed at the attractive blonde who'd entered the house. A brief look of longing crossed his face before a mask of indifference settled across his features.

"Jinx?" Harley looked shocked, and her wide eyes darted to Mark.

The woman paled, and she took a step back, her hand reaching for the doorknob. "I didn't realize…Uh, hello."

She spoke to Harley, but her attention and whiskey-colored eyes remained fixed on Mark and the monster-sized dog.

"Why are *you* here?" Harley asked.

Tension crackled in the air, and an uneasy sense of foreboding shivered down Damien's spine.

"I'm here to see Angel...I understand now why he called off the meeting..."

Damien looked around and realized Angel and Graffiti had disappeared.

"But we can discuss our plans for The Phoenix Rising later." Jinx gave a sharp whistle, and Winston scrambled down the stairs to her side. He obediently stayed put, but he stared at Mark with profound doggy love.

Looking decidedly uncomfortable, Angel reappeared and took Jinx's hand, pulling her away from the door. "I should've explained why I canceled. I was going to tell you later...This is my brother, Damien. He's on the board and the one who's going to help us understand all the legal stuff. You know Maggie, and, er, of course you know Mark, and I guess you know Harley. Shit, I'm sorry, Jinx..."

Damien nodded at the woman, and she offered a nod and strained smile in return. He couldn't shake his unease. It felt like his recurring nightmare of being late for court and not knowing a damn thing about the case when he arrived. It was obvious the woman didn't want to be here, and that Harley and Mark were also uncomfortable.

Jinx stared at Harley and then looked away. She ran a hand over her dog's huge head, but whether it was for his benefit or to comfort herself, Damien couldn't say. Her hair was a dark, honey-blond color and a diamond pierced one nostril. A long, paint-splattered sweatshirt hung low off both shoulders over her leggings.

She appeared to struggle with her words as she faced Harley. "I...Now is as good a time as any to make amends. I'm, um, still kinda new at this. We've never formally been introduced. I-I'm sorry for any pain I may have unintentionally caused you. I promise, at the time I didn't know you and Mark were married..."

Nobody moved or spoke as the words hung suspended in the air like the blade of a guillotine. The decapitation of Damien's short-lived dream was swift and painful. The silence became a sizzling, snapping roar of static tension as his world collapsed. It felt like being shot all over again, and no matter how hard he tried, he couldn't seem to catch his breath.

What?

He turned to Mark and shoved him to a sitting position on the staircase. "What the hell is she talking about?"

Mark slowly stood back up and stuck his hands in his pockets, not saying a word.

Damien shoved him again, but it was like hitting a brick wall. "*Tell me!*"

"I think we all need to sit down and talk," Mark replied. He flinched, but he didn't raise a hand in self-defense.

Angel took the stairs two at a time and pulled him away from Mark. "Calm down, Damien. I'm not having a knock-down, drag-out here. Somebody's going to get hurt, and you're upsetting Maggie."

Damien shrugged out of Angel's grasp, picked up his suitcase, and grabbed Harley's arm, pulling her with him toward the front door.

Calm down? Like hell!

"Sin?" Harley struggled to pull away. "What are you doing?"

"We're going home. Don't say a word. I can't talk about this right now."

"But I need to get dressed and pack." She shook free of his grip.

"Pack and get in the goddamned car. You have ten minutes." He didn't raise his voice, but he made it clear he meant what he said.

Mark raced down the stairs. "Don't get in that car with him. Not if he's acting irrationally." He raised an accusatory finger and pointed at him. "And *never* talk to her like that again!"

Damien's temper exploded. "Irrationally? You motherfucking sonofabitch, I'll show you irrational." He dropped the suitcase and lunged for Mark, who came back with a vicious punch to the gut that brought him to his knees. Mark was a bigger man and all muscle, but unadulterated rage fueled his own anger. He jumped back up and shot a right upper hook, enjoying the satisfying sound of his fist connecting with the asshole's hard chin. His satisfaction was short lived when he took another blow that landed him on his ass. Angel jumped between them, but it was Winston's angry snarl that diffused the situation. The dog moved to Mark's side, growling at Damien.

Sobbing, Harley fell to her knees, covering his body with her own. "Stop. Please, just stop. I'll explain everything. Just stop..." She brushed the hair off his face and kissed him over and over, her warm, sweet breath a cooling fan to his hot temper.

He kissed her back, tasting the saltiness of her tears. As his adrenaline dropped, his aches and pains increased, and his anger dissipated. She was kissing *him* after all, not Mark.

"Okay…Okay. Just pack and let's get out of here."

Mark stood frozen, staring at Jinx as he rubbed his swelling jaw. With Angel's help, Damien got to his feet, holding his aching side. He winced as his body protested his lack of judgment. Dammit, he'd forgotten Mark was such a strong sonofabitch.

Harley stood and paused before Mark. "Are you okay?"

Seriously? What the fuck? Damien wanted to rip his shirt and howl with pain, but his innate sense of control took over, and he brushed himself off.

Mark gave her an almost imperceptible nod, never removing his eyes from the mysterious, silent Jinx.

Jinx snapped her fingers, and the dog stopped growling and collapsed to the floor. Still confused and just wanting the hell out of here, Damien glanced over at her, finding pain in her eyes.

Who is she?

He turned and glared at Mark and Harley.

Harley was speaking. "I'm not coming with you, Mark. At least not yet—"

"I figured as much. Just remember, I love you and I'm always here for you."

A small, strangled sound tore Damien's angry gaze from Mark back to Jinx. Red splotches stained her pale cheeks as she flew out the door with Winston on her heels. She was in her car and peeling out of the driveway before anyone could react.

"Dammit," Mark hissed, looking defeated.

"Please, everyone. Let's have breakfast, calm down, and talk," Maggie offered, twisting the dishtowel in her hand. "Angel, should you go check on Jinx?"

Damien shook his head. "I'm sorry, Maggie. I just…I need to go. Your inn is lovely, and I'm very happy for you and Angel. This…" He motioned toward the tense people in the room. "I don't know what the hell this is. I can't think, I can't breathe…I have to go." His gaze locked with Harley's. "Are you coming home with me or staying with your…*husband?*"

"He isn't my husband. He's my *ex*-husband. And yes, I'm going home with you. I need five minutes to pack."

Damien watched her run up the stairs to her room and turned a wary eye toward the source of his frustration.

Mark stood with his hands on his hips, looking at the floor for a moment before raising his eyes. "I meant what I said; don't hurt her. If you can't handle what she tells you, let her go. And for what it's worth, I'll repeat it again. It was you she loved, all along."

Mark turned to Maggie and Angel. "I'm going to check on Jinx." With one last warning look, he shrugged past him and left.

Good riddance, asshole.

"I'll be in the kitchen if you need me." Maggie stood on tiptoe to kiss Damien on the cheek and gave his arm a firm squeeze. "Drive safely, and stay calm. I'm sure there's a reasonable explanation for all of this."

"Maybe we should rename this place The Heartbreak Hotel." Angel sank to the stair and rested his elbows on his knees. Clasping his folded hands in front of him, he looked up into Damien's eyes for a split second before lowering them. Angel's leg began to bounce, his tell when nervous.

A sick understanding dawned. Damien closed his eyes for a moment and pinched the bridge of his nose in frustration. The dull roar in his ears blocked all sound except the pounding in his head.

"You knew. You goddamned knew," he croaked.

The press is wrong. I have a heart. How else could I feel this horrific pain?

Angel let out a deep breath before raising his guilt-ridden face and nodding.

"You knew, and you never told me." Damien paced with frustration. Unmitigated anger burned through his soul. "Why? How could you keep this from me? Who else knew? Am I the only chump who didn't know Harley and Mark were married? Did Mom and Dad know? What about her parents? When was this?"

"It wasn't my story to tell, and I don't know all the details. I know some of it because of an incident with Jinx that occurred several years ago. I was in New Orleans and in a bad way. Jinx and I were friends, and we were there for each other. I don't know who else knows. Maybe Claire since she's Harley's best friend and Mark's sister."

"Yet you couldn't confide in me, your own damn brother." He wanted to punch a wall, Angel, something…

"Look, dumbass, we weren't even speaking at the time. And you just now figured out she loves you. Cut everyone some slack." Angel stood and grabbed his arm. "Put your damn lawyer skills to use and hear her out, without judgment…"

Damien shrugged out of his grasp and briefly revisited the idea of taking a swing at him. Instead, he took himself out the front door, slamming it as he left.

In a record five minutes, Harley was dressed, packed, and downstairs. She found Maggie and Angel waiting for her. As much as she dreaded facing Damien, she needed to explain. Upstairs, while packing her duffel, she'd phoned Claire who'd given her a pep talk and a place to stay if needed.

Why did this have to happen now, when Sin and I were about to be together?

"D-Did Damien leave?" she asked Angel.

"No, he's waiting for you in the car. But he's upset. And I'm worried. Are you sure you want to ride home with him? He'll drive like an Indy driver on meth. I'll be glad to take you home."

"Or you can stay here," Maggie offered, stroking her back.

"Where's Mark?"

"He went after Jinx. They have some unresolved business, too." Angel hugged her tight. "Just be honest and talk to Damien. He's an ass, but he cares about you a lot. He told me so."

"I will. Thank you."

An impatient car horn sounded. Harley pulled away from the safety of one brother's arms to face uncertainty with another.

"I have to go. Thank you for trying to help…No matter what happens, I'll always have last night. I guess even one moment of love is better than nothing. Thanks for inviting me to stay in your beautiful home."

Angel gave her a bear hug. "Call if you need me. Any time."

"Love you." She held on for a minute, drawing strength from him.

After kissing him and Maggie goodbye, she slipped out the door, her heart hammering as she approached the black Jag. Damien sat behind the wheel, his mouth set in a grim line, his eyes obscured by his sunglasses. She threw her duffel bag and coat in the trunk.

Closing the car door, she turned to him. "Sin—"

Staring straight ahead, he interrupted her. "Put your seatbelt on, and don't say one damn word until I tell you to speak."

"Excuse me?"

"Not. One. Damn. Word." Clenching his teeth, he ground out, "For once in your life, you will show some fucking control."

Harley huffed and fastened her seatbelt. "But—"

The car shot forward so fast her head bounced against the head-rest. The anger in the confined space of the car settled around them like fallout from a nuclear bomb. They drove in total silence for ten minutes. The eerie stillness made her nervous, and eventually her regret turned to resentment. *He's not going to let me explain?*

"Wanker," she muttered under her breath as she stared out the window.

The car swerved into the parking lot of Hudson's One Stop Grocery in the center of downtown Pine Bluff. He braked so hard they would've sailed through the windshield if not for their seatbelts.

Damien slammed out of the car in a flash, and she watched wide-eyed as he started pacing. Harley unbuckled her seatbelt and stepped out, keeping the car between them. An interested crowd began to form around them. As he marched back and forth, he swore voraciously, punctuating certain words with a flying fist, never breaking his pace. He spoke in a jumble of English and Romani.

"No wonder you're a lawyer. You certainly have a way with words," she offered, trying to break the tension.

As he spun around to face her, a lock of his hair fell rakishly to his forehead. She really did like it longer…

"You always have to have the last word, don't you?" he shouted, pointing at her.

His black coat whipped in the wind. If he'd possessed superpowers, his burning look of fury would've disintegrated her into a pile of ash. Seeing him so out of control was both scary and sexy as hell. She bit her lip to keep from smiling.

"Goddammit, Harley! I asked you to do one thing. Just. One. Damn. Thing. To keep your damn mouth shut. But nooo, you couldn't even do that for me. Married? To Mark-Ass MacFucker? What the hell were you thinking? Why the hell would you marry *him?* He's a kilt-wearing, motherfucking, goddamned womanizer."

"It takes one to know one," she goaded.

"Goddamnmotherfuckinsonofabitch!"

"Damien, shhh. You're making a scene—" Harley glanced around at the growing murmuring crowd.

"Don't you dare tell me to shush. I told you to keep your damn mouth shut, but you couldn't. Well guess what?" He pounded his chest. "It's my fuckin' turn, and I'll damn well not keep mine shut. *You're driving me insane.* Totally, fucking insane. Jesus H. Christ, why am I surprised? You've done so since you were five years old. Look at you! You walk around looking like that..." He motioned toward her. "Those gorgeous, tempting, untouchable breasts bouncing in front of me. Not to mention those pouty lips that beg to be kissed, that beautiful ass sashaying around in those skintight jeans. Dear Lord, woman, you'd make a eunuch grow balls and want to fuck."

Harley glanced down at her breasts in her *The Untouchables* T-shirt and shivered. Ignoring her sense of self-preservation, she put her hands on her hips and ever so slightly jutted her tempting, untouchable breasts forward. Out-of-control Damien was almost like an aphrodisiac.

A side-glance revealed two police officers leaving the store. When the cops started moving through the curious bystanders, Harley tried to get Damien's attention with a motion of her head. One was an older gentleman with gray hair; his partner looked about thirty years his junior.

"Stop it. I see what you're doing. Cover up those tantalizing tits. Goddammit, Harley, I'm only human. I can only take so much!"

"Nice alliteration, but Damien, please, just get in the car, and we can talk about this—"

"*Shut up, Harley.* I'm the one doing the talking right now! Do you hear me?"

"Sir? You need to calm down. You're being disruptive and using foul language on private property. Now, what's the problem here?" The older officer spoke in an authoritative voice and stood with his hands on his hips.

Damien began to laugh. "Problem? Yeah, I have a fuckin' problem." He pointed at Harley. "Right there is my problem. Her name is Harley Blake Taylor *MacGregor*. She's my problem. She's been my problem since she was five years old and stole my Cheetara action figure."

He whipped around and pointed at her. "Yeah, Harley. That's right. *I know you stole it.* It broke up my Thundercats set. I had the complete damn set until you came along. Tygra needed Cheetara, goddammit!"

"You didn't play with them anymore!" she protested.

"Ma'am? Is he bothering you?" the younger officer asked. A hint of a smile played at the corners of his mouth.

"No, sir. It's just a little misunderstanding…"

A tinge of hysteria surrounded Damien's laughter. "A *little* misunderstanding? Are you fucking kidding me? Oh yeah, it's a misunderstanding, but hardly little. Mark MacFucker is the biggest damn asshole to walk the face of the Earth! She married him and neglected to tell me. What happened? Huh? Did my invitation get lost in the mail? I would've thought you'd at least tap me for a *wedding* gift. Yep. Just a minor misunderstanding…" Sarcasm dripped from his voice like honey in May.

"We're *divorced*, Sin."

"Geezus, don't you ever listen? I told you not to say one goddamned word."

"I'm trying to keep you from getting in trouble—"

"There you go again, having to get the last word in. That's my job." He pounded his own chest. "I'm the lawyer here! I get to have the last word."

The officer stepped forward. "I don't like the way you're talking to the young lady. Either calm down or you're coming with us to cool off…"

Harley looked at the younger officer. "Please, it's just a lover's quarrel—"

"Lover's quarrel? We're not *lovers!* That's part of the damn problem."

The younger officer raised his eyebrows and smirked. The older officer unhooked his handcuffs.

"Sir, you have the right—"

"I know my rights, dumbass. I'm an attorney—"

The officer's eyes narrowed.

Harley didn't think twice. It was either act now, or watch him get hauled off to jail. She launched herself into Damien's arms, wrapped her legs around his waist, and pressed her hard nipples into his chest. Thankfully, he caught her. Cupping his cheeks in her hands, she interrupted his arrest by kissing him long and hard. When he moaned, she moved her hands into his hair. His tongue danced with hers as he returned her kiss. The bystanders broke out in applause and whistles.

The older officer coughed to get their attention.

Reluctantly, Harley broke the kiss and watched as the officer hooked the handcuffs back on his belt.

"I think you two need to mosey on down the road," he said. "If you need a room, you can find one at the Sleep Inn on the Lake."

Harley grinned and winked at the officers. Damien's warm breath on her neck made her shiver even more than the cold air.

"Not one damn word, Harley," he whispered as the officers turned to walk away.

She pressed her forehead to his and inhaled his glorious scent. Locking her eyes on his, she smiled at him and without making a sound mouthed, "Wanker."

The smack he leveled on her butt made her gasp with surprise. Laughter swept through the lingering onlookers.

Damien huffed when the older officer muttered to the younger one, "I don't envy him. He's gonna have his hands full."

He lowered her to the ground, and she grinned, realizing he was as hard as a rock. She stood on her own feet but swayed, grateful his arms were still wrapped around her waist. If they hadn't had an audience, she would've been tempted to jump his bones in the car. Some of the bystanders dispersed, but some remained, apparently intent on seeing the grand finale.

Damien let out a slow deep breath. "Thank you for saving my ass. Now, please get in the car. We'll talk about this at home. I just need some time to process before I hear what you have to say. Okay?"

Harley nodded and walked back to the car, not saying a word. Her heart was full, and her emotions were all over the place. He was right. They both needed time to think. She just hoped he realized her home was in his heart.

Chapter
Eighteen

Damien parked the car and sat for a moment in the garage. Harley had listened for a change and not said a word on the trip home. He was sure the peace and quiet wouldn't last much longer. She looked ready to bust.

Taking his time, he stepped out of the car, opened the trunk, and retrieved his suitcase, along with her duffel bag and coat. She followed him to the elevator, still silent.

Her eyes glittered dangerously and remained straight ahead as they rode the elevator. *The Untouchables* heaved up and down in deep, measured breaths, and her cheeks were flushed.

Damien bit the inside of his mouth to keep from laughing. The words *"we're divorced,"* along with the passionate kiss that had kept his ass out of jail, had lessened his fury.

But he wasn't going to tell her yet. Watching her struggle to keep her mouth shut was the most satisfaction he'd had in days.

With a soft ding, the elevator stopped, and he approached the desk to let them know he was home and collect his mail.

Jerry's welcoming smile faded when he saw Harley. "Good afternoon, Mr. Sinclair. I hope you had a nice trip." The desk clerk handed Damien his mail.

"Quit staring at me, you wanker." Harley glowered back at Jerry.

"Hush, Harley. I told you not to say a word."

"We're *home*, Sin."

"Jerry, please have our things brought upstairs. As you can see, I have my hands full." Damien swooped Harley over his shoulder and gave her delightful ass a hard swat. She squealed her outrage and beat on his back with her fists.

Jerry's face remained impassive, but his eyes twinkled. "Yes, sir."

"Put me down!"

Damien ignored her, spanked her bottom again, and stalked to the elevators. When they arrived at the penthouse, he unlocked the door, stepped inside, and kicked it shut with his foot.

"We're home now. Put me down!" Once again, she beat on his back with her fists and kicked her feet as he marched toward his bedroom.

He gave her ass another hard pop before throwing her down on the bed. He smirked and ripped open his gray shirt. Buttons flew everywhere as he shrugged out of it. Her eyes flashed and darkened, and her tongue licked her full bottom lip. He crawled on top of her, caging her body with his arms.

"I thought you wanted to talk…"

A knock at the front door interrupted.

"Don't move."

He stalked to the door, and Tim handed him their things. Practically pushing the guy out, Damien slammed the door and returned.

Crawling back into bed, he nuzzled her neck and whispered, "Where were we?"

"Not talking, obviously…"

"Right. I've had some time on the drive home to think, and I've decided I don't want to talk with our clothes on."

"W-What?"

She pushed him away and sat up, looking at him as if he'd gone mad. Maybe he had. At this point, he didn't give a damn. Crazy or not, she was his. Damien unbuttoned his black jeans while kicking off his shoes and socks.

"You want to talk naked?" Her huff of surprise blew her bangs out of her face.

"Yes." He gazed at her hungrily and smiled. "Now take off your damn clothes."

Her eyes lit up like liquid fire. "Seriously. Naked?" *The Untouchables* rose and fell.

He nodded. "Naked."

"Why?" She kicked off her shoes and peeled off her socks.

"No more barriers between us, Harley. This is it. No social barriers, no moral barriers, no secrets, no lies, no half-truths, no clothes. I want us stripped and bare, both physically and emotionally."

Her throat bobbled. "I don't know if I can do this…"

He leveled her with a look, and she scrambled to remove her clothes. He wanted to tell her to slow down so he could enjoy the show, but prudence kept his mouth shut. She shimmied out of her jeans and stood before him in her T-shirt and thong panties. Hesitating a few seconds, she swallowed nervously, closed her eyes, and with trembling hands drew the shirt over her head. When she stepped out of her minuscule thong, Damien's mouth went dry and he paused in shedding the rest of his clothes.

He couldn't move.

He couldn't speak.

He couldn't think.

All he could do was stare. She'd been a beautiful seventeen-year-old girl. But the girl of his memories and dreams didn't compare to the woman before him. She quite simply defied description. It would be like trying to explain heaven, or love. Impossible. He drank her in, knowing that just looking would never be enough.

Her hands moved to cover her nakedness.

"Don't," he managed to croak. Quickly shedding his jeans and underwear, he took her hand and drew her to him. "You're even more beautiful than I remembered," he whispered.

"So are you," she replied, her voice low and husky. Biting her lip, she looked away as her fingers clasped his. Her skin was tinged in Harley red.

Damien traced the outline of her jaw with the back of his fingers, and she turned her cheek into his palm. Taking her chin, he tilted her head toward him and slowly tasted her soft lips, savoring them. She kept her eyes open, staring at him. He deepened the kiss, smiling as he teased her. Reaching around her, he pulled the covers down and gently but firmly pushed her onto the bed.

He once again captured her hands in his and held them above her head as he worshipped her with his eyes. Harley Blake Taylor... He mentally corrected: Harley Blake Taylor *MacGregor,* was the definition of sensory overload. And his cock sat up to take notice. He was pretty sure, if given the opportunity, his dick would bitch-slap him for being a fool.

He squelched his horny inner demon and tried to concentrate on being a patient, understanding man—a man who wanted answers and a long-term relationship, not a quick romp in the sack. But it was damn near impossible with the soft, sexy body he'd dreamed about lying beneath him.

"Tell me about you and Mark. Why didn't I know you were married? When? And what happened?" he managed to ask around the lump in his throat.

"N-Now? Can't we first, um, you know..."

"Now."

Harley moved beneath him and smiled as she struggled to free her hands from his. The woman was driving him to distraction. She always had.

"Are you sure?" she purred.

The smell of peaches—which he now found as necessary as air—teased his nose. He kissed her, smiling at the taste of her cotton candy lips. Her skin was soft, warm, and flushed his favorite color. Sweat broke out on his forehead, and he closed his eyes and as he struggled to remain in control and not embarrass himself like a horny teenager.

"Do I have to tie you to this bed, tempting tart?"

She laughed. "Promises, promises."

An uncomfortable silence followed, and he could tell she was dreading this as much as he was. He tamped down his rising fear.

"Do you love Mark?" He searched her face for his answer.

She blew her bangs out of her face and looked away. Her breasts rose and fell beneath him, as she appeared to struggle to find the words—words he was afraid he didn't want to hear. Her eyes clouded with pain and tears.

"Yes, but not enough. And it's something I regret, because I hurt him…"

He held his breath, waiting for her to continue. Or had all the air been sucked from the room? *Talking* is *way overrated. I don't want to know…*

She held his cheek in her hand, her thumb tracing his lip. "I never loved him the way I love you. I've loved you for as long as I can remember and will love you forever."

He hadn't prayed in years. But with her simple declaration, he closed his eyes, exhaled, and thanked God. *She loves me.*

Rolling off her to his back, he pulled her in close. "Tell me everything."

Her finger traced the healing scar on his shoulder. "I've always loved you. Since I met you, I knew in my heart we were destined to be together. You may not remember, but you kissed me long before that summer…"

"On the rollercoaster. You were crying."

"You do remember."

He grinned. "I felt bad for teasing you and wanted you to stop. Your lips were so soft and sticky and tasted like cotton candy. It's a better memory than what you did afterward. I think I sang soprano for a month."

She giggled. "I didn't know what to do, how to handle my emotions. I knew even back then not to show you how I really felt, that it would push you away. And my brothers would have teased me if I'd acted like a ninny. But I didn't want to wash my face when we got home. And when I was old enough, I bought cotton candy lip gloss to remind me of that day…"

He chuckled. "I know. I like it. And I can't imagine Elise letting you get by without bathing. In her eyes, cleanliness is next to godliness."

"She didn't. The next time we kissed was spring break, my senior year in high school…"

He smiled and stroked her cheek. "You'd grown up. You were all I thought about, dreamed about…We couldn't keep our hands off each other."

"You were my first, Damien."

He winced, knowing he'd done her wrong. "I know."

He had to strain to hear her whispered words.

"It meant something to me, but you left without even saying goodbye…"

"I'm sorry." He sighed, remembering the long ride to the airport with his father. He'd been hung over, furious, and scared.

"I waited, thinking you'd at least call, or communicate somehow. But you never did. I got angry, thinking you'd used me, that I was just one in a long string of girls."

Knitting her brows together, she hesitated. "A week or so after you left, your mother spoke to me as I dusted her room. She told me you needed to focus on school and making good connections. She was happy you were dating Lauren…And there I was, cleaning her room, the daughter of the help. Did she tell me this stuff on purpose? I don't know. But I realized I'd been dreaming. My parents had basically told me the same thing, that I didn't belong in your world."

Damien sighed, staring at the ceiling. "My mother was very conscious of class. Maybe because she was trying to overcome her own past. Her mother ran off with a Rom—a gypsy—and the family disowned her. Running off with her gypsy lover was my gran's favorite story, but I think it embarrassed my mother. After we were caught, my father gave me a lecture. But when Mom got involved it was…brutal, to say the least."

She shrugged and looked at his chest, not meeting his gaze. "Since you never gave me a second thought, I tried to forget you. And it wasn't in a healthy manner."

He could hear the hurt in her voice, and guilt washed over him.

"But you're wrong," he told her. "I did give you a second thought. You were all I thought about. My parents manipulated both of us. From the time we hit puberty, Dad gave Angel and me the hands-off lecture regarding you. After he caught us, he took me into his study and gave me a sterner version. He said he knew it was you I was with. I denied it, but looking back, who were we kidding? Our feelings were probably stamped on our faces. I protested, vehemently, but Dad's a helluva good prosecutor, and I caved. I told him I cared about you, that you were important to me. He might've relented—he wasn't happy, but he *was* listening to me. But then Mom got involved and forced my hand."

"How?"

"She threatened to fire your parents."

"What?" Harley's eyes widened.

"Your parents meant the world to me; they still do. They were almost more like parents than my own. I couldn't risk it. I was miserable, but I planned to contact you, to try to explain. You didn't have a cell phone. I called your house to talk to you, but your Dad told me you didn't want to hear from me and it would be best if I left you alone. I knew you had every right to be mad, so instead, I wrote you a long letter of apology. But you never answered me."

She raised her head and stared at him, shaking her head. "I never received a letter…"

"I know. I found it after Mom died—hidden in her Bible, of all places." He shook his head. "Anyway, a few weeks after I returned to school, Mom sent me some prom photos of you with Mark. She said you and he were serious…I was angry, but then I thought maybe it was for the best. Maybe it had just been hormones fueling the connection between us. I never realized the depth of your feelings for me. I don't even know why you still love me. I've been a complete ass."

"You have a nice ass," she quipped with a slight smile. "I wouldn't know how to *not* love you. It's just the way it is. I think I was born to love you. I moped around, and my parents eventually sat me down and told me it was just a schoolgirl crush that would never amount to anything. They thought I needed to be realistic about our class differences. Do you think our parents were in cahoots to keep us apart?"

Damien shrugged. "I don't know, maybe. We *were* young. I guess they thought they were doing the right thing."

"Things would've been so different…" Harley whispered.

"We can't dwell on the past."

"And yet, we have to discuss it." She exhaled, staring at the ceiling. It was a full minute before she continued. "As for Mark, we weren't serious, and your mother didn't know the whole story…No one did but Mark and me. This is where it gets complicated."

"Complicated how?"

"After you left, I was devastated, like any moonstruck teenager suffering from unrequited love. Mark was there to pick up the pieces. He'd had a crush on me long before I thought of him as anything but Claire's brother. I know you think you know him, but Mark's different than the way he seems to most. He doesn't let people in for fear of being hurt or abandoned. You can't be kicked around to thirteen foster homes and not have some serious issues with relationships. He was needy, and I was heartbroken. Take those two factors, combine it with availability and alcohol, and you have a volatile, disastrous combination."

Damien stilled. "Disastrous how?"

"He asked me out, and we—"

He placed a finger over her lips and begged, "No details. Please, no goddamned details. I can't take it."

She sat up, pulling her knees to her chest, and wrapped her arms around her legs. "Mark was attending a local college but planning to transfer to Tulane. Not long after you left, I was washing the breakfast dishes. Your mother came in and casually mentioned to Mamma that she expected you to announce your engagement to Lauren any day. I assumed it was true. I mean, you'd left me without a word, and you dated her in high school. Plus she went to college in the Boston area…"

"What? That was an outright lie!"

Her lower lip trembled. "And yet until a few weeks ago, she was still in your life."

He didn't say anything for a minute. "Truthfully? I don't know why. Early on it was family pressure, then the connections I needed. In the end, I just didn't care. She was familiar and convenient. I've told her for years I wasn't going to marry her. I'm not a marrying man. She'd act okay about it for a while, and then start pushing. I'd break it off, and then she'd say she was fine with it, but she never really was. It's been worse the past year. She's not a bad person, just a bit shallow. But I knew I didn't love her. I never have."

Harley snorted. "A bit shallow?"

He shrugged. "She was fine for what I wanted. I don't believe in marriage. They rarely last."

"I think your job has made you cynical. My parents have been happily married for close to forty years. And you're a wanker, Sin. You used her."

He grunted in response. She was right. But he wasn't interested in marriage. "I always made it clear where I stood. Go on."

"After your mom dropped the bomb about your supposed up-coming marriage, I was devastated. It was prom night. I went with Mark, and we got drunk. We were careless…"

He stopped stroking her back, processing what she was saying. "Careless?"

"Very. But we didn't realize it. He moved to Louisiana to start work before school started in the fall. I started cosmetology school, never realizing I was pregnant."

It was like a sledgehammer crashing into his chest. He hadn't been prepared for this revelation. His mind had already formulated a reason for their marriage—a drunken night of passion, a run to Vegas for a quickie wedding, and then an amicable divorce.

Pregnant?

Damien sat up, stunned. He rubbed his burning eyes. "Go on."

"Mark's a good guy. He loved me. And I did him, but not the way that's needed to sustain a relationship. But because of the baby, I agreed to marry him." She turned to face him, and her tear-filled eyes held such unspeakable pain he found it difficult to breathe. "Analiese was born much too early. She only weighed one pound and six ounces. My beautiful baby girl had a head full of wispy strawberry-blond hair…"

Hiding her face in her knees, she rocked and wept. Her despair was so profound and so deep it permeated the air. How had she borne this much grief? He couldn't imagine the pain of losing a child. Damien gathered her in his arms and held her. He didn't speak. There were no words to ease her anguish. His tears mingled with hers as he absorbed her pain.

"She was too tiny, so helpless. We prayed so hard for her to make it," Harley whispered hoarsely. He turned her damp face to his and kissed away her tears.

"I know. I know…" But he didn't. Not really. How could he? "I'm so sorry, darling. Your parents, did they know?"

"We hadn't told them yet. I didn't want to disappoint them. You, of all people, can understand that. We didn't tell anyone, and then everything happened so fast."

"They didn't know? What about the marriage?"

She shook her head. "Only Claire knew. I was three months along before I even realized I was pregnant. I phoned Mark and drove down to see him. Luckily, I'd just turned eighteen, so we didn't need parental consent. We married at the courthouse, and then I came home. I wanted to finish my classes. I mean, we thought we had time. I wasn't showing. We were scared—going to school, working, living in two separate cities and trying to make our relationship work. I spent more and more time away from home, wearing loose clothes, too afraid to tell my parents. I went to visit him one weekend and started cramping and bleeding. In part, I blame myself for her death. Maybe if I'd had prenatal care sooner…"

"Don't. These things just happen. No one is to blame. And Mark? How did he handle it?" Damien kissed her brow.

"He was as devastated as I was. He tried to be supportive, but the pressure got to him. Let's face it, he didn't have a role model for marriage until Claire's family adopted him. And our marriage didn't stand a chance after that. We'd married out of obligation. We were children having a child. After Analiese's death, the pressures of school, living separately…We just drifted apart. And yet if I ever needed him, he was there for me, and I for him."

"But you said you did divorce. What about Jinx? How does she play in to this? Mark looked pretty shook by her arrival."

"We didn't divorce right away. I know that sounds crazy. It was some unspoken feeling we had, that staying married gave our daughter's short existence meaning, made it real. I really can't explain it. We led separate lives, married on paper only. I truly think Mark's bed hopping is his way of handling his fear of abandonment. He leaves before his heart gets committed. And I guess I was his ultimate excuse if things ever got too serious—he was already married, his ace in the hole. As for me? Well…my heart was with you. And you were unavailable."

She sighed. "Anyway, every year we get together and visit Analiese's grave on her birthday…Three years ago, I called and told him it was time to end things. I realized we needed to sever our legal ties. That's when he told me he'd met Jinx. I could tell she was someone special. And he agreed; the time was right.

"I arrived to sign the papers, and it turned into a clusterfuck of misunderstanding with Jinx…"

Her red-rimmed eyes met his. "We divorced, but we're still close. We always will be because of Analiese. But we make much better friends than spouses."

She took a deep breath. "And that's my story. Despite all that, I want you to know, my heart belongs to you, Damien. It's you that I love. It always has been. I'm sorry. I was stupid and careless—"

He placed a finger over her lips. "Don't. Don't apologize. You have nothing to apologize for."

She dragged her eyes back to his. "I have to say this. Mark will always be in my life, like it or not. We share too much history, and he's important to me."

He didn't like it. Not one damn bit. But for her sake, he'd learn to like it, because she was important to him.

He squeezed her hands. "Okay."

Her brows knit together as she worried the bottom lip he wanted to nibble on. "What about Renata?"

He pulled her to him and kissed her soundly. "Renata was just a friend with benefits, nothing serious and no attachments. It was her house where I pulled the ultimate prank, and Chris, her lover, who answered the door. They have an open relationship, which suited me just fine. She agreed to the joke as a favor and then dropped by the club out of curiosity since she didn't get to actually see you. I had another panic attack, and she took me home. I stayed up worrying about you, and she slept in my bed. I was furious seeing you with Mark, and when you didn't come home, I was angry. So instead of being a rational adult, I acted like an idiot. Again, nothing happened that night."

He frowned. "I'm not a good man. I've used Renata and Lauren. I've treated you horribly. How did I get so far off track? All I've ever wanted was to be fair and not risk—"

"Heartache? Why do you act this way?" Harley asked softly.

He didn't answer for a moment. He'd seen the devastation left behind when love went bad. Fear had made him a cold bastard. "Because I've never believed in love." He kissed her hand. "Until you."

She brushed the hair off his forehead and held his face in her hands. "We've wasted so much time apart." Her warm lips found his, and she smiled as she gave him a sweet kiss. "I love you, Damien." A whisper of kisses trailed across his jaw line. "And you're not a total idiot. I see the real you," she whispered.

Gazing into her eyes, Damien had a startling recollection from a moment following the shooting, when he'd become aware of his surroundings in the hospital. His father had been there, but the face that had brought him the most comfort had been the pale, crying, blotched face of the woman in his arms, the woman who was now smiling at him with the most seductive look of hunger he'd ever witnessed.

"I love you, Harley," he blurted.

It was one of the few times he'd ever seen her stunned speechless.

Life, he decided, was a series of mundane events strung together in the monotony of daily living. But what made it all bearable were the colorful moments of uninhibited joy, especially if colored Harley red.

Chapter
Nineteen

He loves me! She straddled his waist. His slow, easy grin and warm, wicked eyes held promises of the future. And by God, she intended him to keep every last one of them. She brushed a lock of his dark hair off his forehead.

"You sure?" she asked.

"Pretty damn positive."

His hands kneaded her breasts, rolling her taut nipples in his fingers. She closed her eyes and threw her head back, moaning as the heat coursed through her body. Her skin tingled with anticipation. She leaned forward and kissed him, exploring his mouth as he opened to her. She tweaked his nipples and smiled into her kiss.

"You're Tygra to my Cheetara," she purred in his ear.

Damien chuckled, and his eyes crinkled. She loved those laugh lines. She wanted to see him laugh every day.

"Nice. Can I use my bolo whip on you? I take back one thing. You do owe me an apology for taking Cheetara. That was just mean." He flipped her over and reached into the drawer of his nightstand.

He tore open the condom, but she grabbed it out of his hands. "Let me."

Taking her time, she stroked him before slowly rolling the condom down his length. Beads of sweat dotted his brow, and he closed his eyes momentarily as his breathing grew labored.

"Having difficulty, Mr. Control Freak? Maybe you should learn to let go."

His dark eyes were fathomless. Grinning, his fingers slowly teased, working magic between her legs. She was more than ready for him, and he was prolonging it to torment her. Not that she really minded. He brought her to the brink of ecstasy and backed off. That she *did* mind.

"Don't stop. Please don't stop."

"Oh, don't worry, Viking vixen. I have a plan, and there won't be any stopping."

"Plan?" What plan? Her brain was fuzzy from frustration.

"I'm going to fuck you like crazy and get it out of our system. Then I promise to make love to you so slowly you'll be begging me to hurry."

She wrapped her legs around his waist and dug her fingers deep into his biceps.

"Is there any room for negotiation, O fearless fucker?"

"No, naughty nymph, keep your hands on the headboard, and don't move them."

"Bossy barbarian, don't hold back. For the love of God, I need this." She reached up and grabbed the wrought-iron headboard.

Grasping her hips, he pulled her up and plunged in deep and hard. *Finally.*

"Yes…" She pulled in a breath as she adjusted to him, her body melding with his as a feeling of completeness filled her.

Damien smiled as he moved inside of her, pushing harder and harder. He wasn't joking; he pounded her with the savage intensity she craved. A need for release ignited within her, and she met his thrusts, wanting more. His muscles glistened with sweat as he drove faster and deeper. She moved her legs to his shoulders, and he nipped her thigh. This was unadulterated, raw, primal fucking. And she'd never felt more alive. She relished it, panting as the tension coiled and built quickly between them. Leaning in, he pinched her hard nipple and rubbed sensuous circles around her clit. A whimper started in the back of her throat and turned into a hiss as one hand slipped off the headboard.

He somehow managed to spank her ass and growl, "Don't let go!"

She grabbed the wrought-iron bed so tightly her knuckles turned white. She needed this. She wanted this. Her climax rose in an exhilarating crescendo until she was afraid she'd pass out from the intensity. She couldn't hold out much longer. Her body hummed in harmony with his, and she met each thrust with wild abandon. Her hands cramped and ached, but she refused to let go. When she came, she screamed his name, and he pumped harder into her until he in turn threw his head back and stilled deep within her.

"Fuck." He lowered her legs and groaned into her neck, sucking in air like a man who'd been drowning.

If he weren't lying on top of her, she had no doubt she'd float to the ceiling. She couldn't have moved even if she'd wanted to. Her muscles quivered in the aftermath as she struggled to catch her breath, and her heart ricocheted triple time in her chest. Their bodies were slick, and his damp hair tickled her nose.

The smell of sweat and musky sex mingled with the scent of peaches and autumn, filling the air between them. A bubble of pure joy swelled within her and burst. It started as a snort, then a snicker, and worked up to a giggle.

He raised his head, frowning.

His confusion made her laugh even harder.

"Damn, Harley. I've had a lot of post-coital responses, but laughter hasn't been one. Should I be insulted?"

"I-I can't help it. I needed this…I can't move…"

"Oh, damn. I'm sorry, sweetheart." He moved his weight to his arms, ready to get off her, but she grabbed him by the hair.

"Yeow."

"No, don't move." She laughed until tears streamed down her face. "I think I'm possessed. I've got a Demon inside me."

He looked quite pleased with himself. "Why yes, you do." He lowered his mouth to hers, kissing her tenderly as he stroked her damp hair off her face. "You're so beautiful." His eyes held hers, and she smiled in return.

"This was meant to be, Sin."

"Indeed it was."

After a moment, Damien rolled off her and disposed of the condom. Back in bed, he stretched out and pulled her to him. He stroked her back in lazy circles, and the tension in her muscles relaxed. She sighed into his chest.

"I feel alive and unafraid for the first time since I was shot," he murmured against her hair.

"Me too," she whispered, closing her eyes and giving in to her exhaustion.

He'd kept his promise multiple times over the weekend, making love to her with slow, torturous tenderness. He'd also fucked her silly. They'd ignored all phone calls and only answered the door for take-out delivery. She didn't think there was an inch of her body he hadn't explored, and every muscle protested as she eased out of bed Monday morning.

Damien stirred and mumbled, "Don't leave unless you're starting coffee."

Giving him a quick kiss on his forehead, she slipped on her robe and tiptoed out of the room. She fished her phone out of her purse and was alarmed to find three texts from Maggie, two voicemails from Angel, four texts from Mark, and thirteen texts from Claire asking if she was okay.

Too happy and too tired to deal with the concern, she sent a mass text — *everything is perfect, love you all*— to everyone. She started the coffee and began making breakfast. Her phone rang with the Care Bears theme song.

"*Bitch! It's a good thing you took that self-defense class, or I'd hunt you down and beat your ass for not calling me back!*"

Harley laughed. "I love you too, Claire Bear. Everything is perfect. *He loves me.*"

"*It took him long enough to realize it. What a dickhead. I'm off Friday. We're having lunch, and you're spilling the goods. I want every nasty, dirty detail.*"

Harley laughed. If anyone would have her back, Claire Lassiter would.

"He's not a dickhead."

Harley dropped the phone and screamed as two large hands grabbed her from behind. Warm lips nuzzled her neck.

Damien picked up the phone. "I most certainly am a dickhead, and Harley has to go." He hung up the phone.

Harley turned in his arms and hugged his neck, giving him a chaste good morning kiss. "I don't think I want to know how Claire responded to that."

"She didn't call me anything worse than you have. You two can catch up Friday at the benefit."

"What benefit?"

"For the homeless. Claire's mother is on the planning committee, so I'm sure she'll be there. I'm one of the benefactors, so unfortunately, I have to make an appearance, too."

It took a full minute for the implication of his invitation to sink into her brain.

She glared at him. "Are you nutters? I don't have anything to wear to something like that! And isn't this the one Lauren is involved with?"

Damien's eyes grew wide with mock horror as he tied his black tie. "Maybe you'll have to go shopping—or even better, you could go naked. And yes, it is."

"It would serve you right if I did show up naked, you wanker. Why do I have to go?"

"Because I want you to. Speaking of naked, why are you dressed?"

"Why are you? Your hair's getting long again. I like it." She brushed a damp strand off his forehead and cupped his unshaven cheek with her hand. Her thumb rubbed over his jaw as she inhaled the addicting scent of Damien.

"You're doing it again. That's really weird the way you sniff me. I always wonder if I forgot to use deodorant."

"No, your smell is my catnip. *Meow*." She licked her lips. "Why don't we go back to bed, tiger?"

He pulled away, his face set with grim determination. "No. As tempting as your offer is, I have to go to work." He ran a finger under his collar, loosening the knot of his tie. "And if I'm lucky, I'll work an entire week without freaking out. On Friday night I have to give a heartwarming speech to persuade those with deep pockets and guilty social consciences to open their wallets for the homeless. Because if I don't, my father will likely fire me, and then I'll end up homeless. I don't want to move to the park down the street."

"It's okay to admit you need help. If this week isn't better, go see someone who can show you how to work through post-traumatic stress and panic attacks. That's all it is." She straightened his tie.

He brushed her off with a wave of his hand. "I'm fine." He leaned over and kissed her. "More than fine." Taking out his wallet, he flipped her one of his credit cards. "Here, go buy something pretty for Friday night. While you're out, treat yourself to some pampering. Now kiss your hard-working man goodbye. I'm going to stop and see Samson for a shave and haircut."

"Goodbye, dear. And I'm not spending your money. Don't get your hair cut too short. I like being able to grip it when we're snogging." She handed him back the credit card.

He groaned. "You're not making this easy. And don't be ridiculous; use the card." He put it on the counter and pulled her in for a hug and a kiss.

It started as a peck but grew more intense, his tongue exploring her mouth. Liquid heat coursed through her. *Will I ever get enough of him?*

"Are you sure you want to go to work?" She moved suggestively against his erection.

He groaned. "I'm positive I don't. Don't tempt me." He smacked her bottom and stepped back, shrugging into his jacket.

She followed him to the front door. "Fine. Leave me. I'll spend all your money and buy you blue, pink, and yellow shirts."

"I wouldn't wear them."

"Don't you want breakfast?"

"Nope, if I don't have anything in my stomach, maybe I won't toss my cookies. See you later."

The front door closed behind him, and Harley sank onto the couch, worried. She didn't want to embarrass Damien, but attending a function like this benefit was way out of her comfort zone. The only time she'd been to a fundraiser was to work as a server. But like his mother before him, Damien took his charitable work seriously, and this was a cause she supported fully. More importantly, he *wanted* her to go.

After stopping for a trim and shave with Samson, Damien stepped onto the bustling sidewalk and put his sunglasses on, getting jostled in the process. With a happy smile, he realized it didn't unnerve him. He wondered if he was better, or just too damn exhausted to care. Two blissful days holed up in the penthouse making love with Harley might have cured him...

Who the hell am I kidding? Making love? I fucked that girl six ways to Sunday, in every room, on all available surfaces, in positions that could be featured in the best porn. He ignored the niggling thought that it had been the most meaningful weekend of his life.

His self-satisfied grin remained as he headed toward the office. The growling in his stomach grew intense, but he ignored it, not taking any chances.

He nodded at the staff and instructed Mrs. Allen to hold all calls; he wanted to concentrate on the stack of work on his desk. With quiet efficiency, she handed him a cup of coffee just the way he liked it. *So far so good...*

He settled in and went to work.

The door flew open. Annoyed by the interruption, he looked up from the brief he'd been reviewing.

"Ah. You are here. I wasn't sure if Mrs. Allen was covering for you again. Glad to see you back in the office, son." His father stood with his hands on his hips, giving him a onceover with a critical eye.

Note to self: send Mrs. Allen flowers. He stood and nodded. "Thank you."

Dad wasn't one to exchange pleasantries. Knowing there was a reason for the visit, he waited.

"You'll be at the benefit Friday? Brad said Lauren's worked hard on this project." One eyebrow rose as his father waited for the answer.

"I have no idea how hard Lauren's worked on the project. We're no longer together. Harley has agreed to fill in as my plus one."

That isn't a total lie, just a shading of the truth.

Someday he'd have it out with Dad about what had happened in the past — and what was unfolding in the present — but not at work.

"Is that wise?" his father asked.

"I don't see that it's really any of your business." He sat and picked up the brief again.

"I see. We'll talk soon, perhaps over lunch next Sunday?"

Might as well get it over with. "Sure."

His father left.

And the pounding in his head began.

"Don't be so stubborn. The money means nothing to him. You know he'll be furious." Claire stood beside her as she rummaged through the racks of dresses after their Friday lunch.

"I'm not using his credit card. That would feel…" Harley shrugged. "Icky. I'm his girlfriend, not his mistress. I'm even thinking of taking another job — aside from the yoga class. Damien's favorite bakery is hiring. Besides, I don't even want to go to this benefit."

"Then don't. Work at a bakery? Why? You're living in luxury."

"I want to be my own person with my own money. He only has a few panic attacks now; I'm not really needed to 'work' for him. And I need to grow up. I mean, what am I supposed to do? Sit around all day waiting on him to get home? I want my life to have meaning, I'm even thinking about going back to school. As for the stupid benefit, I have to go. He needs me for moral support. He's nervous about having a panic attack during his speech."

She'd stopped by the office to bring him some lunch on her way to meet Claire. He'd been holed up with the door closed, working. Although he'd said he was fine, she could tell by the thin line of his lips and unease around his eyes he was wound up as tight as a clock, despite having worked every day this week and even making it into court once.

"What does Mark say about you being with Damien?" Claire picked a piece of lint off a dress, looking uncomfortable.

Over lunch she'd given Clare a rundown on the weekend's hot bedroom action, as well as Damien's reaction to her revelation about her past.

Years ago, Claire had declared herself Switzerland between her and Mark. Respecting her position, she and Mark did their best not to involve her in their differences — not that there had been that many.

She and Mark had always remained amicable and supportive of each other. But Harley knew Claire was worried about him. She was, too.

"Like you, he's concerned, but he hasn't said much. He has his own stuff to work through with Jinx."

Claire sucked in a sharp breath and scowled.

Harley knew Claire didn't approve of Jinx. She wasn't sure what to make of the girl who'd turned Mark's life upside down either.

Claire smiled sadly at Harley. "I wish you two could've just worked your shit out and stayed married. I would've loved for us to remain sisters."

"Mark and I are much better as friends. I'll always love him, Claire. Just not the right way for a marriage to work."

"I know, I know…" She sighed.

Harley pulled a dress off the rack and held it up. "Perfect. It's Sin's favorite color. You can't go wrong with a simple black dress, can you? Is Charlie going tonight?"

"Yeah, he's kicking and screaming even more than you are. That dress is beautiful, and anything you wear will look great. But Damien's expecting you to spend money—lots of *his* money—on a cocktail dress. He owes you, big time. Look, if you don't want to use his credit card, you can always borrow something from me. You know I don't mind."

Harley knew Claire meant well, but her offer brought up old feelings of inferiority. It had been hard growing up with children of wealth. Not that her middle-class parents were poor, but she'd attended school with kids who lived in an exclusive, gated community. Having been destitute before, Mark understood her mindset about this. Being children of privilege, Claire and Damien never would.

Determined to do things her way, Harley fell back on her mother's adage. The mark of a true lady was not the price of her clothes, but how she carried herself and treated others. She'd wear her off-the-rack dress with pride. Besides, she doubted they would stay at the benefit long…And her money would be best spent on sexy underwear from Southern Unmentionables.

The dress fit like a glove, and before parting ways, Claire reluctantly admitted it looked much more expensive than it was. A sheer panel covered the bare back and plunging neckline, keeping it sexy but not indecent. Red heels completed the outfit, all for less than a hundred and fifty dollars.

Chapter
Twenty

Harley fumed. It wasn't fair. Damien in jeans and a T-shirt caused women on the street to turn their heads for a second look. In a business suit, he exuded powerful confidence that made women catch their breath at the sight of him. When naked—though she didn't like to think about how many women had seen him in the buff—his tan body was sharp planes of defined, beautiful muscle.

However, nothing matched the sight of Damien Nicolai Sinclair in a tailored, black tux. He was make-your-heart-stop fucking beautiful. The man exuded an aura of sex and sin, making her feel gauche and plain. Harley's fingers shook as she took his hand and stepped out of the car. Taking a moment to collect her wits, she closed her eyes, took a deep breath, and smiled.

"You're doing it again," he groused good-naturedly.

"I can't help it; you always smell so good. Wanna skip this stupid benefit?" She nervously ran her hands down her form-fitting dress.

His warm eyes raked her up and down and a smile lingered on his face. "Don't tempt me." He raised one eyebrow, cocking his head. "Do you have on *any* underwear?"

The night air made her nipples hard as rocks, especially since she hadn't bothered with a coat. She didn't have one nice enough for this event and hadn't thought about it when shopping. "That's for me to know, and you to find out."

"Oh, I plan to." He propelled her forward, and she had to take two steps to keep up with his one, which was no easy feat in four-inch stilettos.

"Damien! What's your hurry?"

He shrugged out of his jacket and draped it around her shoulders. "First of all, you're going to catch your death of cold. Second, I want to get this over with so I can find out if you're wearing sexy panties; it's obvious you don't have on a bra. How do you keep from having nipple exposure with that sheer thingie barely covering your boobs?" Ignoring the photographers as they made their way toward the event, he held her hand, but she still lagged behind in her heels.

"Tape. Everyone knows that."

"I didn't know that."

"That's because the women you've dated either have no boobs or would black their eyes without a bra on. I'm average. God, why did I agree to come? Look at all these people. I don't fit in, Sin."

He stopped abruptly, and she bumped into his back. As if there weren't hundreds of people milling around, he turned, cupped her face in his hands, and gave her a toe-curling, heat-inducing, drop-her-non-existent-panties kiss.

"There's nothing average about you. Come with me." As the photographers turned their attention on the next arrivals, he pulled her to the side of the building. They ducked into an enclosed garden, lit by white lights woven through the tree branches.

"It isn't stars, but it's magical, don't you think?" he whispered.

"Yes," she replied, gazing at his handsome face. They could be standing in a garbage dump for all she cared. At this very minute, life was perfect. He was indeed a magician, casting a love spell on her heart.

"Dance with me."

"Here? In these shoes? My heel will get stuck in the ground. And you hate dancing."

Ignoring her protests, he helped her shrug into the coat and took her in his arms as he hummed The Rolling Stones. Her heel did get stuck, but she kicked off her shoes and danced with him—when she wasn't kissing him and giggling into his shirt. He was such a dork about The Stones. But he was her dork.

When he finished, he placed a chaste kiss on her forehead and pulled away, still gazing at her. Staring into his liquid-lava gaze, her insides melted, and her mind turned into a puddle of warm mush.

"Ah, there it is…"

"There what is?" she managed to croak, holding his hand so she wouldn't topple over with the magnitude of the promises that kiss held for later.

"My favorite color, Harley red. The color you turn when embarrassed or flushed with desire."

Whipping out his handkerchief, he dried her feet and helped her into her shoes as if she were Cinderella, and she fell a little more in love with him — if that was possible. Taking her hand, he escorted her into the event through a back door.

"Do I look okay? Are my eyelashes on? Is my mascara running down my face?" She ducked and checked her reflection in a mirror in the hallway.

"You look perfect." His heated gaze met hers in the mirror, sending more tingles through her body.

"Thank you." Her eyes focused on his and found them dark with desire. "I love you. I wish we could just go home and curl up together on the couch and watch an old movie."

"I love you, too, but duty calls."

She handed him back his coat, and they were immediately swarmed by friends and business acquaintances who hadn't seen him since the shooting.

He did his best to introduce her to everyone, but they soon got separated. Harley looked around for Claire, nodding at the few people she knew from high school or recognized from serving dinner parties at the Sinclairs'.

"It's about time you showed up."

At the sound of the spiteful, sarcastic voice, Harley whirled to face Lauren Cuthbert. Dressed in a long, flowing ice blue dress, her snooty gaze swept her from head to toe. Harley lifted her chin, refusing to cower.

Lauren handed her a tray of *canapés*. "I expect the help to be on time and dressed a little more conservatively." She walked away, waving to someone across the room.

Bloody bitch.

An older gentleman grabbed an hors d'œuvre from the tray. "Delicious."

His eyes never left her breasts, making her uneasy. Why hadn't she listened to Claire and borrowed a dress? Or better yet, listened to her heart and stayed home?

Her face felt hot, and tears threatened as she turned and walked away, still holding the tray. More people helped themselves to the finger food as she struggled to get through the crowd. Across the room, Lauren stood near Damien. Harley had an overwhelming urge to shove the tray of *canapés* in her smug face. Damien seemed unaware of Lauren's presence as he listened to his father and Mr. Cuthbert. When Lauren's gaze met hers, she placed a hand on Sin's sleeve and rubbed up and down. The bitch smiled wide like a Kentucky Derby winner—the horse, not the jockey. Leaning in, she whispered in Damien's ear.

Smiling, he nodded and accepted Lauren's hand, hurrying her through the mob. Despite standing on her tiptoes, Harley lost sight of them. Her heart plummeted and her newfound confidence in what she shared with Damien cracked. She spun around and walked away, slamming the now-empty tray on a table.

"There you are!" Claire grabbed her hand. "I've been looking everywhere for you. This is a madhouse." Claire wore a pink silk concoction, and her long brown hair shimmered down her back. Charlie held her hand, looking ill at ease in his tux.

Harley nodded, trying to keep from crying.

Claire's eyes narrowed, and her brow furrowed. "What's the matter? Charlie, go get us all a glass of champagne, okay? We need to go freshen up a bit."

"Sure. Be right back."

The good-natured Charlie disappeared through the throng. Claire grabbed her hand, and together they worked their way through the crowd.

Once they were in the relative quiet of the ladies room, the damn broke, and black tears cascaded down her face. Harley looked in the mirror and cried harder at the image of the tragic goth girl staring back at her.

"Great, now I'm a mess," she wailed, blowing snot into a paper towel.

"It's not that bad…Well, yes, it is…" Claire wet a paper towel and dabbed at the smeared mascara. "How many times have I told you to use waterproof?" she chided gently. "What's dumbas — er, Damien done this time?"

"N-Nothing. It wasn't him. I mean it was, but it wasn't." She took over repairing her makeup. "Lauren handed me a tray of food like I was the hired help and told me I was dressed inappropriately and late for work. Then some creep stared at my boobs, and Lauren draped herself all over Sin like cheap curtains, looking entirely too comfortable doing so. Then they went off together somewhere, and I just need a moment to collect myself."

"What? That bitch! I'll go open up a can of whoop-ass on her skanky self." Claire whipped around to leave, but Harley grabbed her hand.

"No, it'll only make things worse. It isn't Damien's fault..." *Except for him looking so pleased at seeing Lauren by his side...and disappearing to God knows where...* "I'm okay. I just needed to get out of there for a minute."

Harley checked her image in the mirror and smoothed a loose wave back into her upswept hair. Running her sweaty palms down her dress, she attempted a smile. "Better?"

Claire raised a skeptical brow but nodded. The door opened, and Charlie walked in with three glasses of champagne.

"Charlie! This is the ladies room!" Claire frowned but accepted his kiss as she took two glasses and handed one to Harley.

"I've always wondered what the inner sanctum looked like. Damn, this is much nicer than the men's room. Come on over sometime. I'll give you a tour of the urinals. You okay, Harley? You missed Damien's speech."

Harley laughed. Nothing ever fazed Charlie. Claire's father was convinced he was a stoner, when in fact he was just an easygoing guy and perfect for Claire, who tended to be a little high strung. One wouldn't know it by looking at him, but he'd made a fortune in the gaming industry.

"Oh shoot, I missed it? I'm fine. Thanks. I'll be out in a minute."

Claire gazed at her intently and nodded, taking Charlie's hand. "Okay, see you in a few."

Two other women entered the ladies room. Harley gave them a weak smile and ducked into a stall where she hid until she heard them leave. Taking a deep breath, she stepped out and, with one last check of her makeup, prepared to go find Damien and endure the remainder of the night. As she washed her hands, the door opened, and Harley's eyes met Lauren's in the mirror.

Leaning against the door, Lauren smiled, but her eyes remained cold and ruthless. "Well, well, well, it's the little maid—Damien's flavor of the day. It's no wonder I thought you were the help when you arrived. That cheap dress does nothing for you. What *is* that fabric?" She walked over and tugged on the sheer sleeve of Harley's dress, ripping it at the seam. "Oops, inexpensive fabric rips so easily. So sorry."

Harley looked down at her sleeve and back at Lauren, stunned speechless.

Lauren turned to leave but paused. "I wouldn't get too attached to Damien. He'll never marry you, you know. He's career-oriented and will marry for connections. The type of connections my family can give him. I understand he has needs and seeks pleasure elsewhere, but he always comes back to me. You'll be no different. He'll use you until he's tired of you and then return to the woman who can give him so much more than cheap thrills between the sheets."

"Maybe if you'd tried giving him thrills at all, he wouldn't look elsewhere," Harley blurted.

Lauren shrugged. "Like I said, you're not the first. You won't be the last. I daresay he's been with half the women here tonight. But trust me, men like him don't marry the help. He might keep you on the side like a dirty little secret, but *I* will be his wife. After all, he's known you for years and never wanted anything to do with you until you forced yourself on him."

"You're delusional," Harley snapped.

But Lauren's words had cut with vicious accuracy, slicing open her fragile, recently mended heart. Lauren left, leaving Harley with a tattered sleeve to match her frayed emotions.

Sinking onto the bench, she tried fixing her ripped dress, but the sheer sleeve was torn beyond repair. She could only hope her heart wasn't going to end up in the same condition. *He loves me...* But the nagging truth of some of Lauren's words ate at her soul. She needed to be reassured; she needed to hear it from Damien.

After a moment, with her insecurities tucked away, she fled the restroom in search of the one person who could make this right. The first person she ran into was Damien's father, looking elegant in his black tux. He held a glass of white wine in his hand.

"Good evening, Harley." His face was composed as he took in her appearance.

"Hi, Mr. S." Her cheeks felt feverish.

She scanned the crowd, looking for Damien.

"Damien seems to be back to speed. I think keeping busy has helped him move forward, not dwell in the *past*. I understand you've been helping him out…" His voice trailed off, a typical lawyer fishing for answers.

Harley wasn't sure if his concern was genuine or patronizing. The fact that he'd had a role in keeping them separated years ago still hurt.

"He hasn't been out of the hospital that long, and he's suffering from some post-traumatic stress. From what I've read, you don't just wake up one morning and it's over." She kept her tone even and polite out of habit.

"He's a Sinclair. He'll learn to deal with it. I didn't raise my son to be a coward. Nice to see you again." With a nod of dismissal, he turned to greet Claire's parents.

Harley bit her tongue, reminding herself to be a lady.

Claire's mother hugged her tight, and Mr. Lassiter gave her a quick kiss on the cheek. After exchanging the required pleasantries, she excused herself to find Damien.

Snaking through the mob, she paused when long, red nails gripped her ripped sleeve, and she groaned with frustration. *Why can't all his exes be in Texas like the damn song?*

"*Boa noite*, Harley." The color of Renata's dress matched her claws. It was probably very expensive, and for what it cost, should have provided enough material to contain her ample breasts.

Harley attempted a weak smile but failed miserably. "Hello."

"Are you looking for Dami-en?" Her exotic accent drew his name out with a sexy prolongation that made Harley want to puke.

She tugged her arm away. "That's none of your business."

"He's down the hall. He needs you. He's not feeling well."

The man who'd played the prank walked up beside Renata, draping an arm around her shoulders. "Why, hello there. We didn't really get to meet the other night. I'm Chris." His dark eyes twinkled.

Harley gave him a small smile, scanning the room for Damien. "Where is he, Renata?"

She pointed toward a hallway, and in her eyes, Harley saw only concern for Damien, not spite or jealousy.

"Thank you." A grudging new respect for this woman replaced some of her anger.

With difficulty, she squeezed through the gathering. Ignoring Lauren's burning gaze and hateful sneer, Harley maneuvered her way toward the darkened hall.

She found him in the shadowy vending machine room, gripping the sides of one of the machines, his back to the door. His eyes were closed as he gasped for air. When she walked up beside him, he didn't acknowledge her presence. Lit by the light on the vending machine, his face was void of all color, and sweat dotted his brow. He jumped when she placed a hand on his back, and his gaze darted behind her. There was no need to ask if he was okay. It was obvious he wasn't. Her anger over Lauren's catty comments fled. She needed to comfort and draw him out of his emotional state.

She tucked her hand in his pants pocket. His tired face relaxed into a small, strained smile.

"Find anything interesting?"

Giving him an impish grin, she copped a cheap feel, felt him harden, and pulled out some change. "Nah, nothing much."

"Ouch. That was just plain cruel."

She laughed and gave him a smacking kiss on the cheek. "You know I'm teasing. I love your dangly bits to pieces." Slipping the coins into the machine, she retrieved a package of M&Ms and tore them open. "Chocolate cures everything." She fed him a handful of the candies, careful not to give him the blue ones.

His stance relaxed and finding a napkin, he mopped the sweat off his brow. "I miss the tan ones. Stupid blue M&Ms. You should eat the green ones. And quit referring to the family jewels as bits. You're giving me a complex."

Harley smiled, relieved to see his humor returning along with the color in his face.

"Okay, does samurai sword work for you? And why do I need to eat the green ones?"

"They make you horny. Everyone knows that."

"I didn't know that." She smirked and popped a green one in her mouth. "Mmm, I love sucking off the hard candy shell and letting the ooey-gooey chocolate melt in my mouth." She gave him her best seductive look and slowly licked her lips.

"Geezus, Harley." He shifted, backing her against the wall, and fed her another green candy.

She drew his finger into her mouth and sucked it, holding his heated gaze with her own.

Damien pulled his finger from her mouth and traced her soft lips. "You're not helping my anxiety over being out of control…"

"Good. You need to let go." She wrapped her arms around his neck and played with the damp hair at the nape of his neck.

"I've been looking for you. What happened to your sleeve? No one is allowed to rip your clothes off but me." His warm hand crept up her thigh, pulling her leg up to his waist. Her dress rode up to the point of indecency.

"Christopher Columbus." She exhaled as his hand explored upward with slow, deliberate moves, sending a jolt of electricity to the apex of her thighs.

A knowing smile crossed his face as he watched her. "My, my, Harley…" he whispered. His warm breath tickled her neck, and she felt her cheeks flush as every rational thought in her head evaporated into a mist of sexual yearning.

"Yes?"

"Did you forget something?"

She gasped when one, and then two of his fingers delved inside her, curling toward that special spot. Her inner muscles clenched tight, and his breathing hissed through his teeth.

"P-Panty lines. Not good…" She couldn't string a coherent sentence with her concentration centered on his magic fingers.

"This doesn't feel good? Sure about that?" he teased. His thumb circled and tapped her throbbing clitoris. She ground her teeth, and her head slammed against the wall but the stars she saw weren't from the impact.

"Shit, Sin! No, I meant…I didn't wear…oh God…" She closed her eyes and her hands moved to grip his shoulders as she blew out the breath she'd been holding. Heat infused her body, and the tension inside of her rocketed as his fingers moved in and out, escalating her need for release. He had her pinned—and definitely a captive audience—as his thrusting fingers and wicked thumb worked her toward a quick, intense orgasm, which he hushed by covering her lips with his.

Her legs quivered uncontrollably following her release, and if he hadn't been holding her, she would've slid to the floor in a puddle of orgasmic bliss.

"Now what did you call me? Christopher Columbus? What else can I explore…" His tongue delved into her mouth. At a noise in the hallway, he pulled away and lowered her leg, straightening her dress.

He blocked her from view until she could get herself halfway presentable. She was pretty damn sure she looked a mess after her unexpected sexcapade. Nervously, she ran the hand that didn't have crushed M&Ms in it across her hair and down her dress. Apparently, when crushed during an orgasm, the damn candies *did* melt in your hand. They were also coating Damien's sleeve. Her cheeks burned with desire and mortification.

The light snapped on, and Harley blinked under the harsh fluorescent glow. *Lauren!* Her turned-to-mush, post-orgasmic brain reminded her that less than twenty minutes ago she'd been angry with both Lauren and Damien.

Damn him and his phallic fingers!

Lauren's eyes narrowed, and her gaze darted between them. It didn't seem fair that Damien was the one who'd suffered the panic attack; he didn't look any the worse for wear. He straightened his bow tie and nonchalantly handed her a napkin as if nothing was out of the ordinary.

Am I in some sort of parallel universe?

"I guess I don't need to ask what you two were doing," Lauren said.

The heat in her cheeks hit the record books under Lauren's censorious look.

Damien smiled and winked at Harley. "I was hungry and came back here for a snack. Now if you'll excuse us…"

"You always did like junk food. When you're done with your 'snack,' you'll return to a healthier diet. You always do."

"Not when it's tasteless and boring."

"Yes, but junk food doesn't stick with you, especially when it's cheap." Lauren raised one eyebrow, but it was the impudent smile that made Harley go blind with rage.

Adrenaline pumped through her body, lighting the fuel of simmering fury she'd kept under wraps through years of insults from this bitch. All rational thinking fled, and she exploded, slapping Lauren hard across her haughty face. Lauren stepped back, crying out and holding her cheek.

"Whoa now, Cheetara. Calm down," Damien whispered in her ear, holding her tight.

She shook, and angry tears blurred her vision.

"I've a good mind to have you arrested for assault," Lauren snapped. Remnants of melted chocolate clung to the red handprint on her porcelain skin.

Harley glared and struggled to get loose. By God, if she was going to jail for assault, she'd make it worthwhile.

"You provoked her, Lauren. Just let it drop. Clean up your face and go back to your party. Besides, she has a good lawyer." Damien still held her tight.

Lauren's eyes narrowed, and she hissed, "Your little enchilada is here, too. Going for the full smorgasbord tonight, dear?"

Harley broke free of him, ready to go after her again, but Damien grabbed her hand and pulled her into the hall.

He tore down the darkened hallway about ten feet, and she stumbled behind him in her heels. In less than a second, he had her pinned to the wall, caging her body with his, as he once again kissed her soundly. Lauren stormed passed them muttering about disgusting public displays of affection. He pressed his forehead to hers, snickering like a naughty schoolboy.

"I can't go back in there, and you don't need to. Let's get out of here," he whispered.

"You don't have to ask me twice."

As they walked toward the door, a business associate stopped Damien. Harley stood by his side and looking to her right, caught a look of disgust on Lauren's now-clean face. Self-conscious, she tried to cover her torn sleeve and prayed Damien would cut his conversation short.

To her dismay, the hateful bitch turned and spoke to the woman standing next to her. She gave a derisive nod in her direction as she made a motion down the sleeve of her dress. The woman's mouth dropped open and she turned to the gentleman next to her and whispered something.

Harley watched as the gossip made its way around the room faster than a call girl at a Vegas convention, and her embarrassment deepened. She'd behaved like the cheap whore Lauren said she was. Lost in thought, she didn't respond when Damien placed his jacket around her shoulders. A gentle push on her lower back moved her forward, but doubts assailed her.

Why did Damien do that to me in a public place, where we could get caught? Would he have done that to anyone else?

More importantly, why did I let him?

Damien slammed the door shut with his foot while his hands roamed, lifting Harley's dress. He couldn't get enough of her—her scent, how she tasted, the feel of her body pressed into his. Seeing her anger had made him horny as hell. And he desperately wanted to bury himself within her and forget the embarrassment of having had another damn panic attack.

"You're mine, Cheetara," he whispered hoarsely, tracing the shell of her ear with his tongue.

She pulled away from him, shrugged out of his jacket, and threw it on the hall table. A little irritated, he picked it up and hung it on the doorknob to be taken to the cleaners.

Harley headed into the bathroom and grabbed the toothpaste and her toothbrush. He watched with horror when she purposefully squeezed the tube at the top. She knew he hated that.

When she flung it to the counter and began brushing her teeth, he picked it up and smoothed it precisely, rolling it from the bottom. She spit and rinsed before sinking with an angry huff onto the vanity bench. He brushed his teeth, watching her in the mirror. Glaring at him, she took her fist and smashed the tube of toothpaste.

Dammit. Once again, he rolled it from the bottom before putting it away in the cabinet.

"Sin, we need to talk." Her chest heaved as she yanked the pins out of her hair.

Her tone sounded ominous. Too late, he realized she'd been inordinately quiet on the way home.

"How about I let my fingers do the talking?" He caressed her shoulders and nuzzled her neck. She shrugged away from him.

"Stop it." She glared at his reflection for a few seconds before pointedly ignoring him by rubbing some disgusting white goop on her face.

He tugged his bow tie loose and unbuttoned his shirt. *What the hell is up…besides my dick? Well, maybe not so much anymore…What is that stuff on her face?*

"What? What did I do wrong? Is this about what happened in the vending machine room?" *That was so damn hot…*

"No shit, Sherlock. It was degrading. Would you have ever done that to Lauren? Almost have sex in a public place?" With her face covered in white goop and her hair a wild, tangled mess, she resembled a demented circus clown. Not that he'd make the mistake of telling her that.

"Lauren? She wouldn't know hot sex if it bit her in the ass."

She rolled her eyes. At least he thought that's what she'd done; it was hard to tell behind the gooey mess.

"You didn't answer my questions. No, wait…I guess you did. Your ability to be a first-class arsehole never ceases to astound me."

Stormy eyes the color of struck flint narrowed on his reflection as she finished scrubbing the makeup off her face. Irritated, he pinched the bridge of his nose.

"Why are we arguing? Let's just go to bed."

"Ah yes. So you can fuck me silly and ignore the problem. Is this all I'm good for? Oh wait, no…I guess I'm good for making your bed, as well as lying in it."

He refused to argue with her in her current state. Despite being a lawyer, he hated confrontation in his personal life. Undoing his cufflinks, he marched into the bedroom, stripping off his shirt. Harley was on his heels like a terrier puppy. He placed his cufflinks in his dresser valet and folded his shirt to place in the dirty clothesbasket, ignoring her huffs of outrage and cold looks.

"That! That right there is part of the problem." She pointed at the shirt in his hand.

He frowned and looked at the neatly folded shirt. Her hands moved to her hips, and one foot began to tap. Still not understanding, he shrugged.

"No one folds their dirty clothes."

"I do." *What's the big deal?*

"I know, because you're a control freak who has to have everything in order. It's why you can't deal anymore, why you have panic attacks. You need help, Sin. Your carefully constructed world turned upside down the day you found out you're mortal like the rest of us. When are you going to realize life is a crapshoot? You can't control everything; some things have to be let go…"

He sank to the bed, placing his elbows on his knees, and covered his face. "You don't consider what we did at the benefit losing control?" He rubbed his pounding head. "Not now, Harley. Geezus, don't ruin this."

"Don't ruin this? That's brilliant. This entire night was a fuckin' disaster thanks to that cold reptile, Lauren Lizard, and your happy hands. And no, *you* didn't lose control, *I* did!"

"You didn't think it was such a *damn disaster* or so bad *losing control* when you had that orgasm. I don't understand why you're so upset," he muttered under his breath.

This is worse than the time she backed into my car and blamed me for parking too close.

"I heard that. But more importantly, I saw you."

"You saw me do what?" He made an exaggerated shrug waiting for her to continue, still clueless. "Is it that time of month? Is this a hormonal thing?" Folding his pants, he placed them on the chair to go the cleaners.

"What? My God, you're such an ass!" Harley grabbed the pants and threw them on the floor, jumping up and down on them and twisting them into a wrinkled mess. He sighed, trying his damnedest to remain patient. "Pick them up, quit acting like a spoiled brat, and tell me what the hell this is about."

"Lauren. She was all over you like stink on shit and…" She spun around, her shoulders heaving as if she were trying to keep from crying.

He tempered his tone. "What? When?"

This was ridiculous. He tried to remember any interaction he'd had with Lauren aside from the disaster in the vending machine room. The only thing he'd done was introduce her to a few benefactors and walk to the podium with her, so she could introduce him before his speech.

Harley stormed into the bathroom, slamming the door.

He'd had enough. He pounded on the door.

"Open this fucking door, right now!"

"Fuck you!"

"Open the damn door, or I'll bust it down," he ground out.

She cracked the door, and he caught a tantalizing glimpse of a naked breast. Dammit, she never had fought fair.

"No, you won't. It would make a mess. Guess what? Just like your beloved, archaic Rolling Stones, you aren't getting any satisfaction tonight. Go sleep on the couch."

The door slammed in his face. *Oh no she didn't. Sleep on the couch? This is my damn place!*

He kicked the door open, splintering the doorjamb. She stood before him gloriously naked, her eyes wide. Backing away from him, she grabbed a towel.

He pointed at her as he advanced. "You need to calm the fuck down. And using The Rolling Stones was a cheap shot."

She tossed her hair. "Oh yeah? Well, you need to treat me better than a cheap ho, you bugger." Her chin jutted toward him, but she gripped the towel so tight her knuckles blanched.

"Is that what you think I did? That's what this is about?" He rubbed the heels of his hands into his eyes. "You're mad because I can't keep my hands off your smokin' hot body? Geezus, Harley, you know I'm obsessed with you."

Her mouth opened and shut a few times like a guppy before she looked inordinately pleased with herself. "You think my body's hot?"

"Smokin' hot." He prayed he was back on track.

"Thank you. But still, obsessions become possessions and then they're cast away like toys." Her shoulders sagged.

He wasn't following her logic, but when had he ever understood this capricious woman?

"I think I want to be alone."

"Harley," he whispered, gathering her into her arms. "What's got you so upset? Did something happen I don't know about?"

She turned and pressed her tear-dampened cheek to his chest. Her sobs came out in gulps, and her hands fisted between them as he stroked her hair, whispering comforting nonsense, still unsure what had triggered this crying jag.

"I told you once not to fuck with my heart. I don't want to be your dirty little secret, your fuck *du jour*."

"Why would you think that? I love you. I just took you to a function and introduced you to everyone. Tell me what happened." He cradled her face in his hands and brushed her lips with his. Using his thumbs, he wiped away her tears. "Talk to me."

"Lauren told me you messed around on her, but you always came back…She said marrying her would give you the right connections, that you'd never be with someone like me for long. *And* you'd been with half the women there tonight. I just need to know you won't cast me away, that you're through with other women."

"I have not been with that many women. You're the one that I want. Only you. If you want, I'll sing that stupid song from *Grease* you like. And I never, ever gave Lauren the slightest hint that I'd marry her."

She giggled and hiccupped. "You hate any music that isn't The Rolling Stones. Especially musicals. You'd do that for me?"

"For you, yes. I love you, Harley. You're the yin to my yang, the icing on my toaster tart. You complete me…" He kissed the top of her head. "You're my everything. Never forget that."

"I'm your everything?"

"And some."

She gazed up at him, and sunshine broke out across her tear-stained face. "Promise?"

"Cross my heart and hope to—"

Her hand covered his mouth as her lips moved across his chest. She placed a tender kiss on his scar. "Don't say it."

Her mercurial mood swings left his head spinning. When would he learn nothing was ever black and white with this woman?

She sank to her knees in front of him, leaving no doubt who was in control…But at this moment in time, he didn't give a damn.

Chapter
Twenty-One

"I'm nervous, Sin."

Her knee bounced as she wrung her hands. He placed his hand on her knee to still her and couldn't help himself—he slid it up her smooth thigh.

"Why? It isn't like you've never been here before."

She caught his hand before he reached the delicious scrap of red material that served as her underwear today. In truth, her nervousness was contagious, and he fought to keep the impending panic attack at bay. Damien turned down the long driveway where they'd grown up—he in the mansion, and she in the quaint little house discreetly hidden by the landscaping at the back end of the property.

He cut the engine and blew out a breath. "Ready to face the parents?"

It had been two days since the fiasco at the benefit. The makeup sex yesterday had almost made it worth fighting about, and he'd brought Harley with him for Sunday lunch. Now was as good a time as any to tell their parents they were together. And maybe get some answers about what had happened twelve years ago.

"If I say no, could we go back home and hide under the covers?" She blew her bangs off her forehead and played with the strap of her purse.

"We can't hide forever. Besides, you'd give me hell if I kept you my 'dirty little secret.' Come on, we aren't teenagers anymore. It's time we confronted them. We're adults; we can face our parents without fear. What are they going to do? Send us to our room? Oh wait, that might be kind of fun…" He pinched her cheek and laughed when she slapped at his hand. "Oh yeah, Mistress. You know I love it when you smack me around." He stepped out of the car and opened her door for her.

"Liar. You like it when *you* can spank *my* arse."

He did just that, and she yelped, rubbing her bottom.

"That's true." He frowned, peering at the smudged fingerprints on his car. "Hold on, let me get this…" He buffed out the prints with his handkerchief.

"Oh brother. I'm going on in." Harley disappeared through the back door.

Pocketing his handkerchief, he followed.

As he found his way into the kitchen, the inviting smell of Elise's roast greeted him. Harley's mother was hugging her tight.

"I didn't realize you were coming. Your father will be pleased. We've missed you. You can't pick up a phone and call your mamma?"

Harley patted her mother's back. "I've missed you, too. I do call; it isn't like I moved across country. I'm only thirty minutes from home."

"Living with Claire has given you a sassy mouth!" She shook her wooden spoon at Harley before giving her another hug.

Damien raised his eyebrows at Harley, amused by her lie about her living arrangements. She frowned and put a finger to her lips behind her mother's back.

Elise turned to him, giving him a onceover before patting his cheek. "And how are you feeling? You've lost weight, *søt gutt*." She was the only person in the world who dared to call him a "sweet boy."

He hugged her warmly. "Why, thank you, Elise. Someone not too long ago said I was fat." He grinned and winked at Harley.

She cut her eyes to the ceiling in a poor attempt at looking innocent.

"Fat? Who would say such a thing? But your hair, it's longer than usual. Have you not seen Samson? Go. Get out of my way and go see your father. Your company will be here soon, yes? Mr. Sinclair's in his study. He's had an emergency call, but he's expecting you." She shooed Damien out of the way as she moved back to the stove, checking on the boiling potatoes.

"Harley, set the table."

"Yes, Mamma." Harley frowned and bit her lip, looking at Damien.

"Elise—"

"*Gå!*" Elise shook the spoon at him, and he instantly felt like he was six years old again.

Harley motioned with her head for him to go on.

He shrugged and went to find his father.

Harley looked up from arranging the flowers when her mother walked into the dining room. Mamma frowned and looked at her watch.

"Miss Cuthbert is never on time! Luncheon is ready, and I'll not have my food served cold. It isn't like she eats anyway…"

"Uh, Mamma—"

Her father entered the room and gave Harley a kiss on the forehead. "It's so good to see you. How's Claire?"

"Fine. Daddy—"

She was torn. She loved her parents, but what had been their role in separating her and Damien twelve years ago? Just then Mr. Sinclair and Damien walked in, discussing restraining orders and other legalese.

"Harley, go get the salad." Her mother gave her a gentle push toward the kitchen.

Not knowing what else to do, she did as she was told. She hurried back with the salad and stood still, uncertain what to do next. Damien walked over to her.

"Did you talk to him?" she whispered.

He shook his head and pulled out a chair for her, taking the bowl from her hands to place it on the table.

"Not yet. No time. We had to discuss an emergency with a case. Did you?" he whispered back.

She shook her head. He motioned for her to sit, as if it were the most natural thing in the world. Heat flooded her face as all eyes in the room focused on her as she sat. As understanding dawned, her mother's face reddened before she left the room with a dignified nod. Harley didn't dare look at her father's face. Instead, she stared at her hands clasped in her lap. She wanted to throw up.

"Did you enjoy the benefit, Harley? Damien mentioned you were kind enough to be his plus-one." Mr. Sinclair smiled at her and handed her the basket of her mother's homemade rolls.

"Yes, sir."

"I understand close to a million dollars was raised. Lauren did a wonderful job…"

Damien cleared his throat.

Mr. Sinclair moved on. "Sunday dinners. I've missed them. *Bon appétit.*"

Harley's mouth felt like it was stuffed with cotton. Raising her glass with a trembling hand, she spilled her water and rose out of habit to clean up the mess. Her father's firm hand on her shoulder pressed her back into her seat. She hadn't realized he was still here. Tears filled her eyes as he mopped the water off the table and left to replace her glass. She wanted to slide to the floor and die. Her parents shouldn't be waiting on her. She was no better than they were. This was wrong on so many levels…

Damien stood and threw his napkin on the table. "This is ridiculous."

It was difficult to say who was more surprised by his outburst, Mr. Sinclair, who paused with his fork halfway to his mouth; her father, who stood stock still, his hands clasped behind his back; or her mother, who breezed through the doorway with the platter of roast in her hands.

"Taylor, please set places at the table for Elise and yourself. I know this isn't the way to do this, but dammit, this is awkward as hell. I'm officially letting you all know Harley and I are together."

"Sit, Elise, before you fall over. I don't know what any of this is supposed to mean, but we can either eat in here or move to the kitchen. I don't give a damn where it happens, but I'm hungry, and we're eating *now*." Mr. Sinclair drummed his fingers.

Mamma sank into the chair Damien pulled out for her, looking uncomfortable. Harley hopped up and ran to the kitchen to get plates and cutlery. Her father followed her. The plates rattled in her shaking hands.

"Chivvy along, Harley. Mr. Sinclair is hungry," Daddy urged as he grabbed two glasses from the cabinet. "And we all know His Lordship gets a bit peckish when hungry."

She nodded and laughed at their nickname for Mr. S behind his back. "Daddy…"

"Not now, Harley. We'll discuss this later. Do you really want to face your mother if her roast gets cold?" He raised a questioning brow.

"No, sir."

They hurried back to the dining room.

"Ah, here we go. Now we can eat and have a pleasant conversation about our children and their plans for the future." Mr. Sinclair motioned for everyone to have a seat.

Harley handed her parents their dinnerware and sat down, accepting the roast from Damien. She was grateful when he gave her leg a reassuring pat under the table but jumped when he goosed her knee.

Damien cleared his throat. "Hey, Dad, any news from Angel? Have they set a wedding date yet?"

"You know damn well Angel doesn't call me unless Maggie makes him. So I have no idea. Now, why don't you tell us what this is all about? You're a damn fine attorney. I'm sure you have your opening statement prepared. And I, for one, would like to hear it."

Mr. Sinclair turned his attention to her with a frown as he looked at her untouched plate.

"Is there something wrong with the food, Harley?"

She quickly picked up her fork and stabbed a piece of lettuce. "No, sir. Of course not."

Her mother sat staring at her plate, her head bowed. Next to her, Daddy gripped his water glass.

Damien cleared his throat and pushed his plate back. "Years ago, Taylor, er, John and Elise came to our home with their three children and moved into the little house at the end of the property. And while they *worked* for our family...they *became* our family, at least to Angel and me. And the little girl with stars in her eyes became my shadow."

Damien looked around the table. "Harley is no longer my shadow. She walks beside me and supports me like no one else. Twelve years ago, things between us changed. Granted, we were young. Was it love? Were we too young?" He shrugged. "I don't know. Because we never really got a chance to try. And I think you..." He looked at each parent individually. "Owe us an explanation."

While Harley secretly applauded Damien's delivery, it was plain by the crumpled look on her mother's face that it had upset her.

She tugged on his sleeve and whispered, "Not now."

"Yes, now. I want to know what the hell would've been so wrong with us being together when we were kids."

Her mother jumped to her feet, tears spilling down her face. "I need a moment..."

She ran from the room. Her husband muttered an apology and followed.

Harley put her elbows on the table and covered her face. *What just happened?*

Mr. Sinclair stood. "Damien. In the library. *Now.*" Throwing his napkin on the table, he walked out, his mouth pressed into a thin line.

She blew out a deep breath. "I thought you were a top-notch lawyer. You just botched this up royally. Now what do we do?"

He smiled. "It's called divide and conquer. I'll see what Dad says. You go tend to your folks. He kissed her forehead and left."

Harley sighed and stood up. *Adulting sucks.*

Damien squared his shoulders and entered the library. He found his father staring out the window at his mother's rose garden.

"I miss your mother."

Damien weighed his words carefully, wondering where the random thought had come from. "I know you do. We all do. Sometimes I come home and halfway expect to hear her playing the piano..."

"At night is when I miss her most. Even if we weren't speaking, or in different rooms of the house, I was aware of her presence...This house is empty now...lifeless. But I can't bear to move..."

"Dad, why did you...?"

"Why, what?"

"Why did you, Mom, and the Taylors work so damn hard to keep me and Harley apart? And why the sudden change of heart lately? Was it all Mom's doing?"

He braced for the answer, eyeing his father like an opponent in the courtroom. His father moved behind his desk and motioned him to sit. Was it a ploy to let him know his place? Or was Dad using the desk as a barrier? Regardless, he sat and waited.

"It was a difficult time. You were young. Harley was younger. Your mother and I were fighting a lot about your brother. Angel was having his problems, and all of our energy was focused on him. We didn't worry about you…until I caught you with Harley.

"I should've seen it coming. As you said, she was your shadow, and I suspect she's loved you a very long time. Reasoning with you was futile. Your hormone-fueled defiance needed to be dealt with swiftly. Your brother was making a mess of his life, and we refused to allow you to do the same. We wanted you to focus on school, your future. Not a girl."

"I wouldn't have ditched school. You know me better than that. You took the decision out of my hands when Mom threatened to fire her parents!"

His father folded his hands and looked him in the eye. "And you allowed it to happen. Have you ever asked yourself why?"

If his father had struck him, he wouldn't have been as taken aback.

"What? I tried to call her, I wrote her, but you and her father blocked my communications."

"You phoned, and you wrote. And then what?"

"I, well…I g-gave up…" He stammered like a witness on the stand.

"What does the future hold for you and Harley?"

"What do you mean?"

"Marriage? Kids? I wouldn't mind having grandchildren. I doubt Angel and Maggie will go down that road."

"Whoa. Wait. Marriage?"

His father's eyes zeroed in on him, and he leaned forward. "If you're not ready for a commitment now, what makes you think you would've been ready for one at age nineteen?"

"Are you fucking kidding me? I was just a kid!" *What the fuck is he doing?*

His father shrugged. "A kid with a car, a credit card, and any means pretty much available if you'd been serious about Harley. I think you need to consider what you were afraid of."

Damien stood and paced, trying to stay one step ahead. His headache was returning. *Maybe I have a brain tumor…* "You're turning this back on me?"

"I'm going to ask you again, son. What were you afraid of? What are you still afraid of?"

His heart raced, and it felt hard to breathe. "That I won't be enough! That she'll leave me," Damien blurted.

He sank back in the chair, feeling ill. A memory swam before him. On his sixth birthday, his parents had given him a party—complete with pony rides, a magic show, and bouncy houses. It had been exciting, and he'd eaten way too many sweets.

Harley's parents had just started working for them, and she and her brothers had been at the party. Harley had dressed up like Cinderella and insisted he put her shoes on for her. When they'd told her it wasn't her party and she couldn't blow out the candles, she'd thrown such a crying fit, her father had taken her home.

That night, he'd felt sick to his stomach and went looking for his mom. He'd heard his parents fighting behind their bedroom door. Knocking on the door, he'd called to his mother, telling her he didn't feel well, but they'd continued to argue. Opening the door, he'd peeked in.

His mother had been flinging things into a suitcase and crying. He'd wondered why she wasn't folding them neatly. Dad had reached out to stop her, and she'd slapped him, screaming, "You can't stop me! I'm leaving!"

"Stop fighting!" he'd yelled. And then he'd vomited on the floor.

His mother had stormed from the room, and his father had picked up the phone and called for help. It was Elise who'd come to get him and helped him clean up, giving him something to settle his stomach. But then she'd left him alone…

Abandonment.

That was the night his mother had left, without even saying goodbye. She'd returned five months later, but things were never the same, even after the birth of his younger brother.

He rubbed his eyes. "Shit, I'm more fucked up than I realized. I thought Mom left because of me. Because I got sick after my party. Because I wasn't in control…"

"Son, I know you blame your mother for the problems in our marriage."

Damien didn't deny it. And he bit his tongue not to blame her for his current problems.

"It wasn't all her fault," his father confessed. "I wasn't there for her when she needed me. She left because of me, because of my failings as a husband. I was too focused on my career and getting ahead.

"You need to forgive your mother. I did…Many years ago. She returned to us, and despite our marital problems, we ended up having good life together. Do I have regrets? Of course. But staying married to her is not one of them. Unfortunately, you and Angel suffered the most for our selfishness."

He hung his head for a moment before facing Damien. "Learn from our mistakes, but don't be afraid because of them." He sighed. "I'm sorry. I've placed entirely too much expectation on your shoulders. The future starts now. And I think it's time you take a good, hard look at yourself and decide what makes you happy. Then do whatever it takes to make it happen.

"When you passed the bar, you told me you did it to be just like me. At the time, it made me proud. What father doesn't want his son to do well and follow in his footsteps? But don't follow too closely. Don't end up a lonely old man. It's not any fun…And not that my opinion matters at this point, but I think Harley is good for you." He squeezed his shoulder and left, shutting the door behind him.

Damien sighed, emotionally drained. *Marriage.* Did Harley expect that? He shuddered. *Fuck.* Did they stand a chance even now?

Chapter
Twenty-Two

Harley followed her parents into the kitchen. Her mother sniffled, wiping her eyes with a dish towel while her father held her.

"I'm sorry. This is a mess…" she offered, hesitantly. "Please, can we sit and talk?"

Her mother dried her face and placed a kettle of water on the stove. "I will make some tea." Tea was Mamma's answer for everything.

"Did you know Damien tried to reach me after he went back to school?"

Daddy motioned her to sit and sat across from her, taking her hand in his. "He called, but I told him you didn't want to speak to him."

"Why?" Hearing this from her father hurt more than she'd anticipated.

"You were so young, and like we told you at the time, first loves usually lead to heartbreak. It's part of growing up…"

Her mother put the teapot on the table and sat, her face lined with sadness as she poured them all a cup.

"But you and Mamma…" Harley protested, looking at one and then the other.

"We married when we were in our thirties, after life experiences." He squeezed her mother's hand, who nodded in agreement.

"What does that have to do with me? It was my life, and I was devastated…"

Her father stirred his tea, taking his time before answering. "Harley, being in service is a strange place to be. Our lives are enmeshed with those we work for. Your mother and I love Damien and Angel, but we see their faults, just like we see our own children's. Angel was self-destructive and full of rage. Damien was controlled but self-absorbed. And being our youngest, and only daughter…you were spoiled and impetuous."

Her mother nodded. "That night I heard you crying in your room… Damien had left early to go back to school. As a mother, and a woman, I knew…things between you two had…" Mamma glanced at her father.

"Progressed a little more than we would've liked," he interjected.

"Damien said his parents threatened your jobs. Did they say anything like that to you?"

Her parents shared a look that spoke volumes.

"Over the years, Mr. Sinclair and I have discussed the future of our children," her father hedged.

"Harley, your father and I emigrated here to have a better life," Mamma added. "We had nothing. I was a poor farmer's daughter. Your father was an orphan. Working for the Sinclairs has given us a good life and hope for an even better one for our children. We had such dreams, and still do for you, Byron, and Keats. Please try to understand; we had to do what was best for our family…" Her mother bit her lip and stared into her tea cup.

"Byron was able to go to college because of the Sinclairs' generosity," her father continued. "Mr. Sinclair wrote letters of recommendation for both boys. You were only seventeen. Damien was away at school. I really didn't think it was more than a fling," her father added. "Besides, you moved on fairly quickly. You dated Mark, and that's lasted on and off for years."

Harley felt her heart breaking all over again. She covered her face and sighed. "Oh Daddy, it was so much more…"

Tears filled her eyes, but if she was expecting honesty from her parents, it was time for her to offer it, too.

"Mark and I…We married."

Her mother's tea cup rattled in the saucer, and her father sat back, clearly shocked. "Married? When?"

"I, uh, found myself pregnant right after my high school graduation."

"Pregnant?" Mamma gasped. She reached out and held Daddy's hand.

"What happened?" her father asked, quietly. "How did we not know?"

"Mark and I married, but he was in New Orleans, and I was in beauty school here. We planned to tell you, but I was ashamed and scared of disappointing you. And then things went bad before I started really showing. I went to see Mark one weekend, and our baby was born too early. S-She never made it…Her name was Analiese."

"You never told us?" her mother cried. Tears spilled down her cheeks and she sprang from her chair to pull Harley into her arms. Stroking her hair, she murmured comforting words in a mixture of English and Norwegian.

Harley shook her head and hugged her mother, offering her comfort in return. "I-It hurt too bad. And it happened so fast…To this day it almost seems like a dream—a nightmare."

"And Mark?" Daddy asked, wiping his eyes.

"He was devastated, too. We remained married but lived separate lives, and eventually we divorced. But we're still close and always will be."

She took a deep breath. "I've accepted that part of my life for what it is, but I have to wonder if any of that would've happened if things had just been allowed to occur naturally…Damien and I were *young*, but we should've been allowed to make our own mistakes. However, I have no room to cast blame. I should've told you about Analiese and Mark. I'm so sorry this has been such a mess." Harley wiped her eyes.

Daddy stood. "Mistakes were made all around. I, too, am sorry, Harley." He kissed her forehead and left the room, looking older and tired.

Harley hugged her mother. "I think I need a minute alone, Mamma."

"I think we all do. But we are a family. Nothing is stronger than the love we have for one another." Still tearful, her mother busied herself cleaning up the kitchen.

Harley grabbed her jacket and stepped outside, headed to her favorite spot from when she was a little girl.

"Rapunzel, Rapunzel, let down your golden hair." A voice drifted up from below her.

The branches rustled as Damien made his way up the tree to the old platform. Lying on her back, hands behind her head, she stared at the treetop and waited for him.

He collapsed beside her, looking worried.

"Hey! Get off my cloud," she teased. Years ago, she'd meticulously glued cotton balls all over the open platform, declaring it her castle in the clouds. They'd lasted one day before the rain ruined them.

He grinned and leaned in for a quick kiss. "Good one, but you misquoted." He stretched out beside her, propping his head on his fist. "You okay?"

"I guess so. I'm just trying to sort out my feelings. You?"

"Same."

"I almost feel like we're on a repeat."

He looked puzzled. "A repeat? Of what?"

"You and me. I mean, everything's happening so fast—just like when we were teenagers. And I now I have this uneasy feeling that it's too good to be true. Something's going to happen."

"We're adults now. We make our own destiny."

"I told my parents about Analiese." A tear slipped down her cheek, and Damien kissed it away.

"I'm sorry. I know that must've been hard for you and them…"

"Sin?"

"Yes?"

She sat up and wrapped her arms around her knees. "I love you, but I think we need to back off a bit."

He sat up, running a hand through his hair. "What? What do you mean?"

"I love you, but I need to figure out what I want to do with my life, and it doesn't include scrubbing your toilets."

"I'll hire someone to do that," he offered with a smile. "I just want you to keep my sheets warm."

"Do you want to get married?" She watched his color pale.

"Now?" He looked like a deer caught in the headlights.

She shrugged, waiting.

The wind blew his hair, and the tree gently swayed.

"I, uh, we could think about that if you want…I mean, I don't want to lose you. We just found each other again…"

"But?"

"Can I plead the fifth?" he croaked.

She smiled. "Me neither," she whispered.

"Fuck." He let out a deep breath. His eyes narrowed. "Wait, is this a trick? I love you, Harley. I can't imagine my life without you. It's just—as you said, everything's moving so fast…"

"Ditto. But I want you to know, I'm not interested in marriage right now. I've been there, done that, got the T-shirt. I want to grow up and find myself. I've been lost for a while. I want to do something meaningful with my life. I want to help people."

"Where do I fit in?" A rare look of vulnerability shadowed his face.

"Hopefully beside me?"

"I can do that. And I understand your need to help people. You're good at it. Look at Mr. Gavosovich—and Carl."

"Thank you."

He grinned. "I help people too, you know."

She pulled her brows together.

His smile widened. "I get them get out of misery." The color had returned to his face.

She laughed. "Cynical, Sinclair. If you enjoy your job, that's great. But not all marriages end up unhappy. Look at my parents. And I do believe in the happily ever after; I just don't want to rush into anything." She squeezed his hand. "So you're okay with us just taking it day-by-day?"

He stroked her cheek, looking into her eyes. "Day-by-day, minute-by-minute…As long as you're by my side, the rest is just technicalities to work through. Can we go home now? Because I wanna make love to you."

"We could do it here…" She gave him a searing kiss that made him growl. He rolled over on top of her, his erection pressing between her legs.

He grinned. "Um, aren't you the girl who told me she didn't want to have sex on the back of a pickup? This is a rickety-ass platform that sways every time the wind blows."

"It was cold that night, and Daddy built this to last. If I'm not afraid up here, I wouldn't think you would be."

"It isn't the height that bothers me. Your dad has a shotgun. We're in his backyard. I'm pretty sure I'm not high on his list at the moment. I don't want to risk an ass full of buckshot, 'kay?"

She laughed. "Life without risk is boring. But I agree. Let's go home."

Damien helped her down from the tree and hugged her once they were on the ground.

"You're my obsession, my girl, and my rainbow, Harley."

She laughed. "Can you try a little harder to get more Stones titles in?"

He chuckled. "Let's go home. I need a little T and A."

She groaned.

Hours later, Damien rolled over and stared at the beautiful girl sleeping beside him. *How did I get so lucky?* Twelve years ago, their relationship had evolved from friends to lovers. Fate, meddling, and stupidity had forced them back to being friends. Now here they were lovers again, a full circle.

A part of him still feared it wouldn't last, that she would leave.

Harley didn't want to get married. The relief he'd felt when she said that had been profound…And yet…For some reason, the thought seemed less scary than it used to.

This crazy, whimsical, beautiful girl loved him in spite of his quirks and hang-ups. She was the most giving, loving, funniest person he'd ever known, and he was damn lucky. They'd had more than their share of ups and downs, and with her mercurial mood swings and his need for order, it would always be one helluva wild ride. He'd just have to hang on tight, because he never wanted it to end.

Chapter
Twenty-Three

Warming air blew through the bakery as the bell on the door jingled. Even though it was May, the scent of a crisp autumn day snapped Harley to attention. She'd been working part-time at Damien's favorite bakery for a couple of months now—it was one of her three part-time jobs. She still filled in as a yoga instructor and also helped Miranda out by taking care of Mr. Gavosovich and Shaney when needed.

Damien stopped and spoke to two men sitting at a table, looking relaxed and confident. She glared at two women giving him an appreciative onceover from across the room. *Back off, sisters. He's mine.*

Though she didn't truly worry about Damien and other women, she did wonder if he wasn't growing wedded to his job as he recovered.

Of course she wanted him to get over his panic attacks and fear of crowds, but maybe he could stick to eight-hour days? His hours in the office had slowly crept up and up over the past few months. And this past week, in particular, he'd been distant and secretive. Old insecurities had wormed into her subconscious. In April, they'd gone to see Angel and Maggie again. Seeing Maggie's excitement as she discussed their wedding plans, Harley found herself longing for something more...permanent. But she hadn't dared voice it, not wanting to rock the boat. After all, she and Damien had both made their views on marriage perfectly clear.

Instead, she'd thrown herself into her jobs and started taking an online class with hopes of eventually pursuing a degree in social work.

When Damien approached her counter, it was as if the air in the shop evaporated. She knew in her gut he was pretending about something. Even though he gave her a melt-your-thong-off smile, it seemed forced. There was something worrying him, she could tell.

"May I help you?"

"Harley." The husky need in his voice was nearly her undoing.

"May I help you, *sir?*" she repeated, trying to be professional.

He leaned forward and whispered, "I like it when you call me *sir.*" He wiggled his eyebrows and grinned.

She smiled. "I know."

Out of habit, she smoothed his gray, patterned tie. No man should look that good in a suit. She wanted to rip it off his body, ask him what was wrong, and have him kiss her worries away.

He straightened. "One coffee, black, and a strawberry muffin."

"*Coming* right up, *sir.*" She chewed on her lower lip and gave him her best sexy look before turning to prepare his order, adding a little extra sass in her walk. Feeling devious, she placed a blueberry muffin in the sack and with a fake smile, turned around and handed him his order. Her eyes bugged when he tossed a hundred in the tip jar.

"For the gracious and expedient service." He winked, leaving her feeling guilty for giving him the wrong muffin.

Ten minutes later he returned.

"May I help you?" she asked.

"Yes, there seems to have been a mix-up with my order."

"Oh? Did you save your receipt?" She crossed her arms.

"No, but you know I don't eat blueberries."

Harley bit her lip to keep from smiling. "If you didn't save your receipt, how do I know you didn't order blueberry?"

One eyebrow rose, and he pointed at the order pad. "Check your orders."

Out of the corner of her eye, she saw her boss.

Trumped, she whispered, "Don't be ridiculous, Sin. It wouldn't kill you to eat a blueberry muffin."

Another customer walked in, and she relaxed her frown into a smile.

"I'd like to speak to the manager." Damien smiled. The man standing behind him groaned.

She quickly grabbed a strawberry muffin and placed it in a bag for him. "Here, now go! Sorry for the mistake." She looked around him at the next customer and whispered for his ears only, "Wanker."

Damien slowly opened the bag and looked inside. "Are you sure it isn't stale?" The irritated gentleman behind him turned on his heel and left in a huff. Mr. Harris hurried over.

"Is there a problem, Harley?"

She dropped her head to hide the death look she wanted to shoot at Damien. Dammit, even her cleavage was crimson.

"N-No sir." She prayed he'd believe her and go back to the kitchen. No such luck.

Mr. Harris looked at Damien. "Everything okay, sir?"

"Actually, no. Everything is not *okay*."

Harley snapped her head up, silently beseeching him to just leave and not complain about her to Mr. Harris. Risking her job would take the prank too far. Devilment danced in his eyes. He turned his attention to her boss.

"Everything is *outstanding*. Because of…" He pretended to read her nametag, but she recognized a leer when she saw one. "*Harley's* gracious help. As a matter of fact, I think I'd like to place a standing order for my office on Fridays: two dozen of your delicious muffins; no blueberry, please. An assortment would be wonderful." He handed Mr. Harris his business card as he smiled at Harley. "Let me reiterate: please make sure there are *no blueberry*. We'll start tomorrow."

She rolled her eyes. *I get it. No damn blueberry.* "Of course, Mr. Sinclair."

Mr. Harris beamed at her, and she foresaw her name on the Employee of the Month plaque in the bathroom.

"Thank you. We'll be happy to accommodate you. Well done, Harley." Mr. Harris snatched the debit card out of Damien's hand and rang up the order before he could change his mind.

It was after seven when Harley finished her shift. She texted Sin to see if he wanted her to pick up a pizza on the way home.

Already ate. Another late night at the office.

It was the fourth night in a row he'd used that excuse.

Determined to remind him there was more to life than work, Harley headed to his office instead of home. Everyone was already gone except for the security guard, who let her in.

She rode up in the elevator, and then without knocking, threw open his office door.

Damien jumped, but then smiled. "This is a nice surprise. Even if you did damn near give me a heart attack."

He put down his pen, shuffled some papers into a folder, and slid it into his desk. He looked mildly guilty as he hurried over to her.

She let out a deep breath, frankly relieved he was alone. Her thoughts had briefly gone dark on her way over here. "I, uh, I've been a bad girl. I need to see if you can *get me off*, counselor…"

His eyes crinkled, and his grin widened when she copped a feel.

"Is it a penal offense?" He chuckled against her mouth. "Can I sue your pants off?"

"It is, and please do. Is this what's called a hung jury?"

"More like a firm offer."

Kicking off her shoes and socks, she unbuckled his belt and dropped his pants around his ankles. He laughed, and she giggled as he picked her up and shuffled her toward the desk with his clothing-shackled feet.

Finally making it, he helped her out of her jeans and panties and leaned her back onto his desk.

"I've dreamed about this," he confessed.

"Me, too…Yeow!" Reaching behind her, she moved the stapler.

With a sweep of his hand, he cleared the desk. Papers, paper clips, pens, and sticky notes scattered everywhere.

"Oh my God!" she yelled.

"What? I haven't done anything yet," he said, panting.

"The mess," she said with a gasp, giggling.

"Shut up, I don't want to think about it." He pulled her butt to the edge of his desk. "This is fucking phenomenal."

"Well done. Now get busy."

Smiling, he teased her entrance, but she was more than ready.

He gave her a quick kiss. "We have a split decision to make. Want me to make this brief?"

"Sure, but my lawyer better not withdraw at the last minute."

"I'm going to be the judge, too, and give you a stiff sentence."

He plunged deep, causing her to scoot backward, and he pulled her back to him.

"How come the movies make this look easy?" he groused as she wrapped her legs tight around him.

"Ahhh. This feels so good…" Her worries receded. This was where he was meant to be. With her. Forever. Her inner muscles clenched with each thrust.

"Shit, yeah!" he agreed, hammering her hard.

"Because movies are allusions, and we're the real deal," she said. "Dear God, why are we talking? I can't even think…Yes, there…" She dug her nails into his biceps and closed her eyes when he circled her clit with his thumb.

"Illusions," he corrected with a grunt.

All her fears fled as he drew her closer and closer. The sounds, the smells, the feel of his grip on her hips collided as she went over the edge, screaming his name.

"Fuck! Harley," he yelled as he followed before collapsing on top of her.

Winded, he rested his forehead to hers, grinning. "I love you. Goddamn, that was fun."

"Uh-huh." She grinned, lazily stroking his back, still unable to think.

Damien kissed her again, leisurely. He looked around his office. "Such a mess we made."

A knock sounded on the door.

"Shit," he whispered, eyes wide. He muffled her giggle with his hand.

"Everything okay in there?" asked the security guard.

"Fine, thanks!" Damien hollered. To her he whispered, "I bet he thinks I'm wanking off watching porn."

They heard him leave.

"See? This is why I'm not spontaneous. I always get caught." He stood and helped her off the desk.

Harley laughed. "You may have a point, prosecutor."

As they dressed, Harley asked hopefully, "Are you done for the night? There's lots of world outside this office…"

"After I clean up this mess, I have about an hour more work to do. I'll walk you to your car."

She bit back her disappointment. "No, it's okay. I found a spot out front. Security can see my car through the glass door."

"Okay." He gave her a kiss and smacked her butt as she walked out the door. "See you at home. Thank you for the office visit." He grinned and waggled his brow, still looking deliciously unkempt despite now being fully dressed.

Fuck, that was close. Fiona had just left ten minutes before Harley's surprise visit. He knew she was getting suspicious about all these late nights. She rarely dropped by the office unannounced. Damien quickly put his desk back to right. He had too much at risk. He didn't want to explain Fiona to Harley.

Maybe he'd just go on home now and take a half day tomorrow. Yep. Better to endure the wrath of his father than Harley.

Chapter
Twenty-Four

Harley wiped down the counter and stretched her aching back. Damien had arrived home almost immediately after she had last night, and her mind was somewhat eased. Perhaps she'd made some progress in reminding him of the merits of life beyond the office. She counted down her drawer and gave the money to Mr. Harris.

"Good night, Mr. Harris."

"Good night, Harley. You'll have to go out the front door; a delivery truck is blocking the back."

"Do you need me to help unload?" *Please say no, please say no...*

"No, Larry and I have it."

"Okay. See you Monday." Thank God she was off for the weekend.

She slipped out the front door and frowned when she noticed a crowd gathered in front of the shop. Someone was pointing up toward the rooftop across the street. With difficulty, she squeezed through the crowd, eager to get to her car. Then notes from a violin filtered from above. She looked up.

She blinked and looked again. It wasn't her imagination. Although it was dark, the streetlight illuminated Damien playing a violin on the rooftop across the street. The fact that he was perched precariously on a roof was unsettling, but she'd seen him do this before. After his mother had coerced him into playing the fiddler in his high school production of *Fiddler on the Roof*, it had become his favorite place to practice.

And it wasn't even that shocking that he wasn't playing a classical piece or something by The Rolling Stones, but "Without You," one of her favorite songs. Instead it was the billowing red pirate shirt that spread a smile across her face.

When he finished playing, the crowd around her applauded.

"Harley Blake Taylor," he shouted, pointing at her with the bow.

His hair ruffled with the wind, and he looked like the pirate of her dreams. All eyes turned toward her, and warmth filled her cheeks as she became the center of attention.

"What?" she shouted back.

"I want more than spending the night together. I need you, baby. And I'll even be your beast of burden because love is strong. I know you can't always get what you want, but I promise, no more mixed emotions. I know you live with me and gimme shelter, but I ain't too proud to beg. Please have sympathy for the devil. Will you marry me?"

A collective *awww* rippled through the crowd.

"Is that the best you can do? Have you run out of stupid Rolling Stones songs to string together?" She crossed her arms in front of her chest and tapped her foot, grinning up at him.

"That's it. You've left me no choice," he shouted back.

Then he jumped.

And her world went black.

Damien zip-lined across the street, nearly losing his grip when he saw Harley faint. Thankfully, the man standing next to her caught her before she cracked her head on the concrete. Breathless with worry, he reached her side and pulled her into his arms just as her eyes fluttered open.

"Dammit, you missed the best part," he grumbled as he kissed her forehead.

"Y-You're okay?" she asked.

"Of course. I told you I'm not dying anytime soon."

She shoved against his chest. "You nearly gave me a heart attack."

"But I was being spontaneous," he protested, taking her lips with his.

Her hands wrapped in his hair, and her soft moan stirred him. He wanted her home, in his arms, in his bed, in his life forever.

"Am I dreaming?" she whispered.

"More like a nightmare. This shirt is ridiculous." Still holding her, he managed to struggle to his feet. He grinned as everyone clapped and wolf whistled around them.

"Marry me, Harley."

"Okay," she whispered with a smile.

"You sure? Wait, is this a trick? That was too easy..."

She smacked his chest. "No trick. I'd really like to do this. Let's go home, sexy pirate."

"Okay. The event planner who set this evening up is on board for wedding planning, too. It's tight, but I told her probably June, right? Isn't that traditional?"

She struggled in his arms. "What? Are you nutters? And when have we ever been traditional? June weddings are too cliché."

He put her down but kept his arms around her waist.

"Well...uh, shit. Did I do something wrong?"

"Cut the poor bastard some slack," a man yelled.

Everyone cheered.

"Besides, you can't plan a wedding in just a few weeks!"

"A small ceremony shouldn't take much planning..."

"Small ceremony?" Her lower lip poked out. "I've had the small courthouse wedding. It didn't end so well."

He swallowed. "So, you'd like a gigantic wedding on the date of your discretion?"

"Can I get a big-ass ring, too?"

"Are you marrying me for my money?" he teased.

"Of course. That's what attracted me to you when I was five. You had a five-dollar bill; I only had a quarter." She smiled. "I don't really care about the big-ass ring. But I do want a real wedding this time..."

He laughed and pulled her ponytail. "You can have every damn dime I've got *and* the huge-ass wedding, as long you're mine."

"I've always been yours. Can I have your car, too?"

He frowned. "Okay, I have to draw the line somewhere."

"Seriously? You'd give me a gigantic wedding, a big-ass ring, and all your money, but not your car?"

He tugged her hand, grinning. "I'm open to negotiation, but don't count on it."

Harley narrowed her eyes when Jerry waved and smiled at her as they made their way to the elevator.

"Do they have mandatory drug testing for the employees here? I'm not too sure about Jerry…" She squealed when Damien pushed her against the wall of the elevator and lowered his lips to hers as soon as the doors closed.

"I will never tire of kissing you. I love the way your lips always taste like cotton candy, and you smell like coffee and muffins. Why, Ms. Taylor, you're good enough to eat." He nibbled on her neck, his hands roaming down her body.

"I think they were blueberry muffins," she replied with a giggle.

He captured her hands and nudged closer, letting her know it didn't matter one damn bit if they were blueberry.

The elevator dinged and opened. Holding hands, they walked toward the door when she had a sudden, horrible thought.

"Oh my God, what about your violin? You left it on the rooftop."

"Don't worry about it," he murmured as he swung the door open. With a growl, he swept her off her feet and carried her into the penthouse. "Fiona handled it."

"Who's Fiona? Sin, what are you doing? You're going to throw your back out. It isn't like we're married yet…"

She blinked and then pinched him to see if she was dreaming. His violin was on the couch, the room lit by white candles, and red paper hearts made a trail toward their bedroom.

"Ouch! What did you do that for? Fiona's the event planner I hired to coordinate the proposal and the wedding I'd thought we might be having in a couple of weeks. I'll text her and tell her to adjust things to whatever date you tell me."

"You did this for me?" she whispered in awe.

"No, I did it for Jerry." He rolled his eyes. "Of course I did it for you. Well, I had a little help, believe it or not, from Jerry, Tim, your boss, our parents, Claire, Shaney—who cut out the red hearts, and Mr. Gavosovich. He lent me the red pirate shirt."

She laughed and kissed him. "Pretty damn sure of yourself, weren't you? What if I'd said no?"

"Not a chance. I always get what I want. Plus, I had an alternate plan."

He walked her in to the bedroom, which was also lit by candles. The linens had been changed to red and strewn with white rose petals.

"And what was the alternate plan?"

He laid her on the bed and cupped her face in his hands. "Argh. Why to kidnap you, lass. And tie you to my bed until you said yes."

She laughed outright at his poor imitation of a pirate.

A shiver of excitement pebbled her already hard nipples. "In that case, can I change my mind? That sounds like fun."

"The question would be: *May I change my mind?* And only if you tack on *sir* at the end." His dark eyes crinkled.

"May I change my mind, *sir?*" she purred in his ear.

Epilogue

"Relax, there's nothing to it. You get up there, promise to obey her, acknowledge she'll forever be right, and it's done." Angel slapped Damien on the back and frowned when their father handed him a shot of Michael Collins.

"Everything's going according to plan," Fiona, the wedding planner, affirmed. "I'm off to check on the bride." She breezed out the door.

"Just a little shot of liquid courage," Dad muttered as Angel shook his head no.

Ignoring Angel, Damien downed the shot and handed the empty glass back to his father.

"Hell, you had less than fifty people there when you married Maggie. Half the damn state of Georgia is here." He motioned expansively toward the closed door. From behind it, the orchestra could be heard tuning their instruments in the cathedral. "Is Bridezilla here yet?" Damien paced with nervous energy.

"Yes, she's here and bossing everyone around like the militant despot she's been for the last few months. I was even told precisely how many steps to take to the altar. I told her to let up or I'd tag the bottom of your shoes to say *Help Me*." Angel grinned.

Damien lifted each shoe to make sure nothing was written on them.

"Angel, you'll do no such thing," their father growled.

"Dad, why don't you go greet the guests?" Damien suggested, walking him to the door.

He still played the role of peacekeeper. His dad gave him a hug and reassuring pat on the back and left.

"Asshole," Angel muttered.

"Please don't argue with him today." Damien fastened the cufflinks Harley had given him for a wedding present. "At least Harley settled on a formal wedding and didn't make me wear some ridiculous colorful getup."

His heart rate was speeding to an uncomfortable rate, but he practiced the breathing technique his therapist had trained him to use to handle his panic attacks. Harley would raise holy hell if he freaked out and fucked up their wedding.

"Only because you and her father refused to pay for a pirate-themed wedding," Angel said with a sigh. "Personally, I think that would've been a helluva lot more fun than wearing these damn monkey suits. I'd kinda like to have dreads again." He ran a finger around his collar and sneered at his tux in the mirror.

The door to the room flung open, and Damien gulped back his fear. There was only one thing scarier than his darling Bridezilla. Claire narrowed her eyes as she swooped toward him like a hawk after prey. He backed away until he was pressed against the wall. He shot a look of help to Angel, who threw his hands up, backing away.

Claire reached toward him, and he flinched. She smirked as she straightened his bow tie. Damien let out the breath he'd been holding and relaxed.

"Just making sure you didn't back out," she said. "Angel, if you have to handcuff him and drag his despicable ass into that church, you make sure he's there."

"Yes, ma'am."

Turning her attention back to him, she pushed her index finger into his chest, and Damien swore her eyes were glowing a fiendish red to match her dress.

"Because if you do anything to mess this up for Harley, I will hunt you down and serve you your balls on a silver platter for breakfast," she hissed. "*Capiche?*"

She gave him a kiss on the cheek, whirled around, and left.

This must be what it feels like to get the kiss of death from a Mafioso.

"Damn." Angel looked at him with wide eyes. "She's kind of scary."

"No shit."

"Is he really here?"

Harley paced back and forth and ran her hands down the full, white satin skirt. She stopped and eyed herself critically in the mirror. Her wedding dress was a traditional ballroom style but had an overlay of red lace that formed cap sleeves and swept diagonally across the bodice. It was, after all, a Christmas-season wedding, and one of the sweetest things Damien had ever told her was that Harley red was his favorite color.

"Yes, and I put Angel in charge of making sure he stays put," Claire replied, straightening the full skirt of Harley's dress.

"That wanker better be there."

"Harley, such talk from a beautiful bride…" Her mother fussed as she placed the veil on her head, attaching it with a ruby-and-diamond comb that had belonged to Damien's mother. She gave Harley a kiss on the cheek.

"You are my treasure," she murmured as she wiped at her eyes with a handkerchief. "I can't believe how beautiful my baby is."

"Please don't cry, Mamma."

"Okay, none of you cry. You're going to ruin the makeup." Claire rounded up the three bridesmaids and flower girl, effectively doing Fiona's job for her. "It's time to go."

Harley gave her mother one last kiss and smiled through her tears when her father walked in the room carrying her bouquet.

"'Have I not seen the loveliest woman born,'" her father murmured, quoting his beloved Yeats. He cupped her cheek and gazed into her eyes. "May you be blessed with the happiness I've known with your mother." He wiped her tears away with his thumbs and kissed her forehead. "My sweet child, you have brought me so much joy…" He chuckled and tweaked her nose. "And a few gray hairs. I love you, and it's extremely difficult to give you away. But I know Damien loves you." He gave her another gentle hug and kiss, careful not to muss her hair or dress.

"Thank you, Daddy." She reached for a tissue and dabbed at her eyes.

"Now chivvy along, before the poor boy thinks you've changed your mind."

"As if!"

"As if, indeed. You've dreamed of this since you were a little girl. That poor man never stood a chance." He winked and handed her the bouquet of cascading red and white roses before lowering the veil over her face. As he held out his arm, Edvard Grieg's "Wedding Day at Troldhaugen" began to play.

Slowly they made their way to the narthex. The church was lit by hundreds of white candles and filled with family and friends. Shaney preceded them down the aisle, throwing white rose petals on the red carpet. The wedding party which included Claire, Maggie, Miranda, Angel, and both of her brothers, stood at the altar waiting for them. As they made their way down the aisle, Mark gave her a wink and wide smile. Damien stared at the carpet, his hands clasped behind his back, shifting back and forth on both feet until Angel nudged him. He looked up, and a devastating smile swept across his pale, sweaty face.

This is it. I'm actually getting married.

Harley was breathtakingly beautiful. Through the sheer veil, he could see the blush of Harley red on her cheeks, reflecting her nervous excitement. Carefully, she and her father made their way down the aisle. The closer they got, the more labored his breathing became, and his heart pounded at an uncomfortable rate. A trickle of sweat worked its way down his face, and he wished someone would blow out the damn candles. It was entirely too hot in the church.

Pulling a handkerchief from his pocket, he mopped his brow and gulped when Harley's brows knit together. She used her super-power death gaze to pin him to the spot. She shoved the veil over the back of her head and mouthed, "Breathe."

He took a deep breath and felt somewhat better. Running a finger around the noose-like collar, he tried to give her a reassuring nod despite the stars dotting the periphery of his vision.

Harley shoved her bouquet into her father's hands and, hiking up her skirt, ran toward him. He caught his bride-to-be with both hands and a mild grunt of surprise. Her dress added a good ten pounds to her weight. She wrapped her arms around his neck and kissed him long and hard.

"Didn't we skip the important part?" he gasped when she finally let him go.

"I just wanted to make sure you didn't back out, you wanker."

The priest behind them cleared his throat, and she blushed.

"Oops, sorry."

She looked anything but sorry as she gave him a mischievous wink. The scent of warm peaches helped his anxiety, and he reluctantly put her down, ignoring his gut instinct to run down the aisle. He wouldn't have made it anyway; Taylor would've blocked his exit—if Claire didn't trip him first. Harley's father tapped her on the shoulder, gave her a quick kiss, and handed her the bouquet, which she passed off to Claire.

"Well now, should we start at the beginning?" the priest asked with a smile.

He began by addressing the congregation.

Damien tried to pay attention, but his heart was still racing like an engine at the Talladega Speedway. *Why is the damn church so stifling hot?*

The priest turned to Harley and mumbled something about forsaking others and being faithful.

She smiled and gazed up at Damien as she answered, "I will."

Damien tried to focus on her beautiful eyes, but inky blackness shuttered his vision, and a dull roaring filled his ears. *Why is the priest mumbling? Who's extinguishing the candles? Is this part of the ceremony?*

The room spun like a Tilt-a-Whirl, and his stomach tossed and turned. *Dammit, if I throw up on her dress, Harley will kill me. I'll have my funeral today as well as our wedding.* The tunnel narrowed, and the last thing he saw was Harley's wide blue eyes.

Warm, cotton candy lips were on his, and he smiled and deepened the kiss. This was his favorite way to wake up, but she had on entirely too many clothes... *Wait, what the hell?*

Angel's whoops of laughter snapped his eyes open, and he realized with horror he was sprawled out like an Old Testament sacrificial lamb at the altar, with pandemonium in full swing around him. The back of his head hurt like hell, and he struggled to sit up, gratefully accepting the glass of water the priest handed him, wishing it was the wine instead.

Harley cupped his cheek in her hand and stage whispered, "You better get on your feet and marry me, my swooning sweetheart."

"I did not swoon," he sputtered in protest. "I'm a guy. I passed out."

"Nope. I agree with Harley; you swooned like a little girl." Still chuckling, Angel gave Damien a hand to stand up.

"Are you okay? Are you having second thoughts, son?" the priest asked with a hint of worry in his kind face.

"No, sir. I do, I will, I promise—whatever it takes to get me out of here as a married man."

Claire smacked him with her bouquet. "You're not getting off that easy. You're going to stand here and take it like a man."

It took Maggie *and* Miranda to get her to back off.

He pulled Harley to his chest and held her tight. "I'm sorry, Harley. I do want to marry you."

She closed her eyes and took a deep breath. "Then let's do it. I'm hungry and want some cake."

He tipped her chin up with his index finger and smiled. "You're sniffing me again."

His heart felt ready to burst. But it wasn't from panic, just love. Harley blushed, and he captured both her hands in his and gazed down at her.

"I love you, Harley Blake Taylor. You've turned my orderly life upside down and made my black-and-white world full of color. I never ever want to live without Harley red. You are my best friend, my lover, my tormentor, and soon to be my wife. From this day forward, I want to spend the rest of my life counting stars with you."

Tears glistened in her eyes, and the priest behind them said, "I pronounce that they are husband and wife, in the Name of the Father, and of the Son, and of the Holy Spirit. Those whom God has joined together, let no one put asunder. You may kiss your bride again, and then we will exchange the rings."

Damien looked at him, confused. This wasn't the marriage ceremony in *The Book of Common Prayer*.

The priest leaned forward and whispered, "Learn to go with the flow. Life's too short to adhere to order all the time. Enjoy the chaos of marriage, and from it you'll gain peace."

"Chocolate cake for breakfast is decadent."

Harley licked the groom's cake frosting off her lips. Her beautiful eyes were hooded as she smiled up at him. Damien fed her another bite, and he licked the icing off her lips this time.

"You taste better than cake," he murmured in her ear. "And it made me happy to see Cheetara reunited with Tygra on top of the cake."

He chuckled and glanced at the bedside table, where they'd posed the two action figures in an obscene position—one they had emulated last night before finally falling asleep, exhausted.

"You're going to have to let me out of bed soon, so we can leave for our honeymoon," she told him.

"Not yet. We have time."

One taut nipple begged for his attention, and he nipped it with his teeth. Her back arched, and she moaned. His hands and lips had explored every inch of her body last night, but he couldn't get enough. Where she was concerned, he was insatiable.

"Do you have any idea how much I love you?" he asked as he kissed her.

A lazy smile crossed her perfect lips. "Enough to marry me after going down like a tree in the forest, O fainting fucker."

He growled and licked her belly button. "It was your fault. I wanted a small, intimate wedding. You know I still don't like crowds. That's why I'm taking the job with Angel's foundation."

Her cell phone rang, and he reached across her to grab it, annoyed. It was Harley's mother.

"Good morning, Elise."

He listened for a moment and with a smirk replied, "I'm sorry she can't come to the phone right now. She's a bit tied up. Yes, ma'am, I'll have her call you before we leave for Bali." He hung up and grinned at her.

Harley tugged at the silk ties around her wrists and grinned. "Wanker."

The End

The series will continue with Mark and Jinx's story.

What Is PTSD?

PTSD (posttraumatic stress disorder) is a mental health problem that some people develop after experiencing or witnessing a life-threatening event, such as combat, a natural disaster, a car accident, or sexual assault. It's normal to have upsetting memories, feel on edge, or have trouble sleeping after this type of event occurs. At first, it may be hard to do normal daily activities, like go to work, go to school, or spend time with people you care about. But most people start to feel better after a few weeks or months. However, if it's been longer than a few months and you're still having symptoms, you may have PTSD.

For some people, PTSD symptoms may start later on, or they may come and go over time. Here's the good news: you can get treatment for PTSD—and it works.

Get help if you're in crisis

If you feel like you might hurt yourself or someone else:

Call 1-800-273-TALK (1-800-273-8255) anytime to talk to a crisis counselor. The call is confidential and free. Or you can chat online with a crisis counselor at any time at:

www.suicidepreventionlifeline.org

You can also call 9-1-1 or go to your local emergency room.

Where to find help

If you're a Veteran, check with the VA about whether you can get treatment there. Visit www.va.gov/directory/guide/PTSD.asp to find a VA PTSD program near you.

If you're looking for care outside the VA, ask your doctor for a referral to a mental health care provider who specializes in PTSD treatment, or visit findtreatment.samhsa.gov to search for providers in your area.

For more information and resources, visit the National Center for PTSD website at: www.ptsd.va.gov.

Information presented here was obtained from the media kit www.ptsd.va.gov/about/press-room/Materials_for_Printing.asp.

Acknowledgments

Thank you to my parents for raising me with love and a sense of humor. I'm sure you needed the humor while raising me! And to my sister, who knows me better than anyone, and still loves me. May our love of reading never wane and our sense of adventure continue, even if we collapse before the 6 PM news.

Thank you to my husband who cooks, cleans, and runs errands to the PO as I write. When we fell in love we thought we were grown up. Now we realize we were just kids. He truly is a saint to have put up with me all these years. And thank you to my daughter who is my greatest cheerleader.

Jessica Royer Ocken, this book took more work than usual and was hard. Really hard. When I wanted to call it quits, you encouraged me to keep pushing. Your guidance kept me going and I can't imagine working with anyone else. This book is dedicated to you because you always believe in me.

Shannon Lumetta, this beautiful cover is perfect for this crazy story and your graphic skills amaze me. Thank you for not screaming at me when I bombard you with a gazillion images.

Coreen Montagna, you pick up on the small details and iron out the tiny bumps I've overlooked plus make the interior of my books beautiful, thank you.

Thank you to Stephanie Phillips of SBR Media for being my conscience as well as my agent.

Thank you to Jennifer Lane for letting me bounce ideas off of you and for sharing your expertise.

Christina Santos, PA Extraordinaire, your organizational skills put me to shame. I'm sorry that I tend to buzz you at ungodly hours, I'm trying to do better! Thank you for keeping me on the straight, if not the narrow.

Cain Raisers, your support means the world to me and I love that we can have fun and talk books, lift each other up, and be silly without drama. You are the best, ever. I especially want to thank Jo, Michele, Eunice, Chris, Chantel, and Ashley for being the first to read and give me honest opinions of my books.

To all the bloggers who have taken an interest in my books and helped spread the word, I couldn't do it without you. You truly are unsung heroes/heroines.

And to my SLOBS, you keep me honest, you make me laugh, and you lift me up.

Gel of Tempting Illustrations, you bring my story to life with your beautiful teasers, thank you.

And last but not least, Carrie…thank you for putting up with me going on and on ad nauseum about my books at the day job.

About the Author

During the day, Nancee works as a counselor/nurse in the field of addiction to support her coffee and reading habit. Nights are spent writing paranormal and contemporary romances with a serrated edge. Authors are her rock stars, and she's been known to stalk a few for an autograph, but not in a scary, Stephen King way. Her husband swears her To-Be-Read list on her e-reader qualifies her as a certifiable book hoarder. Always looking to try something new, she dreams of being an extra in a Bollywood film, or a tattoo artist. (Her lack of rhythm and artistic ability may put a damper on both of these dreams.)

Website: nanceecain.com
Blog: nanceecain.com/blog
Goodreads: goodreads.com/Nancee_Cain
Facebook: facebook.com/NanceeCainAuthor
Reader's Group (Cain Raisers): facebook.com/groups/Cain.Raisers
Twitter: twitter.com/Nancee_Cain
Pinterest: pinterest.com/nanceecain
Instagram: instagram.com/nanceecain
BookBub: bookbub.com/authors/nancee-cain
Newsletter: eepurl.com/bhFMtX
YouTube Channel: bit.ly/2xsU6Ad
Spotify Playlists: open.spotify.com/user/12184539074

Books by Nancee Cain:

Paranormal Romance (Angels)
Saving Evangeline
Tempting Jo
Loving Lili (novella)

Contemporary Romance (Pine Bluff Novels)
The Resurrection of Dylan McAthie
The Redemption of Emma Devine
The Rehabilitation of Angel Sinclair
The Redirection of Damien Sinclair
The Reinvention of Jinx Howell
The Reintroduction of Sammie Morgan
The Realization of Grayson Deschanelle

Contemporary Romances

pinebluff

Although each of the titles in this series can be read as standalone stories, this is the preferred reading order:

The Resurrection of Dylan McAthie
A Pine Bluff Novel

Maybe You Can Go Home Again

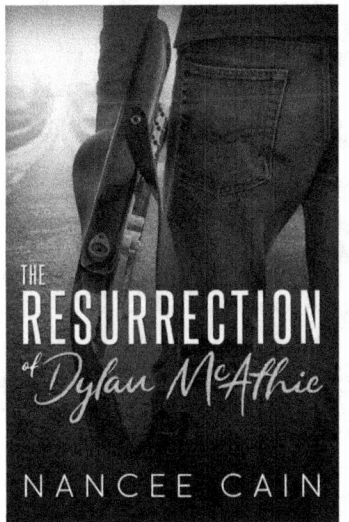

Hounded by paparazzi, Dylan McAthie — the former lead guitarist for Crucified, Dead and Buried — craves quiet anonymity to regroup and sort out his life. An accident leaves him dependent on the family he once ran from, with no choice but to return to the small town of Pine Bluff, Alabama.

Hired by Dylan's estranged brother, private-duty nurse Jennifer Adams remembers the charming boy Dylan was before fame and misfortune. And she notices he's developed a knack for blaming everyone else for his problems, rather than bothering with introspection. She's not having it.

Despite their clashes, as her patient heals, the chemistry between them grows undeniable — until scandal finds Dylan again, threatening to destroy the progress he's made and the couple's growing respect and affection. Can Dylan fix what fame has so easily broken? Or will his public resurrection mean the death of any relationship with Jennifer?

The Redemption of Emma Devine
A Pine Bluff Novel

A Little Shake-Up in Life Can Be Devine

Emma Devine is on the run and fighting to survive. Her tortured past makes trust difficult, especially where men are concerned. But she has no choice other than accepting the help of the man who catches her shoplifting on Christmas Eve.

When not stopping shoplifters, David Patterson leads a quiet life in Pine Bluff, Alabama, working as a high school teacher. His random act of Christmas kindness brings unexpected joy to his life, as he finds himself drawn to the mysterious Emma. When she leaves, his world is turned upside down, and his dreams are changed forever.

Four years later, Emma returns in search of long-overdue redemption. But despite an undeniable attraction between the two, trust is an even greater issue now—for both of them. Can they find their way to a place of understanding? Or have yesterday's mistakes destroyed their chance for a future together?

The Rehabilitation of Angel Sinclair
A Pine Bluff Novel

Love—the Hardest Addiction to Kick

Angel Sinclair arrives in Pine Bluff, Alabama, determined to make amends for his past and move on. But that changes after a chance encounter with a beautiful inn owner, and instead he finds himself pursuing two things that haven't been in his life for years: love and trust.

Still reeling from a bitter divorce, Maggie Robertson wants to focus on making her business a success. Getting involved with anyone in this gossipy little town is the farthest thing from her mind…until she finds herself tempted by a younger man.

Neither Angel nor Maggie can ignore the sizzling heat between them. But Angel's secretive nature soon fills Maggie with doubts about the man she's allowed into her heart.

Was she wrong to believe love could conquer all? Is their age difference an obstacle they can't overcome?

The Redirection of Damien Sinclair
A Pine Bluff Novel

Sometimes You Get What You Need

Acclaimed divorce attorney Damien Sinclair has witnessed more than his share of love's ugly aftermath. He keeps things black and white, preventing anyone from getting too close. But his illusion of control fades when an attempt on his life leaves him struggling with PTSD.

Enter Damien's childhood friend, the free-spirited Harley Taylor. Shrugging off the awkwardness of their teenaged fling and her broken heart, she appoints herself his caregiver. The man needs to learn not to take himself so seriously, and she's hellbent on snapping him out of his brooding funk.

After a decade apart, Harley and Damien find their attraction is stronger than ever. Could Harley's sunny disposition be the bright spot Damien needs in his life? Or will their differences overshadow any hopes of a future together?

The Reinvention of Jinx Howell
A Pine Bluff Novel

Can Love Unmask Their True Selves?

Hiding behind her wigs and heavy makeup, Jinx Howell masks her insecurities — which even she doesn't understand — with bravado, slashing through life with reckless abandon. Lonely, but unwilling to get close to anyone, she finds the ideal solution: a hook-up with the campus's most notorious heartbreaker.

In similar fashion, Mark "Two-Time" MacGregor protects his heart and keeps himself unencumbered through a string of one-night stands. A chance meeting with the edgy Jinx in a dark alley seems like destiny. She claims to want sex with no ties, making her perfect. *Like attracts like.* But this girl with a switchblade has more hang-ups than he does, which is a hell of a lot.

When tragedy strikes, Mark's hit-and-run lifestyle takes a backseat to his need to protect the broken girl whose secrets are unraveling. Along the way, both of them will find their truths unmasked. Can they forge a real relationship, or will they give up on their romance as jinxed?

The Reintroduction of Sammie Morgan
A Pine Bluff Novel

Can Life Get Any Crazier?

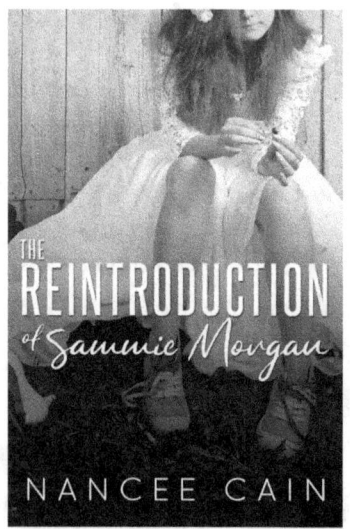

Still reeling from the tragic deaths of his wife and daughter, Matt Tyler trudges through life, caring for his young son, managing his cantankerous father, and working as much as he can. Despite his best efforts, bills are piling up and his vindictive in-laws seem determined to take Luke away from him.

Things change when he stumbles upon Sammie Morgan — with a car that won't run and her mother's ashes in the backseat. Best friends growing up, Matt and Sammie have spent years apart following very different paths. Now they've both run out of options. Without a dime in her pocket, Sammie has nowhere to go. And Matt lacks the stable home life he needs to fight his former in-laws.

Their hasty solution? A marriage of convenience.

But how convenient will this reintroduction be if it means Matt and Sammie have to relive the most painful parts of their past?

The Realization of Grayson Deschanelle
A Pine Bluff Novel

Sex, No Strings Attached

Despite a high-profile clientele, fashion photographer Grayson Deschanelle prefers being behind the lens, away from public scrutiny. After his movie star girlfriend dumps him, he flees to his stepbrother's remote cabin to hide from the paparazzi.

Caught by surprise, Grayson finds Lissy much different than the girl he's known for years. She's no longer a child — though her teen-aged crush is still very much intact. Snowed in with her, he tries to fight his growing attraction. But being with Lissy brings what his life is lacking into sharp focus.

The ice melts, and they return home. When their families discover their secret, Grayson must decide what kind of life he truly wants — and whether he'll fight to keep Lissy by his side.

Paranormal Angel Romances

Although each of the titles in this series can be read as standalone stories, this is the preferred reading order:

Saving Evangeline

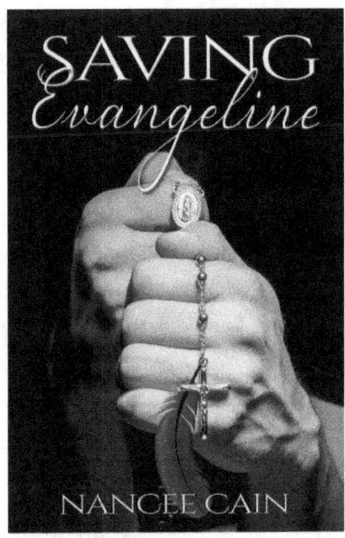

Evangeline is the town pariah. Everyone knows she's crazy and was responsible for the death of her last boyfriend. Even her mother left her and moved cross-country. Lonely and desperate, Evie decides to end her life.

Rogue angel Remiel longs to return to Earth, but there's just one problem. He tends to invite trouble and hasn't been allowed back since Woodstock. The Boss sends him to save Evangeline, but there's a catch: he can't reveal his angelic nature, and he must complete the task as *Father* Remiel Blackson.

Forced together on a cross-country trip, a forbidden romance ignites and love unfolds. A host of heavenly messengers tries to intervene, but Remiel and Evangeline are headed on a collision course to disaster. Will his love save her, or will they both be lost forever?

Forbidden love is hell…

Confident and quirky, Jo Sanford thinks her boss is God's gift to women — and she couldn't be further from the truth. Devilishly handsome, Luc DeVille will stop at nothing to lure his administrative assistant right into his arms — and bed.

Over Rafe Goodman's dead body…

Rafe, Jo's best friend, refuses to sit by and watch as Luc tries to win the heart of the woman he's always protected. After all, Rafe is her guardian angel. Suddenly, Jo's caught in the middle of a battle between good and evil. But the closer she gets to the fire, the hotter it burns. Now, Jo's going to learn that when love battles lust, Heaven and Hell collide.

Loving Lili (novella)

Their lovemaking is hot and dirty. Their break ups are nasty and epic.

Tired of taking the blame for every wicked thing that happens on Earth, fallen angel Luc DeVille decides to write a tell-all-book exposing The Boss.

Sharing a long and passionate history, Luc is shocked when Lili Nix arrives to interview for the job as editor. Immediately the verbal sparring begins, but the sexual chemistry remains combustible. Fascinated by this heavenly creature, Luc changes his game plan. After all, she's the only angel who has ever held his attention and understood his intentions.

Being in this world, but not of this world, is a lonely business. Can two lost angels connect and make it last this time?

www.ingramcontent.com/pod-product-compliance
Lightning Source LLC
Chambersburg PA
CBHW071234260626
47161CB00003BA/941